Premonition of Terror

Kathryn Orzech

Premonition of Terror

~ *Part One* ~

Northeast U.S.A.

ONE

MASSACHUSETTS
Sunday Night

YUSUF LAID HIS KNIFE on the counter. Temptations of the West had lured his Brothers into wicked acts, and now *his* hands were stained with murder.

He ripped and dampened a wad of steel wool from a tattered wrapper he found in a dusty cupboard, muttering words of repentance while he scraped off the crusted blood he had left too long. He raked with steady strokes until steel gleamed, reflecting sun rays with blinding streaks. A bucket half filled from the outdoor pump set in the kitchen sink. He rinsed the blade in the pail, stirring the water like a lamb stew.

The cabin should have been vacant until the warm months. Set back from a little used road between Boston and Worcester, it was an ideal location to squat until his part of the mission was complete. He had ditched a stolen car in a distant woodland and hiked twelve kilometers back to the cabin where he had stored provisions to last a week; he could live on much less, like he had while training with mujahedin—*Brothers of the Eastern Flame.*

Treetops rustled in a stiff gust and dried leaves slid across the floor when the back door blew open. The breeze smelled like moist earth. Not like Cairo where the air could choke you.

Yusuf braced against the frame, pulling the door where it

stuck. Rough wood snagged the sleeve of his jacket. His forehead pressed against the glass pane as he glared at the distant mound where soil and brush had settled and animals had grown more curious. His tongue clucked with disappointment about his carelessness. He had accomplished so much in past months. He should have completed this small task with greater resolve. Perhaps his Brothers had correctly named him, *The Arm*. He had once heard them speak of him as a "man of lesser intellect." No matter what they believed of his mind, he was clear about himself and knew he would not come out of this alive.

Tomorrow I will fix.

Hide the truck parked alongside the cabin, run it into the ravine and cover it with brush.

Dig a deeper grave.

Again the door blew open as if God had whispered permission.

Once a source of peace, a mural of Paradise on the salon wall of his family home in Giza could have been photographed where he now stood—a landscape of heaven—full of life, with more greens than he could have imagined. "They live in Paradise, and look what they do."

Angry. Bitter. More determined than ever. *Something happens to me and it becomes stronger than myself.*

The sudden blast of a horn exploded the silence.

Yusuf scrambled across the room and peeked out the front window as tires crunched on the gravel road. A small SUV with Connecticut plates parked at the deck. A hard crash, and another, as something heavy hit the steps.

The driver called out, "Hey, buddy. Give me a hand with these tools."

Yusuf hid behind the front door, pressing against the wall—the knife with the polished blade clenched in his fist.

TWO

CONNECTICUT
Sunday Night

KATE KASABIAN SHUDDERED with a chill. Maybe it was the weight of the comforter rising off her body that woke her. Perhaps it was the sudden cold spilling onto the other side of the bed as if someone had crawled in. "Todd?" Her whisper was so soft she barely heard it herself. "You're back?" She rolled on her side half asleep, slipping her arm outside the down quilt. Her hand traced his shoulder and slid up the back of his neck. Her fingers combed through his hair with gentle strokes like so many times before.

The bedroom was too quiet. No fabric rustled with her movements. No psychic voices played in her head.

No lover sighed at her touch.

Her eyes shot open.

Todd!

Her body lurched against the mattress as if her soul had crashed into her physical self. She bolted from the empty bed, sprinting so fast to escape she stumbled against the door.

"What the hell!"

Kate stood shaking in the hallway, her arms hugging herself as she stared into the dark room looking for movement.

Listening for breaths.

Pain stabbed her left temple, the first sign of migraine. Her fingers pressed against the throb as she ran downstairs. "Todd, is that you? Damn you if it is." A room-to-room search proved fruitless. Windows and doors remained secure and nothing had been disturbed.

She'd rather face a room of demanding clients than confront a paranormal pest alone in the dead of night, though that wasn't always her way. She once was so brave. So confident. So sure of her supernatural skills. That old Kate had been gone so long, she scarcely remembered her. She inched back upstairs, gripping the rail with hands that had touched spirit.

I felt his hair. Wavy. Silky. His body pressed against me. I know what I felt.

A red scarf nearly tripped her when she crossed her bedroom's threshold. *Must have fallen when I bumped the door.* She snatched it from the floor, glared at her hand and wiped her palm with harsh strokes to scrape off uninvited energy. Scraping. Scraping. More than was needed. Spectral light gleamed with each stroke as if sparking off fingers of steel. She shook her head to sever the psychic connection and drew an energy shield around her while murmuring, "White light. White light."

Clutching the door frame supported an illusion of sanctuary. She leaned inside and flipped a switch; the room seemed harmless in light. Tucking her hair behind her ears was a lame attempt to regain control. She returned the scarf to the belt tree hooked behind the door, inhaled a deep breath to fuel her courage and tiptoed across the carpet. Her head snapped to one side where she saw movement. A silk Chinese wall hanging rippled in the stirred air though no one was there. She grabbed the quilt, flipped it onto the floor and felt the mattress in slow, smooth circles.

The spot where she had lain remained warm.

The other side felt cold—colder than the room.

A trace fragrance lingered on the sheets with the chocolaty musk of a Ralph Lauren body spray Todd often wore.

"If you're coming back, then dammit, bring your body and use the front door."

She backed away from the bed, grabbed a blanket from the guest room and headed downstairs to the living room couch. Her phone sat on the coffee table at arm's length, a fireplace poker propped beside her.

Curled into a tense ball, she clutched the blanket to her chin. *What the hell was that about? His attempt to make amends?* It wasn't a dream. Most of the time she knew the difference and of this she was sure. The ghostly visit was alarming—and strange enough to post on her website, *Dreamwatch.com ... true paranormal experiences of ordinary people.*

The way people used Dreamwatch was nothing like Kate had imagined—a registry for premonitions to warn of disaster —grounding a plane *before* faulty wiring failed, evacuating a town *before* a mudslide smothered it, closing a bridge *before* it collapsed. But it decided what to be when it grew up and the result wasn't earth-changing like she had hoped. People wrote about shared dreams, saving themselves from harm, and more than a few visitations by loved ones back from the dead.

Except for purple business cards printed with white Gill Sans type, Kate did nothing to promote her site, yet visitors found it like sinners flocked to a confessional. Friends and family called them crazy and most feared they were. They craved validation from anyone who might believe their story, because they hardly believed it themselves. Something had happened to them, mysterious and frightening. Something bigger than they were. Something bigger than all of us.

The sudden fragrance of flowers in winter ...

Movement in another room when home alone ...

Or the spirit of an absent lover lying in your bed, so real you could smell his cologne and feel his hair between your fingers.

A shiver ran down her arms, so intense not even pure light could warm them.

Damn. This wasn't supposed to happen anymore.

THREE

Monday Morning

AN EERIE THUNDER seemed to cut through all of creation. A frightening metallic rumble sounded like mountains collapsing or earth's crust breaking apart. Vibration trembled through Kate's body, scaring her like a house cat caught in a storm. She bolted to the picture window to confirm the nearby traprock range remained standing and was stunned to see it unchanged. Not even a tree branch lay on her lawn. *But, it was so real.*

Can reality crack? Did I hear myself pierce the other side? What did I see?

Sleeping on the couch had been quite comfortable until the apocalyptic weather front smashed her dreams into fragments, recall and interpretation now made more difficult.

Kate rubbed her eyes and squinted as daybreak colored the walls a peachy pink. She loved her little house on Summary Road. She had to. It was all she had left since Todd Avery stormed out two nights ago with most of his belongings, that, and her guilt for not loving him enough. *More guilt. Just what I need.* Feeling Todd's presence last night stirred sentimental longing that surprised her. She sat on the sofa's middle cushion and mindlessly picked at her hair to unravel snarls one by one. *I love him. I love him not.*

She might have said *yes* to his proposal in a month or a year, but her heart wasn't there yet. Careening toward her thirtieth birthday a mere nine months away, not even desire for children had swayed her to accept his ultimatum: Marry me or I'm outta here.

Damn him. She might have said *yes* next week.

Though she didn't believe he'd leave forever, it was looking like he had. *Okay. Clean slate. Been here before.* In love and out. Hired and laid off. Counting savings, pinching pennies. *Not so bad. I've been through worse.*

Todd had planned to finish a family room in the basement, maybe rebuild the utility shed into office space, big plans for her and her house. She tried not to dwell on him, but she had to decide about their planned vacation to Prague.

A departure date in five days would be a week since he'd left, which should be enough time for him to chill. Yesterday she poked with voicemail, asking where to forward paper mail, but he didn't return her call. Her choice should be obvious, yet apprehension smoldered deep inside, deeper than her bruised heart.

She must decide by tomorrow and hoped for a sign. A helpful sign. A useful sign. Not a spirit slipping between the sheets scaring the willies out of her.

Ask for guidance and let it go. Trust fate.

Kate turned on the four-cup coffeemaker on top of the crammed kitchen counter after maneuvering it around a container of wooden utensils, strategically placed between the electric outlet and the sink's faucet, where a feng shui consultant advised a barrier. She was good at constructing barriers. Bad at making commitments. Forming protective walls was her nature, like the crab symbol of her Cancer sun sign. *Another reason she should go ... to crack her self-imposed shell.* Life had become too cozy, but that was Todd, easy, predictable and oh so comfortable.

She passed through the back room, a sunroom in name only, draped a shawl across her shoulders and stood at the screen slider where the veil between here and there seemed most thin. Morning mist masked the forest preserve that bordered her lot. Southwest winds could carry the sound of traffic on the interstate, while gusts from the east amplified train whistles from across town. When the air was windless, like now, the silence seemed unnatural. Like a movie scene on mute. Not nearly as creepy as hearing the killer's footsteps, the thumping music of a hungry shark or alien eggs hatching in a distant planet's dark cave. Still eerie because the lack of sound defied reality, and skirting the fringe of reality held far less appeal than it once did. Yet, the forest drew her. If she didn't resist, it would pull her psyche into the otherworld. She rubbed her arms as last night's cold clung to her skin.

Danger is close.

She stared at the tree line as if it were meaningful, as if in her dream she'd wandered there, seen something there—as if she should *know* about it but had forgotten. Her psychic vision had become as foggy as the trees. Faded, as if she used Photoshop to adjust transparency to forty percent.

It's what you asked for.

She poured a mug of coffee and set it on the back porch table, grabbed her Nikon and clicked half a dozen shots of the hazy landscape growing more ethereal as warm daylight met cool ground air.

Kate transferred the photos to her iMac, opened them in the editing program and clicked through a slideshow. "Nice." Someday she'd use them to dress her website. *Forget the forest. Don't get distracted.* She stored the images in a new folder titled Spooky Forests, but even as she typed, spooky didn't seem ominous enough to describe her feelings. She moved the cursor to open the thesaurus, knowing she could easily spend half an hour searching for a more accurate term. She had to decipher the dream and the pall it left behind—and she had to get it right. Was she drawn *to* the forest or warned *away* from it? Did she dream of *her* forest or *a* forest? The slightest error could result in danger ... in death. *Stop.*

KATE HOPED to knock off her to-do list by early afternoon, beginning with positioning images in the medical center brochure. With those files in production, she'd be clear of work commitments and free to travel. Her client's final copy changes were due the next day, so tomorrow became her milestone. Finish and bill the brochure. Decide about Prague.

With Todd's unexpected exit, Kate finally understood her brother's hit-and-run strategy with the women in his life. *What would Jack do?* If his vacation plans veered off-road, he'd have steered onto Plan B. He seemed to have a strategy for everything. Navy. College. U.S. Marshal Service. FBI. Made Mom and Dad proud—unlike her three-year curriculum in a non-accredited art school. She'd supported herself, self-employed for three years, and they still didn't understand what she did, but then, they didn't ask.

At 7:00 a.m. Jack was sure to be back from his run, showered, dressed and on his way to work.

He answered his cell phone on the second ring. "Kate? What's wrong?"

"Todd's gone."

"Again?"

She flapped her arms like a flightless bird. "No. Still."

"I know. You told me on Saturday."

"But—"

"I can't talk now. Call me if something important happens."

Kate ignored the dial tone and continued the conversation as if Jack were supportive and sympathetic—as if he were still listening. "I think Todd wants to come back but doesn't know how, so his spirit came to smooth the way." She imagined Jack affirming that her idea was clever and perceptive. "I thought I'd stopped that extreme paranormal intrusion, the scary stuff like visits from spirits and ghosts and real life drama. I thought I'd sealed the door to the other side, ever since ... well, you know. I can't bear the responsibility.

"But it's happening again. I don't know who or what will creep into my dreams, and I don't want them lurking in my house." She cinched her shawl tighter.

Be calm. It won't be more than you can manage.

Back at her computer with a second coffee warmed in the microwave, she checked e-mail and her site's form mail. With work slowing, redesigning and maintaining *Dreamwatch.com* had become her only diversion.

Prague will change everything.

The Dreamwatch mailbox held one new message, a familiar plea. "I had that dream again. What does it mean? Please help."

That dream had been submitted by Evelyn, screen named LittleEv, a forty-year-old mother of three who lived in South Carolina. Not a stranger. Their online friendship began the week Dreamwatch went live. They hoped to meet one day. Kate *knew* her and the woman couldn't be more normal. LittleEv's disaster premonitions—Katrina, Haiti, Japan—were spot on. As accurate as her own, before she stopped them.

Guilt for not responding knotted at the base of Kate's skull. LittleEv's first message about the vision was still in her inbox after two weeks. *Two dreams in two weeks.* She rubbed her neck as she opened the original form mail and read it again—like she did almost every day.

*Hundreds of dazed people stagger up concrete steps
from underground. Drooling. Vomiting. Mouths
foaming. Their clothes stink of urine. People drop to the
street, twitching and jerking, screaming they're blind,
pupils constricted to pin holes. They lie on the ground
unable to breathe while police rush into tunnels wearing
gas masks that hide expressions of fear.*

*People panic. I see lights everywhere, a sparkly
bridge and orange tree leaves. The only name I get is
Charles Charles. I hear it twice. I don't know why.*

*I sense flowing water like in a river or stream, or
through a pipe or hose. Could that symbolize something
passing through a confined space like trains moving
through tunnels or cars on bridges?*

*I'm frightened and don't know what to do. I feel this
is a premonition of a future event. What does your sixth
sense tell you?*
—LittleEv

The threat of LittleEv's vision deserved more than a guess at
its meaning, and the doubled name confused evaluation even
more. What did it mean? There was a time she would
immediately understand complex symbols and meanings, but
Kate couldn't dissect the vision any better than the day she first
read it.

Insight will come when least expected. Words in your head.

She should have sent a polite "Thanks for your story, but
I'm concerned it may incite … incite some—" *Some heinous
thing.* She could have filed it with the others, forgotten it or
tried to, but the vision didn't fade from her thoughts.

Kate's recent dreams confused her, so how dare she attempt
to explain LittleEv's? Her own clairvoyant visions made even
less sense. Bright silver lines reaching to the sky. Fire and

bridges and snow in September.

She underscored phrases in her dream journal and added punctuation. _Silver lines. Snow in September???_ Doesn't happen in Connecticut, nor in Prague. That wasn't a sign she needed. It must represent something else. Something white? Pure?

Words in her head answered with clarity.

No. Something chilling.

FOUR

NEAR WORCESTER, MASSACHUSETTS
Tuesday, Early Morning

A SINGLE COMPUTER SCREEN glared in the darkened offices of Crime Scene Services. Trooper Leigh Danner flipped open a notepad where she had described a business card found near the body of her newest case. A purple card with only a Web address: *Dreamwatch.com.*

Danni entered the URL, hoping to find a clue to the victim's identity. She didn't expect to spill her guts on a paranormal website, but stranger things had happened this night to lead her here at 4:45 a.m., in dead silence, except for quiet tapping under her desk where her foot twitched against the tiled floor.

No one was on the road but me.

She typed her experience on the site's Submit Your Story form:

> *I'm still shaking. I can't believe what just happened or that it happened to someone like me. I'm a state trooper … almost made it through my on-call shift when my pager signaled. My heart raced like it always does when a call comes in, or the microwave beeps, the alarm clock or any repetitive sound resembling the pager's buzz. I called the shift commander for my assignment.*

The police chief of a small town near Worcester had requested Crime Scene Services. I was to rendezvous with local police off the highway exit, eighteen miles away. The officer would escort me to a cabin off a wooded country road where a body had been found.

Rain had stopped hours earlier and the night was warmer than most. It was a moonless sky and dense ground fog in the valley slowed me down. By the time I arrived, it was 2:36 a.m.

I drove the narrow road until I spotted the cruiser then stopped on the opposite side, but the officer didn't do anything. All my lights were on and I waited, but nothing happened. So, I got out of my SUV and crossed the road. The officer exited his cruiser and asked if I was Trooper Jane Smith (not my real name). He said he'd lead me to the scene and retuned to his car. I turned to run back to my vehicle.

One step onto the road and headlight beams blinded me. I froze. A blast of cold air hit my face as I closed my eyes to certain death. My vest jerked behind me, its zipper cutting into my throat. I stumbled backward to the shoulder. Gravel spattered my legs like shotgun pellets as a pickup roared past. Inches away.

I turned to thank the officer for grabbing me, only he wasn't there. I could see by the interior lights he was seated in his car.

No one was on the road but me.

I know what I felt on my shoulder. A firm hand gripped me. Stronger than humanly possible. One step forward and I'd have been killed.

I sat shaking in my SUV, angry at the jerk for nearly flattening me.

I don't believe what can't be proved. I process crime scene evidence to document events. I don't know how to process this, but I know what happened and I know what I felt.

Someone or some ... thing saved my life.

I never gave much thought to fate or destiny, but I can't help thinking, I wasn't meant to die tonight.

Anyway, I found your site and needed to unload. It helps to know I'm not alone.

—Anonymous Trooper

Danni's hand quivered over the Submit Your Story button, heart racing as if her pager had buzzed. Recalling the incident and typing the details made the experience difficult, if not impossible, to deny.

No one was on the road but me.

I know what I felt on my shoulder.

The submission form didn't require an e-mail address. Not even a name. Several stories in the site's archives had been posted anonymously. No detail could be traced back to her, yet she hesitated. The incident wasn't something to talk about at work where ridicule was sure to follow.

She *had* to tell someone. *Oh, what the hell.*

She clicked the button.

FIVE

CONNECTICUT
Tuesday, Early Morning

KATE HELD HER BREATH. Memories of a dream were fading too fast and anything but stone-like posture would disturb the link between this world and the next. She gasped as the dream's details slipped from her spirit's hold. *A misty river. Statues silhouetted along a bridge. Spotlights cast on horrified faces.* The gray and the blue and the red. And then it was gone.

How long had she sat in darkness? Asleep? Or lost in a trance on a mystical road?

The clock on the DVD player read 5:46. The table lamp's soft radiance lit a circle around her like the white light she often summoned to form a psychic shield, a rite that had replaced bedtime prayer. A practice that of late, had earned an impressive failure rate.

The last images from another place and time flashed in her mind. Menacing and terrifying. Kate collected her energy to reestablish her presence. In her body. In her home. In the here and now.

There was something comforting about the quiet empty house, like when your car stops spinning out of control. You brace for impact but come to rest on the side of the road heading in the right direction, frozen like she was now. Stiff and cold. A shadowy silhouette of yourself like a statue on a bridge

… while your mind catches up.

Then the shaking begins.

You've eluded damage or danger and can continue your journey, if only you knew where you were going. *Or where you had been.*

Her eyes darted around the living room to familiar things, cherished things—a brass palm tree from Rome, Canopic jars from Egypt, lava rocks from an ancient volcano. Vacation mementos and scrapbooks of daring times. She was adjusting to being alone and felt more like herself than she had in two years, as if doors had opened and air had cleared, like that first day after winter when you raised windows and smelled spring. Dormancy ended.

Her car had stopped spinning. Her journey began.

KATE WAS ALMOST FREE. The medical center brochure was all but complete. Copy changes had been finalized and approved, and she'd sized and positioned all the photos, except one.

She launched the page layout program, InDesign, and opened the image in Photoshop to balance the color before placing it on the inside front cover. A slight adjustment of the cyan level corrected the staff's flesh tones, but the picture's blue tint triggered a memory of last night's bridge dream, though not enough to recall specifics.

It'll come back.

She enlarged the photo to six hundred percent, magnifying two white specks on the front lawn. *Rats.* A Dunkin' Donuts bag and discarded paper cup. She swept the cursor over the debris and hit it with the Clone Stamp tool, replacing litter with unspoiled grass.

Kate had arranged for the hospital grounds to be mowed, trimmed and raked until flawless and posed the staff at the main entrance with no faces obscured. *No small feat.* She hadn't noticed windblown litter in the frame, nor would anyone spot a couple of white specks in the printed piece, but she'd know they were there. She scrolled the image from top to bottom and side to side, correcting every imperfection in mindless rote.

Her hand stalled as she stared. She would have missed the distant bridge at normal size, but enlarged— Its bluish tint contrasted against the sun's cast on the crowd of faces. Images from her dream rushed into consciousness, replacing the shot on the screen.

The dream. I remember the dream. She strolled on the Charles Bridge in Prague where a man emerged from a crowd of tourists. He passed nearby, walking in the opposite direction. A slight limp marred his gait. A shadow concealed his face. Though his presence was familiar, she sensed an aura of danger about him. She waited for him to step into the lantern's light, but was distracted by a glow on a nearby hill. People bumped against her and she almost dropped her camera. She bent to clutch her belongings and nearly collided with the man. When she looked up, he was gone.

Kate jotted notes in her dream journal: *Sunset. Bridge. Crowd. Dark stranger on Charles.* Got it.

Was Todd the mystery man? It didn't matter. The dream showed *her* on the bridge and left her feeling she'd soon collide with change. *Don't need a dream to show me that.*

Decision made. She'd go to Prague as planned.

In a way, she was already there.

KATE HAD TO REMIND her brother about her travel plans.

Jack answered his cell, "Kate, what's wrong?"

Why did he always assume something was wrong? "I'm going to Prague."

"Todd came back?"

She hesitated as her lips parted and swear words ran in her mind. *Don't.* She couldn't tell him what happened on Sunday night … could never ever tell him about feeling Todd in her bed. "No, but the trip's paid for and I finished the hospital brochure. I'll bill the job today and if I watch my expenses, the money will carry me to the end of the year." She left her computer in search of her coffee mug, nuzzling the phone between her ear and shoulder. "Timing couldn't be better."

"You're flying to Eastern Europe by yourself?"

"I dreamed I should go." She paused for the tirade that didn't come. *Quick, change the subject.* "What are *you* doing this weekend?" She rummaged around the art taboret and the low shelves of the bookcase, the spots where her coffee often hid. Shifted clutter on the dining table, kitchen counter …

"Not inviting trouble by traveling alone to a foreign country."

There's the Jack I know and love.

He breathed into the phone. "Can't you postpone until I can go with you?"

She couldn't recall when she'd last heard an offer so insincere; she choked back a laugh. "You're kidding, right? I love you, but I can't see us traveling together. Ever."

"Can't one of your friends go with you?"

"None have traveled out of the States and I don't want babysitting them to cramp my experience. Coop was my only good traveling companion." Her throat tightened when she said her name. Elizabeth Cooper, Kate's best friend since grade school, had gone MIA two years ago—her mind and maybe her soul were missing. Her body remained in coma at a nursing home down the road.

Kate's head throbbed and her stomach wrenched with a sudden queasiness as a migraine was born. "I'd rather just go by myself."

Jack's silence seemed to shout disapproval. He wouldn't dare talk about Coop.

No one would.

"My flight leaves Saturday."

"*This* Saturday?"

"I hoped to see you, but I'm not up to a four hour drive to Vermont. Too much to do." She wandered to the back porch. "*There* you are."

"Who's there?"

"I'm talking to my coffee." She took a cold sip that might have been from yesterday. "Can you come down here?"

He paused too long. "Call before you leave for the airport."

"I will, but not for a last minute lecture. Remember *almost Special* Agent Kasabian, you can't scold me like some FBI rookie. We sit at the same table on holidays."

"Ouch."

"Seriously, any plans while I'm gone?"

"Hanging out with Dante."

Dante Benard, Jack's college roommate, was like a favorite uncle. She and Jack affectionately called him Crash for all the cars he'd demolished, including three cruisers during a short-lived cop career. "I wish I could be there. I need a good laugh."

"Yeah, well, lately he's not laughing. I'll fill you in another time."

"I'll come up when I return. After my jet lag. Tell Dante so we can plan something fun."

The phone clicked. A dial tone replaced Jack's good-bye.

Kate held the handset at arm's length, smirking with a sense of accomplishment.

She'd told Jack she was going. There was no turning back.

SIX

MASSACHUSETTS
Tuesday Morning

THE BARRACKS WASHROOM smelled of pine disinfectant, an odor Danni had learned to love. She washed her hands, even though she'd scrubbed them an hour ago when she first returned from her call-out.

The office wall clock read five fifty-nine. Several hours might pass before the District Attorney's office secured a search warrant for the cabin, the scene of an apparent homicide.

Danni slipped out of her utility vest and smoothed the fabric over the back of her chair, tucking in the neckline tag that read, Target Boy's Size 16. The vest's right side bore the State Seal and white type on the left identified her mission: Crime Scene Services.

Sleeves pushed to her elbows, she scanned and entered John Doe's prints, but didn't find an immediate match, nor had she found the vic's wallet. No problem. She'd identify him soon enough. In five years she'd not failed and wasn't about to start now.

She checked and replied to department and personal e-mails. Anything to pass time. Anything to avoid revisiting her crazy experience on the road. She had to put away that incident like she'd put away the barbaric slash across John Doe's throat.

Where's the warrant?

She had checked the URL listed on the business card, her only clue, intending to skim the entire site. Quick. Fast. Looking for a lead to John Doe's identity—or to the killer's.

Even during her early check, the glossy card was out of place in the rustic cabin, though she resisted forming conclusions. There was something compelling about Dreamwatch.com. Easy colors and soft-edged graphics seemed crafted by a feminine hand. *A woman couldn't kill like that. She'd lack height and strength.* Later she'd ask digital services to track the webmaster.

Danni clicked through links to the archives. It was a curious site. Small and simple, with stories written in plain language by ordinary people like the card stated. Several claimed experiences similar enough to hers so hers wasn't that strange after all.

Earlier, she'd submitted a short version of her impossible episode, before reviewing fluff pages for any connection to the crime, checking links to: About, Bio, News and Resources.

Nothing.

The Glossary was briefly distracting, but no one word defined what had happened to her.

Her quiet office. The incident on the road. Ghost stories. The site's mysterious images lured her. The longer she looked, the more detail she saw. Eerie faces emerged from backgrounds. First one, then another. Her muscles tensed.

A loud screech made her jolt against the chair, roll it far from her desk and from the images on the screen. The janitor's pail had scraped against the file cabinet behind her. *What the hell am I doing?* She tiptoed the chair back to her desk and shut down the computer.

Where's that damn warrant?

THE PHONE RANG at seven ten. "Wake up. Get to work." Lt. Mike Riley's voice was as shrill as the screech of the janitor's pail.

"It's about freakin' time. I've been waiting since five. Hours, Riley. Hours." She stashed evidence bags and print lifters in compartments along her pant legs. "Meet you there."

"Now. Don't make me wait. You know how I get."

"Yeah, yeah, I'm on my way." She slipped her vest on and grabbed her briefcase, weapon and purse. The sun eased around the building as she crossed the parking lot to her state Ford Explorer, arms wrapped around extra supplies: a box of latex gloves that nearly matched the purple business card from the cabin, and a cardboard evidence box to safely transport a big knife if she found one. Her briefcase nestled on the front seat and her laptop on the passenger floor. A SIG SAUER pistol was locked in the glove box.

She was on the road within ten minutes of receiving the detective's call, time enough for McDonald's drive-thru. "Sweet iced tea, large, and a breakfast burrito." She handed over a five stashed in her pocket and tucked the food bag into the console on top of a cache of peppermint gum and sanitizing hand wipes.

She twisted to check for an opening, pulled into traffic and drove toward the cabin. A lovely fall day. Perfect weather to work outside. Riley won't mind waiting. Summer had been quiet. Too quiet. Only three deaths, all from natural causes and all older adults. Danni didn't like that. It meant fall would bring disaster.

Danni exited the highway, driving past the patch of ground she'd stood on last night. It seemed foreign in sunlight as if she'd never been there. She doubted that last night's incident happened, because … How could it? Only a miracle could have saved her life. Was she destined for something great? To solve this major crime? Or tomorrow's crime? Or the next?

She turned onto the gravel road leading to the cabin. Daylight exposed the ruts she was unable to avoid last night, but the smell was the same. Moist earth. Rotting leaves. This was why she didn't like fall. Bright colors and robust scents teased with excitement before striking with death and decay.

Last night's fog had been clammy against her collar. Even now her neck felt a chill. Her shoulder ached from the grip. She'd been yanked backward, the clench painful, like a vise, pulling her from the rush of wind, away from calamity. Away from death. The more she thought of it, the stronger the grasp.

Her cells held its memory as if the cold hand still seized her, its hold tightening, its icy fingers reaching to her bones.

SEVEN

CONNECTICUT
Tuesday Morning

I'M FREE. Kate had uploaded the brochure's digital files to the printer's FTP site and a PDF invoice to the client. They were happy. She was happy. She showered, dressed and scrambled the next to last egg for breakfast, toasted the third to last slice of rye bread, and mixed tonic water from last Christmas to make the orange juice stretch another few days. If the dining table was clean, she'd have sat down to a real meal with flatware and napkins, paper and pen, but the mess forced her to stand on the back porch with the egg plate balanced in her hand while she organized the day's tasks in her mind. Clearing the table soared to the top of her list.

She set the plate in the dishpan then hauled from the basement a medium size suitcase on wheels and her favorite carry-on that served double-duty as a footstool while she waited in airports. A light spray of Lysol and a dose of fresh air would rid their musty smell. Tomorrow she'd select a travel wardrobe and still have time to launder what she needed.

Bills set on the table in piles to pay, the old-fashioned way with written checks and Forever postage stamps. Several weeks of direct mail advertising found its end in the kitchen trash. Last week's laundry was finally folded and put away. The table surface was visible for the first time in a month, leaving room to organize paperwork: passport, plane ticket, hotel confirmation, a list of must-see destinations suggested on tourism sites, a currency converter and a city map she'd burned into her brain. Todd's ticket and passport were gone.

Four days to departure. She could have squeezed in a visit to Jack's after all, but it was better not to push the clock. Clean up. Chill out. Catch up on site maintenance.

The Dreamwatch mailbox held two new messages.

A note from LittleEv read, "Just checking in. No pressure." Kate laughed aloud.

Two of LittleEv's dreams in two weeks. Two pieces of litter on the hospital lawn and two new site messages. *Better pay attention to twos.*

She opened a new entry sent earlier that morning by a Massachusetts state trooper:

> *… I'm still shaking.*
> *No one was on the road but me.*
> *I know what I felt on my shoulder. A firm hand gripped me. Stronger than humanly possible. One step forward and I'd have been killed.*
> *I know what happened and I know what I felt …*

Don't I know it. Kate gaped at the screen, heart pounding as if she were there. Smelling the forest. Seeing the headlights. Feeling the rush of wind and the surge of fear, culminating in deliverance. *Like a driver whose car spins out of control and comes to rest by the side of the road.*

Then the shaking begins.

The state trooper in the forest. An image flashed in her mind; the trooper was small and stretched to see over her vehicle's steering wheel. Traffic, then trees. Was *this* the forest in her subconscious? A foreshadowing of this submission and the cause of her forest fixation? Why she shot forest photos filed as Spooky? Was this *the something* she should know?

Her fingers trembled as she clicked the Dreamweaver icon to launch the site software. She copied the trooper's story, pasted it onto the Fate & Destiny page, ran spellcheck and the Clean Up HTML function, in case she messed up the code by mistake. Her technical ineptness to navigate a steep learning curve sometimes brought her to tears, but she'd rejected tutoring and outsourcing to preserve a sacred bond with her visitors, like the connection she felt to the anonymous state trooper.

From years online, Kate knew which submissions would come to haunt her, like LittleEv's predictions of catastrophe and this trooper's, who wrote of a remote road in Massachusetts where she was touched by a warm spirit or brushed by a cold ghost. Plucked from certain death to salvage her destiny. A rare paranormal experience even among the rare.

Their stories weren't finished.

Somehow. Somewhere. Their lives would intersect—hers, the trooper's and LittleEv's. She knew they would. Deep inside her soul, she knew the truth of LittleEv's dreams, the truth of the trooper's fate and the truth of her own foreboding premonition of terror …

Like she knew Todd was never coming back.

EIGHT

MASSACHUSETTS
Tuesday Morning

DANNI PARKED IN FRONT of the cabin at the road's end. Eight o'clock and Lt. Riley eyeballed his watch. His lips pursed as if she were late. She climbed out, opened the passenger side door and set her breakfast on top of her briefcase, popping open the sipping hole of her iced tea cup and checking her fingernail for damage.

"Manicure run late?" Riley smirked.

Danni bit into her burrito. "Got the warrant?"

"Where's my coffee?" He opened the van's rear door and pulled a handful of booties from a plastic bin.

"I'm not your office girl. Get your own damn coffee."

He turned toward the crime lab chemist. "She sets up breakfast like we're at a Patriot's tailgate party."

Danni muzzled a smile. "Hi, Lisa."

"Don't let him get to you." Lisa adjusted the strap of her supply bag. "He just got here."

"Get off my case about breakfast. I was here till after four, remember?" She chewed the last of the burrito and tossed the wrapper into her car. "And the vic's not getting any deader." After a gulp of tea, she set the cup in the console and grabbed her camera.

Riley waved the warrant in her face and stashed it in his breast pocket.

Danni aimed her lens at a jumble of hand tools piled on steps rising to the front deck while Riley named each as he wrote in his notebook.

"Hammer, nail gun, pry bar …"

The same local officer from last night yawned and greeted them on the deck while they slipped on booties and gloves.

Inside the cabin, the stale air smelled like the sealed rooms and basements of past crime scenes that reeked of blood and death. Danni's flashlight panned across the beamed ceiling, knotty walls and wide floorboards. "Stop." She held out her hand like a traffic cop. A dozen mud-dried boot steps circled the body and laid paths to and from the front door. She shot photos with and without numbered markers. "Mud and blood. Come in but keep off the prints."

"We'll float to the body if it makes your job easier." Riley rose on tiptoes as if levitating.

She shined a magnifier lamp. "These sole patterns are *not* identical. They're different sizes, too. It looks like we have one … two … three people here."

"Cripes. Tell me *one* of them is the vic." Riley backed out of the way and leaned against the far wall on the cabin's east side where he cracked open a window.

Danni squatted, angling her flashlight on the bottom of the victim's boot. "Sure is. He matches some of these, plus that clear print by the door." She wiggled the light.

Riley glanced out the window, pinching his nose. "You know it smells more like an August body than late September."

Danni's brow furrowed. "I smell it, too, but not down here. Not where the body *is*." She circled the room in a slow motion. "We've got a good one here." Her torch lit a bloody fingerprint on the doorknob. "This guy was in a hurry to leave. Sloppy,

sloppy boy."

"That's gold. If he's that careless, he doesn't give a crap if we know who he is." Riley noted the bloody print. "What's your gut tell ya?"

She shrugged. From several hundred crime scenes, you learn what should or shouldn't be there. Some cops called it instinct while some said hunch. The person who managed the Dreamwatch site might argue it was more. Lingering energy? Unsettled spirits? "I don't know, but something's off."

"I feel the same."

Danni moved beside the body with her arms drooped at her sides, ignoring the living souls beside her while she absorbed the sense of the cabin. "This is a great spot to hide out." She peered through the glass where Riley stood then through the window of the back door. Nothing but forest. "One thing bugs me. We're out in the middle of nowhere ..." She faced the police vehicles in the front drive. "So, how'd he get here? Where's his car?"

Riley called out to the local cop at the front door.

The cop leaned in. "We didn't tow it."

Riley snapped, "We'll deal with the car later. Tell me about the vic."

"No defensive wounds. No calluses, cuts or abrasions. If the deck tools are his, he didn't use them every day." Lisa taped paper bags around John Doe's hands. "No watch, no rings, no tats that I can see. I'll scrape his nails at the lab, but they look clean."

Danni stooped beside the body. An attractive young man, late twenties, well-groomed and dressed in neat khakis from J. Crew and a Land's End flannel shirt. Name brands she also wore. A down vest had absorbed most of the blood. "He sure doesn't look like he lives way out here. Baby smooth hands and new boot tread. A clean-shaven city boy in pressed pants. *He's* what's off. Who the hell is this guy?"

Riley's cell buzzed. He pulled out his notepad. "Spell it. C-a-l-u-m-e-t. Ryan. When did he buy the place?" He pocketed the phone and popped a stick of Dentyne. "Vic's new to the area. Assumed ownership two weeks ago. Ryan Calumet." Riley scanned the room. "Was probably doing maintenance before sealing it for the winter."

Danni asked, "Does anyone in town know this guy? Can neighbors confirm this body is Calumet?"

"What neighbors? Local PD will canvass around town today. Until then, we can't be sure."

"Then he's still John Doe to me. Motor Vehicles must have a license photo and I'll keep looking for Calumet's prints. AFIS didn't have him. No reason for IAFIS until we dead-end here. How'd we get the call, anyway?"

"Two hunters walked into police headquarters." Heads turned toward the officer on the deck. "They gave their account and led the chief here. Said they'd used this cabin last fall. Thought it was abandoned. Turns out the out-of-state owner hadn't been here in years. It's been on the market eighteen months. When the hunters checked it for this season, they found the vic. Never walked through the door. Came right in to report it. Chief verified their story and by the time that happened it was late last night. He called CSS and you know the rest."

"Makes sense. You seen anything like this?" Danni pointed to the fatal wound, throat sliced ear to ear with one hard cut of airway and artery. No hesitation. Trachea cartilage reflected white in the torchlight beam. "Who kills like this?"

Riley leaned over the body. "Military. Butcher. Hunter. Someone who can field dress a deer. Someone not squeamish about close combat." He backed away. "That ain't the work of a typical gang banger, I'll tell ya that."

Lisa plucked and bagged a few hairs from John Doe's head and compared them to a single hair her tweezers pinched off his shirt. "I've got something." She dropped the hair into an evidence bag and tagged it. "Victim has longish, brown silky hair, but this strand is short, black and wiry. I don't need my scope to see they couldn't be more different."

"Maybe it went down like this." Riley twisted his upper torso and pointed toward the front door. "John Doe parks his car, unloads his tools and drops them on the steps, figuring in a minute he'll turn on lights and bring them inside. He enters. It's dark, right? Perp's hiding behind the door and grabs our guy from behind. Never saw it comin'." Riley's forefinger eased the door closed and pointed to the wall behind it. "Check the paneling for fibers."

"Sounds about right, but where's the damn car?"

"You didn't find the vic's keys. Perp took the car. Gotta be. Cast the footprints and tire tracks nearest the tools."

Danni lit the area behind the door at shoulder height where rough timber had snagged a fuzzy filament. She offered her magnifier to Riley. "Looks like grey fleece, like from a running suit."

Riley grinned and gave Danni a high five. "We *are* goood."

The scent of crushed leaves drifted on a northeasterly breeze—along with an unmistakable stench that could only mean one thing.

Corpse.

Danni covered her nose with her sleeve and turned her head away from the window. "What the hell happened here?"

NINE

SOMEWHERE IN CONNECTICUT
Tuesday, Midmorning

YUSUF SHOULD HAVE BURIED the other body, but the man's sudden appearance had been too shocking, and the cabin's location so isolated that months might pass before it was found. Both logical excuses for his carelessness, but he knew the truth. He panicked and he was lazy.

The last stage of his assignment hadn't been as tidy as planned, and he hoped he would not need to explain the casualties or why his money was almost gone. In less than a week he would reunite with Ali and until then he must make no mistake. Success was too close to risk.

He drove the infidel's car from Massachusetts, southbound on the interstate until fuel was low; he abandoned it in a commuter lot between Springfield and Hartford, and walked to Bradley airport where he boarded a limousine bound for New York. When the coach dropped passengers at the Shefford Four Seasons Hotel in central Connecticut, he exited and did not return.

An autumn allergy scratched at Yusuf's eyes, but he could do nothing to attract attention, not even seek relief. No matter. *Malesh.* He had only to endure a few more days of hiding. He hated this place and was desperate to leave—the region, the country, this life on earth.

A mile away, Yusuf checked into a room for two nights in a cheap motel that seemed more suitable than the luxury hotel with limousine service, security monitors and staff. He unpacked all he carried, except for a camera, memory cards and a computer jump drive that were to be shipped to an overseas guesthouse.

The man's wallet and overnight sack held a passport he might someday peddle on the black market and an airline ticket to Prague. He turned on the man's cell phone for a moment, confident no one would be tracking its location so soon. Its screen displayed a photo of a young woman with hair in soft curls that fell short of her shoulders. Rich brown color complemented thoughtful eyes and the light tan of her square face. A compassionate smile invited approach, though he would never act on such temptation with a woman who was likely the man's whore.

He turned off the phone and sat on the creaky bed, rubbing his eyes and forehead, spreading the contents of his billfold on the nightstand. He organized the little cash he had left, the New Jersey driver's license he was given on arrival in the U.S., his sister Sahar's school photo and her crayon drawing of an ice cream cone from the day of the sandstorm. He pushed aside his papers and cash, glaring at the drawing. Tasting the ice cream. Smelling the Nile. Choking on brown dust. *The* haboob *was a bad omen.*

Yusuf doused a hand towel with hot tap water, wiped his face and neck, and held the cloth against his forehead until it lost all warmth. He ran cold water over the short end and pressed it against his eyes before returning to the bed. Feet up and crossed at the ankles, he leaned against the headboard, shifting pillows to prop himself as he held his sister's sketch. Fire burned in his heart as he recalled his last good day with her.

He was busy with studies, but the day was hot and she wanted to watch excursion boats, drink mango juice and eat ice cream at their favorite café across the Nile. Father was working in the south on an Aswan Dam power project, while the family driver, an orphaned man from Sudan who lived in the service quarters, had taken Mother and his brothers' wives to the Port Said Free Shop. They would be gone until nightfall.

Sahar drew the crayon picture and pleaded with Yusuf to take her out, too. So they went. It was the best day with laughter and talk, and she spoke of her wish to someday marry a surgeon doctor, and all the family would live in a house with rooms more beautiful than the Hilton hotel.

Strong winds and a cold rain came upon them. Feluccas sailed to shore when gusts stirred the river, and the sky changed from blue to red then ghost white. All of Cairo and Giza turned yellow from the sands of the Libyan desert.

The trees and heavy things fell, and the fires came. People died.

A week after the sandstorm, university friends came to Yusuf's home to see his family's new colour TV. They told him of trouble at a political protest in Tahrir Square. The National Guard had responded and Central Security Forces assisted to control the crowd. Plain-clothed and uniformed armored police dragged protestors and citizens into building entrances and thrashed them. The violence against both demonstrators and passing pedestrians turned Tahrir into a bloody battleground. It was then that Sahar, whose primary school was visiting the nearby National Museum, was struck by a club and left to die.

Yusuf first learned she was killed while he was in the salon decorated with the mural of Paradise. *Life gives us everything but takes from us the precious thing. Sahar died and I cannot forget her, forever.*

He closed his eyes and tugged the frayed sheet over his head.

No one saw if Sahar's fatal blow had come from the Security Force or from a demonstrator, but Yusuf knew who was to blame—America. The root of all his trouble.

Hurt had built inside and his heart was not relaxed. He worried about everything and could not keep himself to be stilled.

He gave his voice to jihad; it grew strong and reached the ears of Central Security, who kidnapped him. The gang pulled him from the family's Chevrolet Impala while riding to Bani-Suef on the road after Oasis Faiyum. They caged him like a dog at the Cairo Zoo and tortured him for what he knew of Eastern Flame activities.

Early plans failed, but never mind, the day would come.

TEN

AN OILY RESIDUE marred the window of the cabin's back door as if someone had pressed their forehead against the glass. "I've got a sample," Danni said to Riley. "These doorjamb fibers look identical to that strand from behind the front door."

"Let's find the source of the stench. Wrap the whole package so we know what we have." Riley jolted the door, kicking its bottom so hard, it smashed against outside cladding with a booming crash. Birds squawked and twigs snapped as squirrels scurried from ground positions to the safety of trees.

Danni turned her head into the northwest breeze and the odor of rotting flesh. "This way, I think." Her foot slid on moist shale tiles surrounding a well's hand pump; she made a mental note to check its handle for prints when she processed the tools stacked on the front steps. To the right of their path, water had puddled in ruts where tire tracks disappeared into the woods between damaged shrubs. She and Riley followed the stink coming from the opposite direction. Danni lifted a yard-long branch from the ground and flicked off crawly creatures.

"Find something?" he said.

"Walking stick."

Riley pointed forty yards ahead, slightly to their left. "There it is."

She honed her sight toward the buzz of flies. "Oh geez." Human fingers pierced a shroud of leaves like a zombie reaching from its grave. *That goddamn Web site.* She grimaced.

Riley shot a look at her that seemed intolerant of her revulsion.

Unprofessional. Get yourself together. Using her stick, she scattered organic waste from around the hand, tracing resistance that shaped an arm, shoulder, head and torso. "Better call …" Her voice fell to a whisper. "For the cadaver dog."

Like flipping a switch, she and Riley powered their cell phones. Danni called her supervisor. "We found another. Buried. Yeah, I need people."

Riley called headquarters. "Two. Could be more."

Her heart pumped faster and her breathing quickened. "I'm here with Detective Lieutenant Mike Riley." Danni put distance between Riley's phone call and hers.

"No slip ups, Danner."

"Yes, sir." She rolled her eyes.

"And for crissakes, make sure I can find you. The team's on their way."

"Yes, I'll run yellow tape at the main road. I'll do it now."

A single body had become routine, but two killed at different times … few investigators would see. Supervisors would want their names attached. Someone would leak to the media, and reporters and news anchors from as far as Boston, Springfield and maybe even Hartford were bound to appear; she almost heard their choppers overhead.

"Let's check out the ridge." Riley aimed toward the tire tracks and damaged shrubs.

Danni followed like a duckling trying to match his steps. "We shouldn't be leaving foot impressions like this. It complicates the process and now all the suits are coming. No offense."

"Danni, relax. We're doing everything by the book, so ease up. What's with you today?"

She massaged her shoulder to soothe the ache and to erase recollection of the spirit hand. "I must have caught a chill this morning."

Underbrush thickened except where tracks sheered into the ravine. The air was fresher away from the cabin with whiffs of crushed leaves punctuated by gasoline fumes. They stood on top of the hill scouring the overgrowth where a dry brook bed at the bottom of the trench captured debris. Danni focused her camera's telephoto lens, sweeping the gully from left to right, homing in on an unnatural heap of brush.

"What is it?"

"Taillight on a silver vehicle." She pointed with her stick. "If that's the cabin owner's, maybe his license is in the glove box and we can call it a day."

"Hail Mary for that idea, but who's buried in the woods? Or who's lying in the cabin?"

"I'll tape the property before the crowd arrives. Should we have someone grab lunch?"

He burrowed his nose against his arm when the wind shifted. "I know I said relax, but geezus. Lunch?"

"I'm just sayin', we're gonna be here all day." She winked at Riley. "Guess I'll have to cancel my manicure after all."

DANNI PAUSED for a break at her van, her home away from home, and a last chance for a breather. She peeled off gloves and rubbed her hands with a sanitary wipe. Perched on the rear bumper, she sipped her tea, watered down from melted ice. She popped a stick of peppermint gum to overpower the reek of death stuck in her throat.

These few minutes refreshed her, as long as she didn't think about where she was and what she had seen.

She headed down the road, her footsteps startling chipmunks and field mice and some small lizard thing she didn't know lived in New England. Sunlight sprinkled through the tree canopy on moss and ferns bursting from the forest floor. The picturesque environment was too serene and too lovely to be home to such a slaughter.

ELEVEN

CONNECTICUT
Wednesday

PRAGUE'S EXTENDED WEATHER FORECAST was similar to southern New England's, a bit warmer than normal with mostly sunny skies. *Stroke of luck. Makes packing easier.* Kate stacked on her bed orderly piles of tops, bottoms and lingerie. Nothing too dressy. Only comfortable walking clothes and a couple of sweaters for evenings at outdoor cafés. Maybe a nicer outfit suitable for a concert hall. If that.

She shimmied a dresser drawer to coax it open, knocking one of the framed photos to the floor. *How did the glass* not *break?* She turned it over to see which one had fallen. "Coop."

Kate dropped to the carpet and sat cross-legged with her back against the bed. The photo keepsake cradled in her hands commemorated a six-week trip around India with best friend Coop, college graduation gifts to themselves even though Kate had only received a course completion certificate in commercial art. Coop had made it through law school.

India had been a packing nightmare with climate ranging from stifling heat to ice and snow. How carefree and happy they were riding elephants, sleeping in palace hotels, exploring the Taj Mahal, even spotting Elton John at a Chinese restaurant near the monkey temple.

Her muscles tensed. Who could have foreseen what the future would bring?

That's the problem. You did *see her future.*

You told her and look what happened.

Kate's throat tightened as she ran her fingers over the photo where she and Coop had been marked in observance of a religious holiday, one of hundreds. They'd stepped off the Darjeeling Toy Train after a ride along the southern Himalayas, chatting with other passengers about the breathtaking beauty they'd witnessed. An old bearded guy seemed to come from nowhere to anoint them with some oily substance on his thumb that glued a few grains of rice to their foreheads—tokens of good luck, blessings, they were told. Coop worried the gesture might be blasphemy, but Kate convinced her it was merely a cultural tradition and wiping their foreheads would be rude.

They laughed and joked that the head dots made them initiates in the cult of Shiva or some similar god or goddess. So happy. So much fun. A middle-aged woman from Ohio, also a passenger on the train, had snapped the moment and months later sent identically framed prints to both of them.

Coop's photo hung on the wall of her apartment living room until ....

Don't do this to yourself. It wasn't your fault.

Kate returned the picture to the dresser. "Yes, it was."

DARE SHE VISIT COOP?

Go now. The migraines will worsen until I find peace.

Outside Kate's front picture window, her neighbor Donna walked her dog and Art clipped his Japanese maple, the UPS truck delivered a package to Mr. Allen and the school bus ran four minutes early; a typical day on Summary Road.

She couldn't bring herself to imagine what Coop's average day was like, but wondered if any part of her remained.

Kate knew what was eating her, the cause of her migraines and the vagueness of her premonitions, the commonplace life on her street. What she wouldn't give for Coop to return to such routine. She hadn't visited since the medical center transferred her to the nursing home at Westwoods Senior Care. It seemed like the hospital doctors—and she—had given up on Coop's recovery.

But I haven't. You're in my thoughts every day.

I sacrificed my gift for you.

She stretched the five-minute drive to Westwoods to fifteen, with each stop sign another opportunity to stall. Kate parked in the far corner of the lot facing the building like she always did, with the window rolled down and ignition turned off, her left hand flirting with the door latch.

They used to talk with ease about any subject. Best friends forever.

Would Coop be able to hear her? Would she know she was there? Not even the medical staff agreed with each other, so she was hopeful. Her one-sided conversation had better be brilliant.

She could tell Coop she was leaving for Prague, that she wished they were going together, that she missed her and no one could take her place and life wasn't the same without her confidante. She could tell her all that ...

Or she could say she was sorry for what she did.

Kate moved her hand off the door, twisted the ignition key and drove home. Again.

TWELVE

ALABAMA
Wednesday

MATT CHASE, Supervisory Special Agent with the FBI's Counterterrorism Division, entered the Marshall Space Flight Center in Huntsville at ten in the morning. Two of NASA's software engineers had agreed to enhance the image of a suspect, accidentally captured in the dark background of an al-Qaeda training video that Chase held in his possession. He hoped to leave with a clear snapshot of an extremist named Yusuf, though he was prepared to return to New York no better off than he was now.

He had dressed to reflect the casual attire he anticipated from his NASA buddies. His suit was less Armani and more like JCPenney, but even dressed down there was no disguising who he was, Matthew Christian Chase.

He greeted both men. "It's been too long."

"Here's the man. Been what ... more than a year?" With a sly grin and a wag of his finger, the physicist teased, "It's even better than last time."

"Hard to imagine you can top what you did then," Chase said.

"Much better. Think of VISAR super-sized." The other scientist extended his hand. "I'll take that tape. How'd you come by this?" His brow creased up as if anticipating an epic tale.

"You guys have the wrong idea of what my job is like. I spend most of my time at a computer like you do."

Their scrutinization seemed shameless, gazing like digital scanners from Chase's polished shoes to the parted hair he'd crafted so crisply. He raked his hand across his head.

The scientists shook their heads. "No, we don't. You're our James Bond."

Chase didn't feel like a super agent. Far from it. He'd been credited with disrupting the communications network of the militant Eastern Flame, but only because he'd caved to pressure and acted against his intuition, which ultimately sacrificed long-term benefits for short-term goals. The bureau's ability to eavesdrop became collateral damage and he now felt he'd shot himself in the foot.

All signs pointed to an attack. He knew it but had no proof. His gut tensed with growing menace that the Northeast, *his* Northeast, was the likely target. He felt as helpless as watching an accident about to happen and being unable to stop it. But he had to try, every second until they were defeated. He couldn't live with himself otherwise.

He alone believed in a super-cell—the worst of the worst, recruited from criminal cartels, fringe Arabs and disaffected Russians—fighters who made attacking Western interests their life's work. He wondered if this secret cell had formed long ago, longer than even he suspected. Analysts had been criticized for lacking imagination, but Chase's imagination had no bounds, even when it should.

He'd compiled a list of suspects and chased every rumor of a sighting. If Chase hadn't been his family name, it was what his friends at the bureau would have nicknamed him anyway.

The cell's leader, Ali, and his soldier sidekick, Yusuf, topped his personal watch list for reasons only he understood. Rumors suggested the two had partnered with Vasili Chemenko, Ali's

Russian counterpart, along with *his* loyal lieutenant whose identity remained unknown, and a Somali assassin who was new on the scene. Ali's shrewdness and tenacity were bad enough. Add access to Soviet-era weapons of mass destruction and Chase couldn't imagine a deadlier union. If this pitifully inadequate photo of Yusuf was his best active lead, he needed more than FBI, CIA and NSA resources to stop them. He needed to shoot for the stars.

"James Bond, huh." Chase laughed as he opened his aluminum hard case. "Sorry, guys. No mystery here." He lifted a plain white video box. "Navy souvenir from a curiosity shop in a Kandahar market, along with a *hookah*, an antique musket and a pirated copy of *Top Gun*." He handed over the tape.

The scientist said, "*Top Gun* and a hookah. You're a hoot, Chase. Love it when you visit. What were you doing over there, hosting a screening party? Or Afghan Air Force recruitment?"

Chase winked. "There's no fooling a rocket scientist."

"Come on. We have a station set up. We had to dig a video tape player from basement storage, but it still works. Make yourself at home." The scientist gestured to a wheeled stainless steel cart stocked with drinks and snacks. "Then we'll treat you to lunch. We've discovered a new kitchen type barbecue restaurant down the road."

"I thought you discovered planets and black holes." Chase checked his watch. "My ride leaves at three fifteen. I'm all yours until then."

"Plenty of time." The physicist shot a curious look. "What are you doing, flying commercial?"

"Sometimes." Chase smirked. "Today I lucked out. Hitched a ride with a Navy flier with business down the hall." He poured black coffee and tucked a protein bar in his pocket.

The posh computer station fit like favorite slippers. Beta version tech toys inspired envy. Chase rolled his chair behind the two men, rested his arms on their seat backs and peered over their shoulders. "Are you guys ever going to make money on this new software?"

The physicist loaded the tape. "What's up with you? You've never been interested in economics. Got your eyes on a new frontier? Daddy cut you off?" He launched the software and ran the tape.

Chase studied the faces on the screen. Some were masked, and some he'd previously identified, interrogated and detained.

The scientist cringed. "Dang, they're a nasty-looking bunch."

"But not superhuman," Chase snapped. "Remember that. They're just men like you and me."

"Eight years in counterterrorism, you must be feeling the burn."

Chase wouldn't admit their assumption had nailed it. "Not burned out. More like yearning to hang with a nicer group of people. I don't mean the bureau. They're great.

"Stop! Go back, go back." Chase rocketed to his feet, nearly choking on his coffee. "I mean like this asshole." He jabbed his finger at the top left corner of the screen where the shape of a man was barely visible. "That's got to be Yusuf. The dirtbag there, hiding in shadows."

"Yeah. We'll take care of him. Calm down, Chase."

The physicist squinted at the screen. "I don't see a damn thing. How do you know he's your guy?"

"See the masked fool next to him? He ID'd Yusuf during questioning."

"Watch this." The scientist initiated new generation VISAR software, highlighted the suspect area and ran the program to stabilize the shaky video. They stared at the monitor as the shadowed image with blurred features sharpened to a detailed portrait.

"Got 'im." Chase bent over and squeezed the physicist's shoulder, grinning at the screen. "That's a shot I can use. Grab a still shot." He patted the scientist on the back. "I *am* blown away. What made the difference?"

"Merged data from multiple frames, lightened, brightened and we're done. We only need a couple of seconds of footage to get a clear image."

"Sweet. I'll remember this when the next murky problem lands at my door. I'll need high- and low-res JPEGs and an uncompressed TIFF with the file name, Yusuf_01." Chase logged onto the bureau's server and uploaded the photo. He burned the files onto a CD and a flash drive he tucked into his inside breast pocket. He printed hard copies and stashed everything in his hard case, along with the original video, then locked the case.

"Are you sure you have enough backups?" The scientist laughed. "We could shoot a spare to the space station."

Chase slapped his hand over his heart and shook his head. "You mock my diligence?"

The physicist said, "We could use a guy like you to assess requests in the transfer program. A career change might do you good. Hell, Chase, country air would do you good."

The scientist said, "The public would respond to your … well … to you. Admit it, you dressed down today and you're still a goddamn movie star."

Chase rubbed his chin in an *aw shucks* kind of way.

"You grasp new technologies quicker than most of our applicants and we like having you around." The physicist said, "A simplified version might make it to the home video market. You could do that. Start here and get a couple of years under your belt. I see great commercial opportunity if you ever thought about starting a business. Sleep on it, Chase."

FOR A FEW HOURS, Chase relaxed over lunch with his seldom seen friends for a little tech talk and a lot of laughs. He forgot his life and death worries and his burdened past, while dodging sympathetic queries about his personal life.

His shoulders slumped. "No, there's no one special. My job doesn't allow time for—"

"That's crap."

The physicist said, "Your wife's been gone two years. It's time, buddy."

"I haven't worked through that yet. There are still a few—"

"Yes, I imagine there would be. Look, this isn't an FBI case. You don't have to solve everything." The physicist paused. "But you know what still bugs me?" He leaned toward Chase with a sober expression. "Why'd the hospital take so long to notify you? There was something plain wrong about that whole day."

"I appreciate your empathy, but I don't want to talk about it. Let's enjoy the little time we have." He couldn't tell them that when she was hit, she was with another man. He leaned back against the seat. "So tell me, what's up in space?"

THEY WERE BACK from lunch by two thirty-five and Chase met the pilot for his ride, leaving the Marshall Center with Yusuf's face as clear as if he'd posed for a studio portrait. He could now run the photo through facial recognition software and hoped Yusuf was on the bureau's radar with a full name, aliases, background—with a damned clue to his whereabouts. If Yusuf's prints were in the IAFIS database, he'd have clearer insight of his travels, which might lead him to Ali. If he could break Ali, he'd be closer to learning who pulled strings behind the curtain. Part of him feared the curtain was still made of iron, but he didn't want to go there until he had to.

For all of Ali's accomplishments, education and training, why hadn't he surfaced in Pakistan, Yemen or Indonesia? What the hell was he waiting for?

The cell has to be planning something big—for us.

THIRTEEN

MANHATTAN
Wednesday Evening

MATT CHASE'S Upper West Side neighborhood once suited his lifestyle. His one-bedroom apartment was once spacious enough, even for two people, but he'd come to feel confined by the city, as if the towering buildings pressed on him. He longed for open space, imagined trees overhead and a mountain horizon that replaced the skyline of concrete and glass.

He set his takeout bag on the counter of the galley kitchen and his case on the foyer floor; he dropped his keys into a shallow bowl crafted from lapis lazuli that he'd picked up in Jalalabad. Even the damn bowl reminded him of a harsh time wasted on a fruitless chase.

Too many memories haunted him with regrets he couldn't forgive. He shed his suit jacket, loosened his tie and rolled his shirt sleeves, but he still felt like he did every night—fatigued, frustrated, pensive—and today was a good day.

No matter how hard he worked, his efforts seemed futile, and for the small advances he had made, the job was changing him in ways from which he feared he might not recover. He was becoming cynical and more isolated. *A dangerous slide.* He was drawn to dark, but didn't want to *be* dark. He loved the ocean, but he didn't need to hang on a raft in the raging middle of it. *Is this to be the sum of my life?* If something didn't change soon, he'd descend to an even darker place. His thoughts had already begun sinking.

His apartment was still furnished in the way his wife decorated. Her clothing remained stored in boxes on the closet floor, not yet purged. He hadn't even opened the bag of her personal belongings the hospital gave him. It was as if the ugly thing had never happened—as if the wife in his mind, the one he loved and married, would someday return. But that wife who deceived him and lied to him, the wife who took a lover—she was the wife who had died.

Chase turned on the radio and stood at the bathroom sink. Did he look as tired as he felt? He wore his heavy spirit like a mask. Creases at his eyes belonged on men older than his thirty-six years. He washed his hands, strong hands that could kill a man with a taut quick twist; longing hands that ached to touch the smooth skin of a woman.

He opened the Italian dinner of veal, penne and green beans he'd picked up at Café Napolitano around the corner from his building, and poured a glass of Chianti. He set his work laptop on the desk and logged onto the bureau's server to check e-mail and briefing memos. Two extremists killed, couriers with suspected ties to Eastern Flame's super-cell. One in Sudan, the other in Oman near the Yemeni border. "Interesting." He noted their names, clicked to their photos and studied their faces.

Chase chewed a bite of veal while he verified access to Yusuf's image, sent it to his regional list and copied it to his personal laptop. As he was reviewing photos in his various image libraries, his dead wife's snapshot, misfiled among Radical Extremists, popped onto the screen among suicide bombers and jihadi wannabes, just as the radio played Seal's *Kiss From A Rose*. The accuracy of the lyrics startled him, too coincidental with the appearance of her photo and where his thoughts had sunk. She *was* the light on his dark side.

He had not seen this photo of her. No surprise. She was careless with her files. Didn't know the meaning of organizing an image library or labeling CDs. Her haunting stare was aimed at him and her green eyes sparkled. Her expression unnerved him. He couldn't recall that she'd ever smiled at him like she did in that photo, as if she were happier in death than she'd been in their marriage. Did he push her to another man's arms? Could he ever forgive her? Or forgive himself? Perhaps if he'd been home more, supported her goals, encouraged her dreams ... he might have disrupted the sequence that led to her death.

How long had she lived her lie? When did she seek comfort in the arms of a lover? How could he have missed the signs?

She still held power over him—in his pleasure and pain—like the song said. He stared at her eyes, bright on the screen ... so angry he'd been denied the chance to question her, accuse her, scream at her ... tell her how badly she'd hurt him.

He grieved for more than her life.

All he could say now was, "Damn you." He clicked to close her image.

He didn't delete it.

Chase had lost so much—in Afghanistan, in Iraq and even in New York. It seemed everyone he cared about and loved was gone—killed by a Taliban bullet, blown apart by a roadside bomb or crushed by a hit-and-run driver at the corner of Christopher and 7th.

Am I too damaged to ever love again? He yearned to be with a woman, imagined her in his mind. Good. Smart. Someone to protect, but strong enough to lean on. A true partner he could trust—absolutely trust. He craved an ordinary life in a home where they'd sit across a table cluttered with yesterday's mail and converse over breakfast and dinner, where he wouldn't feel pressured to disclose secrets of national security.

It had been so long since he'd talked to anyone outside of the bureau, he'd forgotten how to connect with a woman, with anyone except suspects and insurgents. Why worry about it? His job didn't accommodate personal time anyway, no matter what the rocket scientists believed.

He could see himself in a different life and it wasn't too late. If only he could leave his wife in her grave.

Today's job offer cut close to home, stirred desires he'd suppressed for too long. He dreamed of the day he could transfer from counterterrorism, but not before he claimed a win for the good guys, though he wondered how much more he had to give.

He had penance to pay for losing Ali long ago when their paths first crossed … nearly crossed.

The dream that kept him going was of that other Matthew Christian Chase, the one he used to be, as a boy and in college and in the Navy—innocent, optimistic and hopeful. Did *he* still live behind this mask? Or did a future Matt Chase? One who owned a software company and lived in a cozy home under a star-filled sky, with neighbors who waved when he stepped out to the porch. Could he hope for a wife whose fire burned only for him?

He closed both laptops, set his work computer by the door, switched off the radio and turned on the late TV news. Car bombs and drones and suicide attacks. More of the same. It was time to shake his world, to reach further and take greater risks. His NASA friends were right. He needed change, personally, but first, professionally. He could have Ali's photo in his image library and not even know it, and *that* had to change. Tomorrow while he focused on Ali, he'd assign a Russian specialist to study Vasili Chemenko. His best agent was Marcus Banzik, temporarily assigned to the Czech Republic but due to return within a week.

Tomorrow he'd look with clear eyes focused on Yusuf and Ali.

And the two dead couriers in today's news.

FOURTEEN

CONNECTICUT
Wednesday

AN ACHE OF LONESOMENESS ripped through Yusuf. He had not lived or worked apart from family or Brothers for so long a time, and the third-rate motel made him feel unworthy of more. *This place does not feed my soul.* If he knew how to reach Ali for words of inspiration, he would.

Yusuf pulled a bag of mixed nuts from his backpack. The aroma carried his mind back to Kandahar, to the camp—to the scent of roasted nuts and dust and gunpowder. He had imitated the walk of his father, proud owner of a wire factory, as he carried a coil of power line in his hand—an AK-47 tucked under his arm.

American jets overhead.

Ali had struck the back of his head. "In the dirt. Do you want to lose your life before you are called?"

He and Ali had first met while bombs exploded around them. Both injured, they had fled to Herat where Yusuf's contacts arranged safe housing and medical care until they were able to leave for Iran. Since then, they had reunited in Budapest, Khartoum and Jakarta to assist with operations in Southeast Asia, though they preferred working in the U.S., where no one paid any mind to them and they were free to cross state borders without showing papers.

Yusuf's U.S. assignment was nearly complete with research of logistics; leasing a Boston warehouse and stocking it with water, canned meats and beans for the foreign fighters who would soon come.

The Syrians were due in time to commandeer vehicles; and he wondered if the Russian with his lieutenant had arrived … would arrive. Their contribution was vital and their charge of weapons kept most secret. The Russian was prepared, willing and capable. But Yusuf's trust in them was feeble and it pained him to partner with them. They seemed to have the same goals, so how could he object? He was devoted to Ali whose reasoning proved strong. Yet when Yusuf's mind was quiet, his heart warned he and the other members of Ali's cell were being used for a different purpose.

Perhaps Yusuf's new idea would insure his continued participation in the American mission. Ali had been seeking a secure method of communication. Now he, Yusuf, "man of lesser intellect," might have found one. He was not as versed in technology as Ali, but he could not fault his accidental discovery and was eager to tell what he had found.

Yusuf studied the airline printout he had lifted from the man at the cabin. The most timely transport for him proved to be the same Delta flight operated by Air France, departing from New York on Saturday at five. He smirked. The fool had scribbled his user name and password on the ticket. Yusuf walked to the Four Seasons and entered the business center where he logged onto the airline site, cancelled the stolen ticket then bought a new one. He connected the infidel's phone to the computer and uploaded the whore's photo to a server in Prague where Brothers of the Eastern Flame operated an Internet café.

PRAISE GOD. *Another night passed without capture.* Yusuf called the number he'd been given by Ali. An Arab driver would transport him to Bayonne, New Jersey, where the New York cell maintained a safehouse, a longstanding refuge since the eighties, providing shelter, food, and if approved by leaders, a small amount of cash to any good Muslim man passing the area. The driver should arrive in two hours.

Yusuf inserted into his small tape player a cassette he bought in Yemen. The music, performed by three brothers whose father was a prayer caller, soothed his heart with sounds of a *kanoun*, clay drums and an *oud* imported from Egypt, he was told. Yusuf's head pitched from side to side as the ancient rhythm became more urgent. He longed to be on the desert plateau with his brothers, father and uncles and closed his eyes to imagine the stars, the silhouette of Giza's pyramids against Cairo's lights, the tents and camels and campfire sparks spiraling toward heaven. His outstretched arms had embraced his brothers when they danced and laughed and did a big party in the desert. Thundering drums broke the night's stillness. Cymbals clashed and a reed flute wailed.

Yusuf kicked off his shoes. His body swayed around the motel room like it did long ago in a faraway homeland. Brothers around campfires. Brothers around flames.

He opened his eyes and saw himself in the motel dresser's fractured mirror, his face severed by the cracks … the desert camp replaced by his shattered self.

"Forgive me," he said to God.

He turned off the tape player and tossed it with his favorite Yemeni cassette into a wastebasket beside the toilet.

Yusuf spread his prayer rug with the built-in compass toward Mecca. He prayed he would be chosen to execute the mission's final stage. His passage to Paradise.

At midday, he pulled on his grey fleece jacket, checked out of his motel room and tossed his bag in the back seat of the car that came for him. Blocks away, the car swerved onto the southbound lanes of the Wilbur Cross Parkway toward New Jersey.

Yusuf instructed the driver, consulted GPS and located a convenient shipper in the next town, where he handed over his camera, memory cards and thumb drive for shipment to an address in Prague. The last detail, about which Ali had been most insistent, was now complete. When they returned to the parkway, calm fell upon him as if a burden had lifted. Within two hours, they would pass New York City and arrive at the safehouse, where he would rest and pray until his flight to Prague in two days and three nights.

Soon it will be finished.

FIFTEEN

CONNECTICUT
Friday

KATE COULDN'T BELIEVE how quickly months of travel planning had passed, saving money, completing work and navigating bumps in her love life, namely Todd, and she was bent on having a blast in Prague even if she traveled solo. Tomorrow.

Browsing travel sites, she checked weather forecasts and the day's currency exchange rates for dollars, euros and Czech korunas she'd try to memorize on the plane. The State Department site warned of typical street crime with pickpockets and purse snatchers, but the Republic was a stable democracy. No travel warnings. No internal or external terrorist threats.

She studied an interactive map of must-see city sights, tracing routes to and from Old Town Square and the Astronomical Clock, the Charles Bridge, Mala Strana and Prague Castle; and planned a schedule in her head. *That's only two days.* Travel would account for two days, so she had two more days to kill ... or fill with museums, concerts, shopping and photography.

Everything is still in twos. Doubled like the two visions LittleEv wrote about, and the repetition of her own vague dreams. LittleEv's e-mails had collected in her inbox with another added today. *Not now. Not with leaving tomorrow.* It was hard enough to curb her feelings of dread without adding LittleEv's distress. She finally wrote, "Regrets. Unable to comment at this time. Will respond in a week or so. Try not to worry." When she returned from vacation, she would reluctantly crawl into that dark place she'd been avoiding, because she, too, sensed catastrophe and she *had* to prepare for what was coming.

She called the limousine service to confirm her pickup time of eleven for her five o'clock flight. The service agent tried to persuade her to take a one o'clock pickup, but she'd rather hang around the terminal than worry about all that might delay her. Besides that, her sixth sense pressed for arrival at the airport *before two.*

That evening Kate called Jack, a last good-bye before she was to leave the following day.

"You're going without Todd?"

"Can't get there soon enough."

"Did you check—"

"I'm online now, checking everything."

Jack hesitated. "Has he called since you split? Is this trip a running *from* rather than a running *to* type of thing?"

"Don't do this now." She shoved the mouse across the pad, rolled back her chair and paced to the refrigerator. Squeezing the phone between her ear and shoulder, she poured a half glass of beer. "Where's this coming from? It's not like I haven't traveled."

"It's because you have and your history troubles me."

Troubles him? Her stomach clenched like when they were kids and he caught her going through his secret treasure box. She braced for *the list.*

"Starting with that hijacked Athens flight."

Beer sloshed out of the glass and dripped past her wrist

when her arms flailed. "I wasn't on the damn plane." She rushed back to her office with quick little shuffles as she tried to balance the glass, the phone—and her patience with Jack.

"Same flight a month earlier. It *could* have been you. In Turkey it *was* you. You're always close to disaster, and I'm the one on the phone with State asking if Americans are missing or killed in an earthquake in freaking Istanbul."

"I love Istanbul." Kate set the beer on the taboret beside the computer desk, wiped her wrist on her sweatshirt and leaned into her chair, testing how far back she could stretch before tipping. "I can't believe you're talking about this now. You're such an ass. You know I'm nervous before flying."

"See, you *are* nervous."

"About missing my flight, jerk."

Jack laughed. "You get to the airport before TSA clocks in."

The chair lurched with an odd noise that screeched like metal against metal. "Oops." She sipped her beer. "I had a premonition about the quake."

"You didn't tell me."

"I don't share every thought that crosses my mind."

"I wish Todd was going with you."

Her shoulders slumped. "Me too. He took his ticket and passport; maybe he'll surprise me. If he still insists on marriage, I'll probably say yes." An uncomfortable moment passed.

"Don't say that."

"Maybe it's best. Whatever, it'll resolve itself tomorrow when the plane takes off. If he's on it, I'll take it as a sign."

She could swear she heard Jack's eyes roll.

He slipped in a few more shots about her risky decisions and life choices guided by psychic impressions, his usual rundown. "Just be careful. You don't have to talk to everyone you meet. If anything happens, and I mean it, Kate, I'm your first call."

"Okay. I promise. You're my *only* call. Don't worry. Nothing bad will happen."

For the first time in her life when she said that, the ring of truth sounded more like a shaky prayer.

SIXTEEN

NEW YORK
Friday

MATT CHASE, his number two guy, Special Agent René Vargas, and a team of agents had distributed Yusuf's enhanced photo to all Joint Terrorism Task Force agencies, and TSA had been alerted. If there was more Chase could do, it had to be done now—before the plane, before the train—*before* the hit.

He had to think more like the front line fighter he once was, because the threat was the same: They were determined to kill. He called Vargas into his office. "I know in my gut something is up. Maybe not today or tomorrow, but soon. Do you feel it too?"

"Honestly, Boss, I'm not sensing the same urgency. All new photos are out and we've personally called supervisors at every northeast airport, but it's only been a couple of days."

"Send them national and to Interpol." Chase leaned into his chair, drumming his fingers against its arms. "We're missing something. I can't get a fix on Ali. And I haven't been able to integrate Vasili Chemenko into the cell. Soviet history, Russia and Eastern Europe, the whole Red threat." Chase shook his head. "It's not my area."

"I know you have a past with Ali. We all know. Is that what's getting to you?"

Chase didn't respond. Were decisions he was making now tainted by mistakes he'd made back then? A young and inexperienced captain in Afghanistan during the worst days of the war, he'd been assigned one mission, to find and interrogate Abdul Wahab al-Khalifah, a.k.a. Ali. He had Ali's then number two guy in custody. *How much easier could the damn task have been?* Who could have foreseen it would go so quickly to hell?

"What are you thinking, Boss?"

"That I need a day off." Chase spun his chair and stared out the window. "Think I'll drive to Connecticut this weekend, visit my folks' country home and reboot myself."

"Yeah. Now you're talking."

"Didn't one of our new guys train with the Russian mob task force? Put him on their trail until Banzik returns from Prague. I want to know everything about Chemenko and the lieutenant who shadows him like a puppy. They were spotted last month in Athens with some Syrian and that can't be good."

"On it, Boss."

Chase didn't divert his stare when Vargas left. His mind was otherwise engaged in finding and fortifying connections. Except for the announcement a suspected Eastern Flame courier had been killed in Bonn, the morning Compstat session was disappointing. He needed an active lead and remained aimed on Ali and Yusuf, taking another critical look at their history.

Ali, *The Brain*, was a 42-year-old Saudi national, married with three children and held degrees that matched his own in Islamist studies, computer science and cyber technologies. Physical descriptions conflicted within a range of 5'8" to 6'2" tall, 160 to 220 pounds. Black hair and eyes. Brown skin. He attributed Ali's previous successes to dumb luck, evading capture and serious injury more than once.

Yusuf, *The Arm,* was a low-level soldier trained at an Afghan camp and injured in the same raid. Both escaped. *What are the chances?* He speculated the two men met and trained at the very camp shown on his video tape, though their curriculums would have followed different paths.

Yusuf had once studied at a madrasa then lived in Herat near the western border. Chase checked a map and marked their probable exit route, about three hundred tough miles on a crappy highway. From Herat, they could have crossed into Iran, while he was way the hell off in Jalalabad. Yusuf's whereabouts remained sketchy, but reports from captured insurgents indicated Ali had moved on to Spain, Germany and several Eastern European countries, where he could have hooked up with Vasili and his band of former Soviet loyalists and KGB operatives.

Violence seemed incompatible with Ali's profile; his expertise was in communications. As the group's new-media expert, word was "he didn't take a shit without a mobile Web device." Chemenko would blow up a power station while Ali would hack its computers and upload malware.

Last year Chase had disrupted Eastern Flame's communication network forcing them to limit phone usage, and with Internet security compromised, he had knocked them back to Dark Age methods—handwritten messages delivered by couriers.

He hoped he'd stuck a thorn in Ali's side, slowed his stride or at least pissed him off.

By end of day, agents had distributed Yusuf's new photo to foreign partner agencies.

Chase browsed group photos seeking the one image where he might find Yusuf with the elusive Ali. He was confident Yusuf's starstruck expression would betray Ali's identity as surely as a Judas kiss.

One face after another enlarged to full screen, he studied stance, features, eyes. Some looked doped on khat or coke, but they were low-level guys who blew themselves up.

Damn. The blank stares he'd been reviewing replicated the emptiness he saw in his bathroom mirror. What had once made *him* vital had withered, and nothing replaced it except the hatred and dogged determination fueling his hunt. He'd lived two years in anger and condemnation of his dead wife, and even longer chasing Brothers of the Eastern Flame. *Wow, I really do need a few days.*

SEVENTEEN

Saturday Morning

CHASE RAN THROUGH his daily pep talk: *Today is the day*, a tip he'd learned from an Israeli counterterrorism expert: How to maintain self-motivation? Operate as if *today* is the day of attack.

He lathered his face with the same shave cream his father used. He brimmed with confidence, knowing his dad was proud of him, even if he preferred Chase build his own software company. He'd call his father and visit after a quick stop at the office.

Maybe the night's solid sleep, the intended visit to Connecticut, or last night's full moon moved him to dress splashy. He pulled a taupe colored suit and lavender shirt from the closet, matched a champagne and gray striped tie, and laid them on the bed. Maybe he'd go to a fine restaurant later in the day, or drive out early or ride the train to see his folks.

He took a cab to the office, surprised to see Vargas and his team on a Saturday morning. Did they finally sense the danger or had his obsession bled to adjacent offices?

Chase checked the morning briefing: Another Eastern Flame courier killed, his body found in a narrow alley in Aswan. Sudan, Oman, Germany and now Egypt. Four couriers dead in a week. Assassinated.

Good news, but most compelling was that *we* didn't kill them.

SATURDAY AFTERNOON at one o'clock, Vargas tapped on Chase's open door and leaned in. Chase glanced up from his computer screen and said, "Hey, did you see this?"

"The courier? Yeah. But that's not why I'm smiling. You're gonna love this, Boss."

Chase leaned back in his chair, stretched up his arms and locked his fingers behind his head. "Tell me something good."

Vargas reached behind the door and grabbed Chase's Go Bag. "TSA might have Yusuf on their monitors. Now."

Chase bolted from his seat and slipped on his suit jacket as they ran down the hall. "Which airport?"

"JFK. Terminal One. Air France."

"Tell them I'm there in fifteen. And you're there in thirty. Not the full Task Force, only the linguist, an analyst and you. Who's the TSA Agent-In-Charge?" Chase pounded the elevator button three times with the side of his fist.

"Name's Reyes. Where's your phone? I'll enter—"

"No time."

"Well … here, I wrote it all down." Vargas tucked a 4" x 5" notecard in Chase's inside breast pocket. "They matched the new photo we sent this week. Good call, Boss."

"Remind me later to thank my guys at the space center."

"Will do. See you in a few."

Chase glared at the elevator then flew down six flights of stairs to the parking garage where a white Crown Victoria was gassed and waiting.

Most days traffic was much worse, but he arrived in good time, adrenalin in overdrive. Yusuf might have been sighted, but Ali could also be in the terminal. *Eyes sharp.* He imagined them waiting in a security line as he led his own JTTF SWAT team toward them. The slightest smile of content formed on his face. Was today *the day*? In a few minutes, he would know.

EIGHTEEN

NEW YORK AT JFK
Saturday at 1:35 p.m.

KATE ENTERED TERMINAL ONE at JFK International Airport where the Air France counters were located. She checked in with one suitcase, confirmed window seat 37A and received her boarding pass. Todd would have been in 37B and may yet be. She left the lobby to pass time outside, leaning against a concrete wall to the right of the building, as far from the chaos of the passenger drop-off area as she could get. *What a relief.* She was exactly where she was meant to be. Normal anxiety about flying, crowds and foreign travel was under control. Her research had been thorough, it wasn't flood season and the Czech Republic wasn't prone to earthquakes.

She was ready.

Todd could still appear, late as usual, but not *too* late; the plane didn't leave for hours. She'd listened to a Pink Floyd CD on the drive to the airport; a song played in her mind and she quietly sang the *Wish You Were Here* lyrics, wondering if she'd sabotaged her best chance at love, … until …

The steady rhythm of taxis and limousines ceased when a Crown Victoria screeched into the passenger drop-off area and parked at the curb. *Who would have the audacity to park at the front door of one of the nation's busiest airports? Homeland Security?* She leaned forward to see around the wall, checking the car's registration: white plates, U.S. Government. *Yup, got to be. And Jack says I don't pay attention.*

The driver exited the car and walked toward the door at the end of the Terminal, the door nearest to her. His eyes darted from side to side sweeping the area and glancing over his shoulders. His long sure strides slowed when their eyes met.

This might be one of those moments you remember and relive your whole life, when you wonder what you should have done differently because you let it pass. She'd had similar encounters, but didn't act on them, regretted they had slipped by and imagined how the alternative might have unfolded. *They must play out in parallel universes.*

She'd check her watch if she wore one. Was it two o'clock, the time she felt compelled to be here? She'd bet her life it was.

He wore a perfectly tailored taupe suit with a lavender shirt, a cream and charcoal striped tie. *Gutsy.* Must be a confident man, and movie star handsome, though he didn't seem to have that air. His attire wasn't standard FBI, at least not what she'd seen when visiting Jack's office. He could be a U.S. Marshall or Air Marshall? *Nope, too well-dressed to blend with the crowd unless he flew first class. Hmmm, do they do that?* She couldn't take her eyes off him, nor could she recall when she'd been so drawn to anyone as she was to him.

In the instant they connected, she sensed his nature, not the job or the fancy suit or the face that took her breath away, but all that came to shape him. *Foreign lands. Explosions. Loss.* Scenes flashed in her head. And the same song played, sparking thoughts of trading heroes and hot ash. A cool breeze blew across her face. *Lost friends, lost wife, lost life.* A high price to pay for a lead role in a …. *Change.*

Kate came so close to completely understanding the future and it scared her. She was visually oriented and he was beyond good-looking, but *this* wasn't *that.* And it wasn't her sucker-for-a-pretty-face lust. His easy smile was riveting, so magnetic it pulled her spirit closer to him. She sighed and wondered if she could fall in love with someone like him.

Saturday at 2:00 p.m.

HORNS HONKED, CABBIES YELLED and skycaps directed passengers. Chase pulled into the drop-off area behind taxis, limousines and vans where business travelers, tourists and families were about to embark. They had no idea he was on his stated mission: Defeat terrorism. Neutralize extremist cells and operatives in the U.S. Help dismantle terrorist networks worldwide.

Chase parked at the curb, more like screeched to a halt, and walked toward the terminal. A nearby couple hugged and kissed, appearing distraught to be separating. Several years ago that couple could have been him and his wife. A younger pair beside them attempted to corral kids who giggled and played hide-and-seek between luggage stacks. He envied those civilians who couldn't know that today they also stood on a war's front line.

His eyes gauged the crowd and the attractive young woman standing to the right of the door. She'd been leaning forward, looking around the concrete wall to curbside. Her carry-on bag set at her feet, a boarding pass tucked in its side pocket, a rolled sweater bursting from the open zipper. She peered up and down the drop-off area as if she waited for someone. He noted her features and mannerisms like he did with anyone who caught his attention: Caucasian of northern or Eastern European descent; near thirty; 5'4", 130 lbs. with nicely formed hips; brown eyes; brown hair with red highlights where the sun hit. She wore flat-soled slip-on shoes with loose fitting khaki slacks, a black crew neck sweater with a silver ankh on black cord hanging around her neck; comfortable clothes for an overseas flight. Probably well-traveled. Certainly pretty. Approachable. Not a threat. *Definitely not threatening.* He wondered about her destination and for whom she waited.

Of the thousands of faces he'd study today, hers would be the one he'd remember.

Her eyes traced his figure and seemed to follow his movements. She seemed aware and in the moment, not plugged into an iPod, yet she appeared to be singing. Her arms hung at her sides with her palms exposed. *Nothing to hide.*

His eyes locked on hers and she didn't glance away. Their connection was palpable and irresistible. He fixed on her for as long as he could, even as he proceeded dutifully toward his mission.

She raised her chin and said "hello" so softly he couldn't hear the word, but knew by her lips. He nodded and smiled and dared to wonder if he could someday love someone like her.

NINETEEN

AT FIVE AFTER TWO Chase raced to the TSA Watch Room where Agent-In-Charge Anton Reyes steered him to the monitor displaying the security line at Concourse A. "That's my guy. Which way?"

Reyes pointed and took the lead. "If you hadn't sent that photo and if your agent hadn't called, we might have overlooked him. I'm sure we would have."

"But you didn't." Chase authorized Yusuf's security screening to be completed before interrogation. He entered the private interview room and examined his passport from the Arab Republic of Egypt. "Yusuf Mohammed Hamza." He flipped pages, reading immigration and security stamps. "Spain, Germany, U.K." All lengthy stays, but not one entry justified detention. He peered beyond the book to Yusuf. "Can't make up your mind?" No response.

Chase's cell phone buzzed. Vargas and members of the Task Force had arrived. He handed the passport to Reyes. "Get this to my agents. They'll know what to do. Have the analyst and linguist join me in there with the luggage. Your people can guard our guest. And I mean watch him. He's not to put anything in his mouth, not even his fingers. There'll be no ticket to paradise on my watch, not until I get what I need. I'll inspect his bag before we talk."

"My people can do that."

"I'm sure they can, but I'm looking for more. I want to see how he folded and packed his belongings, and in what order."

"What do you hope to find?"

Chase shrugged. "Insight." He turned. "And send in forensics and your canine team."

In a nearby inspection room, Yusuf's single carry-on had been placed on a long table. Chase unfastened the Velcro straps and zipper. A prayer rug sat on top of rolled clothes. He respectfully placed it to one side before he removed two sets of clean cotton pajamas, four gray T-shirts and briefs; and a pair each of jeans and athletic shoes stuffed with dirty socks.

He ordered the forensics technician to lift fingerprints, and collect hair and fibers. "You know what we need."

She nodded. "Will this search come back as a violation of privacy rights?"

Chase said with a sardonic smile, "Screw his rights."

The technician cataloged a brown hair snagged in Velcro; it obviously wasn't from Yusuf's head. One of the bag's rubber feet had caught a sliver of a leaf. Dried red mud was embedded in the shoe tread; she scraped it into an evidence bag.

The analyst shook his head. "Nothing odd in the passport." He ran a hand scanner over the identification page and across each travel entry stamp.

Chase rifled through Yusuf's uncluttered wallet: almost $400 in small bills, a Jersey driver's license, a photo of a young girl approximately seven years old, and a crayon drawing. "Interesting." He stared at Yusuf in the adjacent room while asking his team, "Sister or daughter?"

They compared the girl's features to Yusuf's and simultaneously replied, "Sister."

Agents lifted prints, scanned the wallet's contents and returned them.

"No computer disks or thumb drives. Nothing ties him to Brothers of the Eastern Flame nor to Ali. We've got zip on this guy. He's cleaner than my mother," Chase said. "But I'm sensing personal motivation. Ten to one the girl's dead and he seeks revenge. Check it out."

The analyst said, "We know he entered the country six months ago at Logan on an Air France flight from Paris."

"Where the hell has he been? Have the Boston Field Office review security tapes from his entry date." Chase's mind processed data like a computer with each bit of intelligence burning a new trail of investigation. "Check the airline. How many bags did he arrive with? Same at de Gaulle and Orly, wherever he boarded; maybe cameras caught him meeting someone at those airports. Was Paris his origination point or did he use connecting flights? Check Logan's car rental agencies. He didn't freaking walk to New York." Chase turned to look for Reyes. "How did he get here today? Have TSA examine footage of the drop-off area and get me the plate number of the car he rode in. Do that first."

"Got it, Boss."

Agent Vargas entered. "I ran his travel history. There's nothing on this passport number."

"Yeah, no surprise. He must have others stashed somewhere."

"What do we do with this guy, Boss?"

Chase planted his hands on his hips, glaring through the window of the interview room where Yusuf stared forward as if in trance. He weighed the value of detaining this one unsophisticated soldier against the benefit of collecting the intelligence that might dismantle the entire cell. He'd learned from previous blunders, and regardless that others considered them triumphs, this time he'd hold out for more—extinguishing Eastern Flame. "We let him go. Have him tailed when he gets to

— Where's he going?"

Vargas glanced at his paperwork. "Paris, but booked through to Prague."

"Perfect. Agent Banzik is on assignment and I have friends there, we partnered in exercises at the National Counterterrorism Center. Meanwhile, we have new leads to pursue." Chase checked his watch. "How much time do we have? Where's the passenger manifest? Who's seated next to him? Could it be another from his cell?"

"Forty-five minutes to boarding, with two air marshals on the flight."

"Excellent. You can brief them. I'll be with our guest, then at the gate." Chase slapped his fingers on Yusuf's stacked clothes. "Photograph and repack. And drop in a tracking bug." He browsed the passenger list. Yusuf was assigned seat 37B, with K. Kasabian in 37A. He pointed to the list. "Who is this? I want a word with him … her."

Vargas checked a more comprehensive version of the list. "Yeah, she's clean. Kate Kasabian. I ran her passport history, plenty of activity. India, China, Turkey. Several trips to Egypt so I gave her a second tier look, but there's nothing suspicious in her background. A commercial artist. Graphics and Web design. A brother in Vermont is her emergency contact. She checked in early with one suitcase TSA searched and cleared—"

Chase shook his head. "Why did they examine her bag?"

"She was first to arrive. The inspectors wanted something to do. She talked to one of the agents who told me even during the search she seemed 'pleasant and very much at ease.' Anyway, she's not at the gate and hasn't passed through any other security points."

"Where the hell is she?"

Vargas shrugged. "Shall I page Ms. Kasabian? Call her to the Air France counter?"

"No. Don't attract attention. I'll catch up with her at the gate. You have a lot to do. Get more people if you need them. Check out everyone on this flight and remember to look for Russian and Syrian connections."

YUSUF'S BLACK DEAD EYES struck Chase like those of insurgent detainees he'd interrogated in his early career. The asshole seemed fit though not powerful. His clothes were sloppy, cheap and out of date. His grooming needed work with untrimmed facial hair and unattended cuticles, but his appearance was not so poor he'd attract notice. He seemed jittery, checking his designer-knockoff watch every other minute. A few words of flawed English sounded like British primary school, but his rants reverted to Arabic with a Cairo accent. He mumbled about missing the plane and visiting his sick mother, typical pedestrian excuses. He seemed angry as if he wanted to strike something—or kill ten thousand Americans.

Hatred exuded from Yusuf like the stench of a corpse. *We can hope.* Chase loathed being in the same room, yet it was exhilarating. He sat across the table, face to face, eye to eye. *There must be something human inside—he valued a child's crayon drawing, for crissake.* He considered asking about the girl in the photo … using her to get a rise from him. It took all he could muster to stop himself, confident a tail in Prague would produce the results he wanted.

He left the interview room, telling one of Reyes' agents, "I'll be at the gate. You can release him. And his ride today … find that damn plate number."

CHASE ENTERED GATE 13 on Concourse A. He leaned against a window with bright daylight shining behind him forcing passengers to squint if they looked in his direction. He reviewed names on the list, occasionally glancing at travelers lined at the kiosk. Yusuf was one of the first to board as if he couldn't bear another minute of Western contamination—or he wanted to get away before Chase changed his mind.

Several minutes later a young woman stepped to the counter and handed her boarding pass to the ticket agent, but he didn't swipe its magnetic strip. He slid it aside and nodded at Chase. Chase couldn't help breaking a smile when he saw her. His warm response turning cold with the sudden realization that Kate Kasabian, the woman he'd noticed at curbside, was seated on a transatlantic flight next to suspected Eastern Flame terrorist Yusuf Mohammed Hamza.

Chase led her aside.

"Hey, it's you." Her flirty smile said more to him than did her words. Her shoulders dropped and she seemed to relax when she saw him. "What's this about?"

He pulled identification from his inside breast pocket. "Matt Chase. I need to ask a few questions."

Kate tucked her hair behind her ear and planted her hand on her hip. "Did *my brother* put you up to this?"

Chase tilted his head. Not the reaction he expected. "Excuse me?"

Her eyes flashed around the concourse and the gate's waiting area, widening as if she'd just become aware of police, agents, TSA—and his legitimacy as an FBI supervisor. "Is this for real?"

"Real as it gets. May I see your passport, please."

Her hand brushed against his for the longest moment when she surrendered her document. He gazed from her hand to her eyes, then flipped through the pages, raising eyebrows several times. "Are you traveling anywhere other than Prague? When do you return?"

"I'm not planning to, but I'm flexible. I'll be gone six days. What is this?"

"When did you book your flight? Why are you traveling alone?"

"I don't know, six months ago. The last blizzard in March when I lost my mind to cabin fever. Do you *have* to know why I'm traveling alone?"

"No." He smiled as he swayed, shifting weight to his other leg. "But humor me."

"My boyfriend … former, er … *ex*-boyfriend and I planned the trip, but we split up."

"Nonrefundable tickets, huh?" The boyfriend's seat opened and Yusuf snatched it.

"Yes, how did you know?" She winked. "FBI training?"

"Common sense." His insides fluttered when a breeze from the air vent blew her gardenia scented perfume toward him. "Where are you staying?"

"The Renaissance Hotel … ah, Hilton Old Town."

"Right, it's now Hilton. Good choice. I hear it's been refurbished and looks like new. Across from the Marriott on V Celnici, a short walk to Old Town Square." He wanted to, but didn't say, let's meet for dinner when you return. He wanted to say, I'll meet you there.

Kate pointed to the shrinking line of passengers. "Look, Agent Chase, I'd love to chat. I really, really would love to. But I didn't get here three hours early to miss my flight."

Chase touched her shoulder. "Please consider this advice." He leaned closer, bending at the waist. "Don't talk to strangers."

"I can't promise." She laughed as she jerked a step backward. "Everyone will be a stranger where I'm going."

He handed back her passport. "Have fun." Their fingers touched. He blinked away the thought of kissing her like the couple at drop-off area, then inched closer and whispered, "Be safe."

In his whole life he had not felt as empty as he did when Kate Kasabian walked down the boarding ramp. Then she suddenly stopped and pivoted toward him, waved and threw a kiss.

He shook his head and felt his cheeks begin to burn.

YOU IDIOT! Kate scolded. What the hell are you doing throwing kisses to an FBI agent. *Restrain yourself.* She nearly died when he asked where she'd be staying, allured by the quiet confidence of his voice. A fantasy he'd join her flashed in her mind. She didn't consider he might be playing her. When he touched her shoulder, she felt safe being near him.

When he whispered in her ear, she felt his heat on her neck while shivers ran down her arms. She was sure she felt his lips on her skin. She sighed. A smile lingered as she boarded the plane.

From midway down the aisle, Kate spotted her seat and the Middle Eastern looking man next to it, in Todd's seat. She pulled out her extra sweater so the bag would zip and struggled to hoist them into the bin. The guy in 37B lifted her carry-on and shoved in her sweater, he didn't ask. He didn't say a word. He didn't even look at her. He stood in the aisle until she settled by the window, seeming annoyed by not merely the inconvenience, but by her very existence. *Too freaking bad.* He seemed angry, as if he wanted to punch something. *I hope it's not me.* She didn't dare request her sweater. She'd freeze her arms off before she'd ask anything from him.

She would definitely heed Agent Chase's advice about talking to strangers, at least for the next seven or so flight hours, but they did speak during dinner, mostly about airlines, hotels and Prague. He said he would "soon be join his small sister," awkward phrasing, but far better than her linguistic skill, so who was she to criticize. *His sister must live in Prague.*

He spoke of a cyber café within walking distance of the old Renaissance on the Western hotels row, and she could save money if she used its Internet and phone service. That was the end of their conversation. It was going to be a long flight. She took two Dramamine, original formula, hoping to remain drowsy all the way to France.

TWENTY

5:05 p.m.

AS SOON AS THE FLIGHT drew wheels up and disappeared in the distance, Chase alerted the Czech Security Information Service and Marcus Banzik, the agent assigned to their Joint Terrorism Task Force, to Yusuf's flight information. In Paris, French National Gendarmerie would ensure that Yusuf continued to Prague where Czech SIS agents would meet the plane and initiate surveillance.

Chase stopped at the Watch Room where he found Reyes and his team viewing video from the passenger drop-off area.

Reyes pointed to a pot on the counter. "Grab a coffee. We don't know what time he arrived so this could take a while."

Chase loosened his tie. "Can I help?"

"We're covered. Your agents are in the office if you want to wrap up your operation."

Chase poured coffee and joined his team. Their conversation abruptly stopped when he entered. His left hand planted on his hip, his suit jacket draped behind it. He sipped the drink. "Don't stop on my account." No one spoke for an awkward minute. "You think we kicked the can down the road?"

"We *did* kick him down the road," the analyst said. "Didn't we?"

"We had him and we let him go," Vargas said.

Chase shifted his weight to a more relaxed posture. "We tossed bloody chum off the back of the boat. We'll get him back. Along with bigger fish."

Reyes knocked on the window. "We got 'im."

"See." Chase grinned. "First bite. Vargas. You're with me."

They followed Reyes to the monitor to see Yusuf standing at curbside. His driver had exited the car, opened the trunk and handed a carry-on to him, the same bag Chase had examined. They'd said their cheek-kissing goodbyes and Yusuf entered the terminal. The car drove away with its New Jersey plate number clearly visible. No words were necessary when he glanced at Vargas.

Vargas was at a computer, framing a still photo of the driver and running the auto registration before Chase finished his coffee. "Here we go. An address in Bayonne. Car's registered to Pavel Korskovich."

"Not our driver. You know what to do."

"Full Task Force surveillance. Identify who comes and goes. Travel histories, associates, photos, taps. Property and bank records—"

"Keep me posted. Yusuf won't get to Prague for twelve hours. I'm taking the night off."

Chase straightened his tie, buttoned his suit jacket, and entered the terminal lobby where hundreds of new arrivals from a dozen countries had cleared Immigration and Customs. Any one of them could be an asset or a menace. *God help us.*

Chase gazed at the concrete wall where Kate Kasabian had stood. It was crazy, but the entire area, even with crowds arriving for evening flights, looked painfully incomplete. He wanted to hit a reset button to replay the last three hours and perfect what had transpired.

The time on his watch indicated Kate's flight would be well off the coast of Cape Cod by now, and because of his decision, she was seated beside the terrorist who occupied the number two slot of his personal watch list. Kate and Yusuf might be conversing, their belongings mingling in an overhead compartment. Coats and sweaters shedding fibers, losing skin cells, remaining with the other long after they disembark. *What have I done!* If his instincts were wrong he'd be tormented by final images of her on the boarding ramp, happy, excited and spontaneous. Looking embarrassed. An empathetic smile crossed his face.

He'd be haunted by his first sight of her standing by the wall, probing his soul—sparking feelings he thought were as dead as his wife.

Kate Kasabian was close to the darkest manifestation of humanity. Their arms may be touching. And his risky gamble had allowed it. The idea struck like a bolt. He walked to the spot where she stood, swiping his hands through his hair as guilt twisted in his gut. Is this what he did to his wife? Extinguished her light with his darkness?

He should have stopped Kate—flat out told her not to go.

She would have listened, changed plans just like that. He was good at reading people. She would have agreed to anything he asked. Chase pushed himself away from the wall and walked to his car. He drove back to the City thinking, Kate and Yusuf must be over the Atlantic by now—breathing the same air.

Kathryn Orzech

~ *Part Two* ~

Prague, Czech Republic

Kathryn Orzech

TWENTY-ONE

PRAGUE, CZECH REPUBLIC
Sunday Morning

AGENTS WITH THE CZECH Security Information Service waited at Prague's International Airport for the Air France flight due to touch down at 9:20 a.m. A three-team, plain-clothed surveillance mission would launch when Yusuf disembarked. Most of the SIS force had completed training in the U.S. with American and British counterterrorism agents a mere month ago, for just such a mission.

Team Two, with FBI liaison Special Agent Marcus Banzik and Czech agents Anna and Roman, sat in an unmarked Skoda Fabia parked at the curb of the terminal exit. Their attention was centered on a suspicious Mitsubishi minibus; its driver seemed lost, yet he had disregarded direction from airport security.

Agent Banzik rattled his head when they confirmed the man, who didn't speak Czech, had been recently hired by an Italian tour company. "Okay, that was for practice. Let's focus." Banzik asked Roman, "Is Team Three in position?"

"Inside the Arrivals terminal like we planned. A couple waits at Baggage-Customs and a third agent at Passport Control."

Banzik fidgeted in the back seat, sliding from side to side while raising binoculars to check the parking area where a white van, sporting cleaning service logos on side panels, housed three Team One agents. Fitted with audiovisual recording and tracking receivers, the van had the capability to distribute data to global intelligence partners. Banzik held his breath as he listened for the tracking transmitter SSA Matt Chase had hidden in Yusuf's bag. "Are you hearing the ping?" He winced when a shrill voice crackled in his earpiece. "This thing shrieks like my daughters' cat when I enter the room."

Anna twisted toward the back seat and smiled. "The cat does not care for you?"

"A sentiment I share. I'm more of a dog man, sadly outnumbered by my wife and girls." He tapped his earpiece.

"It is coming online," a Team One agent said.

A Team Three agent reported he had shadowed Yusuf through the passport checkpoint. Banzik peered out the window. "Baggage, do you have him?"

"No checked luggage. One carry-on. He's with the customs inspector," a voice said.

"The one we briefed?"

"Yes, no worry. He will pass, no problem."

Banzik wiggled his earpiece. "What's happening? Talk to me."

Yusuf was among the first of his flight's passengers to exit the terminal. Banzik checked the damp crinkled photo in his grip. "That's him." He eased back against the seat with shoulders slumped, binoculars balanced on his knee. "We got him."

A private rental car, a blue Nissan Almera, seemed to come from nowhere to meet Yusuf at curbside. He tossed his bag in the trunk and settled in the front passenger seat.

"I don't hear anything. Do we have audio?" Banzik said.

"No one is talking, but we have a steady signal from the bag."

The Almera pulled away, followed by Team Two. Roman had the wheel and Anna rode shotgun. The surveillance van trailed close behind, passing Prague Castle and several embassies, to a residential neighborhood in Mala Strana, the Lesser Town. The Almera slowed along a tree-lined street with well-kept homes and apartment buildings, and parked in the driveway alongside a six-story edifice. Team One parked the van in a spot with good cover under broad linden trees, while Roman eased Team Two's Fabia into a parking spot, two doors down and across the street from the suspected safehouse.

Banzik and Roman assessed the area while Anna clicked a half dozen photos of the targets entering the building. "Not the best," she said. "They didn't raise their heads."

Banzik shrugged. "Not all will go as planned."

The Czechs had scheduled rotating shifts. Anna and Roman would remain at the apartment for the next six hours until Team Three replaced them; personnel from headquarters would relieve Team One in the van in uneven stints. As the only U.S. agent assigned to the Republic, Banzik would see no relief until the following afternoon when his backup was due to arrive from a temporary assignment in Warsaw; something to do with investigating a couple of Russians, he had heard.

Surveillance teams, along with SIS commanders, and two units of the Czech Special Disciplinary Force waited at operational headquarters for Chase's analysis, when they would raid the apartment and secure the hostiles. Banzik checked his watch: CZ: 12:42 p.m. - NY: 6:42 a.m. He transferred to Team One's van.

PRAGUE
Sunday Morning

KATE CHECKED INTO THE HOTEL, dismissing Jack's suggestion to notify the U.S. Consulate. *Prague. Seriously? Look around. He has to get out more.*

She'd changed $200, half each of euros and koruna; and grabbed a hotel map of the city center, as if she didn't have enough maps. A long walk might ease the knots in her legs from sitting all night on the plane. From her room, she collected a hotel matchbook and postcard from the stationery packet in the desk drawer; something she did when she didn't speak the local language—which was always. If she lost her way, the nearby Marriott was a prominent landmark; almost everyone in the city would know its location. She passed the cyber café on the next block, the one the creep on the plane spoke of; it looked a bit shabby and had no customers. *Not a good sign. Keep walking.* Before she knew it she was standing at the Municipal House, shooting colorful theater posters of current and future performances. To its left, the Powder Tower marked a crowded corner that was too congested to be composing photos; she'd been bumped three times during the seconds she'd paused. *Oh crap. Pick pockets.* She checked her purse. *Still there. Billfold safe. Be careful in crowds.*

Celetna was one of the easier street names to read on the lamp post. Quaint shops lined the narrow pedestrian lane that opened to the medieval Old Town Square, "The Heart of Prague," the hotel registration clerk had said. She glanced at the map and rattled her head: Old Town, New Town, Lesser Town, Little Quarter. *It seemed so clear on the computer maps.* She wasn't going to be in the city long enough to ease into its geography, so navigation needed more of a SWAT strategy. The Castle's hilltop site became a must-see for the afternoon, or for tomorrow; she'd inquire at the hotel when she returned. At least she was confident she could find her hotel from the Square: Celetna to the Powder Tower, left to Municipal House, and right toward the Hilton. *Cake walk.*

A few blocks before the Marriott, a brick building's alleyway and a string of small storefronts bordered a secluded courtyard. Construction debris scattered on the sidewalk could be tricky to maneuver at night, especially with no street lights that she could see.

She entered the courtyard and climbed several steps to the landing of an Italian bistro where she cupped her hands against the glass. *Looks nice.* People eating, drinking and laughing like several other restaurants she'd passed, all within blocks of the hotel. The posted menu had been translated into several languages and listed inexpensive meals she hoped to try later in the week, but a food mart next to the bistro would satisfy immediate needs. She studied the package photos and found several familiar brands. A refrigerated bin held ready-made sandwiches, but when printed descriptions failed to match recognizable words, she peeked at the meat and took her best shot, adding a few to her basket along with three one-liter bottles of Pepsi, a bag of chips, cookies and chocolate bars, all for the room. *The room sure has an appetite.* She couldn't recall when she last ate a meal, not that market snacks would qualify.

Sunday Afternoon

BACK AT THE HOTEL travel desk, two American women, who appeared to be a little older than she, maybe early forties, asked about city tours.

"Hi. I'm Kate Kasabian from Connecticut." Her arm jerked forward, but heavy grocery bags interfered with a handshake.

Her lips turned up to an embarrassed smile as she fumbled. "Are you going to the Castle?"

"We're trying. Maybe tomorrow. We're from Arizona. Sedona," said one woman.

"Can we explore on our own? Is it near enough to walk?" asked the other.

The clerk suggested riding a taxi or bus uphill and touring with a guide versed in history.

"Good idea. We're history teachers."

"Sounds good to me. May I join you? I might leave after the tour and walk down to Mala Strana. That's across the river from here, right?"

"Yes. Some call it Lesser Town." The clerk circled an area on a street map and tapped with his pen. "Boutique shops and pubs line these cobblestone streets. It is a lovely and safe area to walk, especially in daylight."

Kate said, "We'll be near the river so we can hang out on the Charles Bridge where there's always something going on, so I've read."

"We like that plan. Let's all do that."

They arranged the same tour for the next morning, exchanged room numbers and set a time to meet for breakfast. Kate raised her grocery bag. "I'd prefer company for lunch. I saw a few cozy pubs near here. Are you hungry?" For the briefest moment Kate remembered the warning, "Don't talk to strangers," but school teachers from Sedona, please—not even Agent Chase would object.

Their city adventure began that very hour at an ancient cellar pub with vaulted ceilings, stone walls, and cart service offering meats, chicken and duck.

One of Kate's new companions nodded towards the hotel. "We were going to have a bite at the coffee shop. We didn't plan for much of anything this afternoon, so this is like getting an extra vacation day."

They feasted on roasted pork and potatoes, and intriguing conversation. Kate felt right at home with food in her stomach and good company at her side—so much easier to relax and be in the moment when you don't have to guard surroundings every second. She learned one woman had been recently divorced, and the other was simply enjoying a break with her friend. They seemed as tight as she and Coop, and watching them interact made her miss her best friend and travel buddy all the more; the four of them would have had a blast. She told the teachers the short version about her breakup with Todd. *Compared to Coop's tragic story, that was her* good *news.* She set her beer mug on the table, leaving it half full. "Are we ready? Let's walk."

They meandered around Old Town Square, wandered little streets, peeked in shop windows, and soon found themselves on the Charles Bridge.

"It's beautiful," a teacher said. "This is so much fun. So many people."

"It's like in the movies," said the other. "But more crowded."

They paused a dozen times as they crossed to gaze down the Vltava River and pose for Kate's vacation scrapbook photos. "I'd like to return at sunrise or sunset for close ups of the statues and the lanterns."

They laughed and said in unison, "Sunset."

"I wonder who the statues represent," Kate said. "I'll have to check my guide book." She knew she wouldn't, but it was comforting to keep it handy.

"I read they are saints," said one of the teachers. "Some with spooky legends."

"Spooky is my middle name." She told them about her Dreamwatch site.

"Now I understand why you came to Prague. Some say it's

Europe's most haunted city. Do you believe in ghosts? Can you communicate with spirits?"

"Communicate?" Kate smiled as she recalled Todd's presence in her bed. "You don't know how funny that is. I talk, but few listen—dead *or* alive."

"Are you psychic? Do you do readings? Can you do ours?"

Kate squirmed. "No, I can't." Her eyes darted as if searching for a quick exit from the situation. "I had a bad experience with my best friend." The teachers looked baffled. "I don't read anymore." She pointed ahead to the Little Quarter where tourists gathered around vendor carts and at cafés, and colorful boats docked beside the bridge. "Let's go."

They strolled along tree-lined byways and browsed the boutiques at Malostranske Square. "We may find ourselves here tomorrow," Kate warned.

"I wouldn't mind coming everyday to see what's happening."

"Nor would I."

A dark pub was the perfect spot to refresh dry throats and tired feet, to cool down and sample local beer. The bartender suggested they visit John Lennon's Peace Wall, located nearby. One of the teachers specialized in world history and knew about the Wall and the Velvet Revolution.

"I've never heard of it," Kate said. "I can get us to the hotel, but not to the Wall."

Distracted by conversation, laughter, and beer—and Kate's insistence that "this way feels right" and she was "being pulled in this direction"—they walked from the pub on a course opposite from what the bartender had suggested. "I'm sure we're supposed to be here on this block. I don't know why, but this street is significant. It means something to me. Come this way." But the Wall wasn't there.

A teacher looked around the neighborhood. "What's next?"

"I rarely share my psychic insight. But I'm telling you this, there's something special about this street." As soon as Kate said the word aloud, she hoped the location wasn't special in the same way her one and only racetrack wager had been special. The one horse she'd waited all afternoon to stake a wager collapsed half way around and had to be carted off the track. Kate spread her arms a few inches from her body; her feet firmly planted on the concrete walk allowing for better energy flow. "It's clear to me. Where we stand right now. Can you feel it?" Kate pointed down the block where two cleaning workers emerged from a driveway and headed toward a service van parked across the street. "Let's ask those guys. They look harmless."

The teachers agreed. "Ask for the French Embassy. Trust me."

Kate waved to the workmen and ran to catch them. They spoke excellent English and aimed her in the right direction.

She asked the teachers, "What's with the French Embassy?"

"I don't know exactly where we're going—"

Kate's laugh interrupted. "But it's near the French Embassy? I like the way you think."

By the time they found the Wall it was six o'clock. The neighborhood was as peaceful and quiet as a Sunday afternoon at home and with dried leaves crushed on the sidewalk slates, it even smelled like autumn in New England.

She shot a dozen photos of the Wall's graffiti and promised to share copies, a bond that cemented their friendship. And after all, what better purpose was there for a retired Peace Wall.

Over coffee and pastries at a pavement café in Old Town Square, they giggled like schoolgirls about the day, and the workmen who had helped them find their way; they lingered in the plaza until the night chilled.

Sunday Afternoon, at the Same Time

SPECIAL AGENT MARCUS BANZIK, in Team One's van, aimed binoculars at the safehouse occupied by Brothers of the Eastern Flame. "Fourth floor. I saw him. Yusuf just closed the curtains. Go. And stay in touch."

Two agents dressed in worker's coveralls left the van carrying plastic hand caddies packed with cleaning supplies that disguised listening devices and flashbang grenades, in case their primary mission went bad.

"We're skirting the building. Crossing a slated courtyard in the rear. A stunted willow partly conceals the service entry."

"That's your entry point." Banzik stroked his chin.

"We're in a stairwell where each apartment has a back service door. All is quiet. We're on the fourth floor."

Banzik pressed in his earpiece and thought he heard a door click open. "Easy." One agent reported tossing in a bugging device. Banzik heard it skip across the floor and rest against a wall.

"We're going down."

They joked and laughed and sounded like common laborers who had completed their task. Banzik ran his hand across his forehead.

The agents stood curbside, about to cross the street, when three attractive women approached. One spoke English with an American accent and asked for directions to the French Embassy. The agents laughed and pointed down the street and the women left, nodding and laughing.

"Hey, forget the girls. Grab Anna's photos." Banzik shook his head, but couldn't help smiling when Anna handed off her camera's memory card and seemed to be scolding them over their distraction, harsher than he would have.

Back inside the van, the agents removed coveralls, slipped on headsets and turned on the recorder.

Banzik asked, "What happened just then? Did we get those women on camera?"

"Lost tourists," one agent said, grinning at the other. "It's nothing."

"What did they want?"

"Americans asking for the French Embassy."

Every agent in the van roared.

Banzik was apparently the only one who didn't understand the joke.

An agent winked and said, "Tonight we will welcome the lovely tourists to Prague."

"We have photos." A second agent teased, "Hold them near your heart ... while you sit all night in the van with four Czechs."

They all laughed, even Banzik. Nervous relief.

BANZIK DONNED HIS AGENT FACE when he called the office of the Counterterrorism Division at 3:00 p.m., 9:00 a.m. in New York. Anna's photos of Yusuf, the driver and the safehouse building, were being uploaded.

"Yes, sir," he said. "Going through now." He glared at the live feed on the video monitor. "Wait. A taxi just pulled up. Two men are getting out."

"Who are they?" Chase's voice had an edge of restrained excitement. "Are you watching?"

"Yes, it's happening now. Hold on, Boss." He turned to a Czech agent, snapping his fingers for attention. "Get video on those guys."

"They're removing luggage. Entering the building." Banzik paused.

"Get me those photos."

"Yup, coming right at ya."

Banzik notified the SIS Command Center that the flat now housed at least four hostiles. "Get someone on your traffic cameras and advise headquarters to backtrace that cab. Start at airport terminal exits. That'd be my guess." He wiped his forehead. "Get flight numbers, passenger lists and passport histories."

"Supervisors agree." An agent nodded and grinned. "We fish with big hook?"

"Yes, we do." Banzik chuckled. "We cast a wide net."

THE NEIGHBORHOOD REMAINED UNDISTURBED for the rest of the day. Team Three relieved Roman and Anna at the end of their shift. SIS and the Special Disciplinary Force had reviewed building floor plans and were refining strategies. Chase had confirmed Yusuf's identity, as well as three low-level operatives, foreign fighters who Interpol had in their database, and KLM Airlines had confirmed the two recent arrivals had boarded in London holding British passports.

SIS was ready to move. Their plan was set—until Chase requested delay at least until the following night.

Team One agents hammered Banzik as if postponement had been *his* decision. "Why must we wait for orders from New York."

"My boss knows this group. And the CIA has new foreign intel suggesting the cell's leader, Ali, the guy we're after, is on his way to Prague. He should arrive in one or two days."

"*Foreign* intel? You mean Israeli friends? Or Saudi?"

Banzik smirked. "We have friends everywhere."

"Why do you do this to us? We could complete arrests and be home for late dinner."

"I won't be getting home to my family for at least another week, so you get no sympathy from me." A tap on the van's door announced two security force agents carrying three paper bags. The two workmen agents squeezed out the door and raced toward the car that had transported the relief agents; it sped away with headlights off.

Banzik introduced himself to the new agents. "Hand over the package." He pulled a sandwich and a Coke from the bag, and checked his watch, 8:25 p.m. His replacement had been delayed.

TWENTY-TWO

Tuesday Afternoon

AFTER A DAY and a half of no activity, two hostiles made a bakery run, returning with three cake-size boxes cradled in their arms; a few hours later at 5:00 p.m., 11:00 a.m. in New York, the Almera again sped away. A Team One agent informed headquarters of the speedy departure, but supervisors resisted sending Team Two to follow.

Banzik scowled and snatched the phone. "He may be the cell's designated airport driver. We've seen low level guys hire taxis, but private cars meet leaders and notable people. The CIA reports Ali is expected in Prague, so Team Two should follow the car. A team should also be positioned at the airport to watch for the car. This is not complicated. I'm telling you, they're picking up our guy."

The reply from the other end of the line wasn't what Banzik wanted to hear. He tossed the phone back to the agent who said, "You worry too much. We will find them. Czech Republic is not so big."

Banzik gulped his cola.

AGENT BANZIK JOLTED from the sudden prod of a dusting wand from the undercover cleaning supplies. "Okay. Okay, I'm awake. Just resting my eyes." He grunted as he sat upright.

"What is it?" He straightened his hair and noted his watch, 6:40 p.m., 12:40 in New York. He'd been on duty nearly sixty hours. "What's happening?"

"See we find him. Driver returns with our package."

"Briefing notes report he travels with laptop." Another agent pointed to a satchel on the monitor. "He could be the big fish. But we have no photo to compare."

"No one has a photo. Not even his reported height and weight are accurate, but this guy fits our general description and he seems the right age."

The Czech agent said, "We wait now for Passport Control to send information."

"Let's hope," Banzik said. "I need a shower and a bed. I need to see my girls." He buried his face in his hands. *I need my wife.*

Within fifteen minutes, he had sent video and still photos of the suspect to Chase along with an audio recording from the apartment that roughly translated, stated: Ali arrives.

PAPER TRASH LITTERED the marble lobby, but Yusuf was unapologetic when he greeted Ali. Compared to the caves and hovels they had shared in the past, any structure with running water was an improvement. He kissed Ali's cheeks. "Welcome to Prague palace." He shrugged. "This way to the lift. Stairway around corner when you prefer. Service door in rear." He pointed down a dark hall. "Fire steps and roof exit on side of apartment washroom."

Ali eyed the vestibule.

The creaky elevator seemed to rise a meter a minute and fit only three or four passengers. A manually triggered interior bulb cycled so briefly, light barely lasted to the fourth floor.

Worn furniture and stained bathroom fixtures sat on cracked linoleum floors like most guesthouses in Jakarta,

London and Jersey. The six-room apartment was as neglected as the lobby, except for fresh paint on two newly plastered walls; Ali ran his hand over them nodding approval. Even though maintaining this safehouse was not Yusuf's responsibility, he felt it was and he craved Ali's approval.

Yusuf pointed to a table where small cakes and Egyptian sweets filled a chipped china platter. He snapped his fingers to attract the notice of a low-level soldier from Libya. "*Cha-y, min fadlik,*" he barked for tea service and pointed to Ali. His tongue clucked. "They are house hospitality yet they do nothing. No good. Only one skillful man works for this important house and he is driver." Yusuf reached for Ali's hand to hold. "Why did you not come before now?"

"I traveled through Athens. It was a bad decision. Sandstorm from Sahara. Too big. Too strong." Ali shook his head. "*Malesh.* It doesn't matter. We are here."

The hospitality soldier carried a brass tray holding two glasses of Turkish tea, and a tarnished silver spoon in a bowl he set beside the cakes. Ali sat in a leather recliner that clunked and groaned but no longer reclined; he stirred two spoonfuls of sugar into his glass and invited Yusuf to drink.

Yusuf waved his hand and the driver handed an envelope to Ali.

"It is good?" Yusuf asked.

Ali examined his new passport, clean of travel visas and immigration stamps. "Good."

Yusuf gave him one of the CDs he had shipped to Prague from the UPS Store before he left Connecticut.

Ali pulled his laptop from its satchel, copied the CD's reconnaissance images onto a thumb drive, and stashed the drive and his clean passport inside the breast pocket of his navy sport coat.

Yusuf briefed him about the images and the information he had gained by observing the American targets. "I sent photos to our server at the Internet café, but distribution awaits your instruction. You understand? The manager can call you about …" He glanced aside at the foreigners. "New developments."

He was confident about his plan, but didn't tell Ali he had already spoken with the café's manager. He would ease Ali into his idea, feeding only critical morsels. He did not tell him about the mess at the airport with the baggage search, nor did he mention his interrogation by the FBI supervisor. He did not tell Ali many things. "Are you pleased about my assignment? I beg permission to return to America."

Ali did not hesitate. "No. Your thinking remains small. You hold onto Sheik Usama long after his death. The al-Qaeda you long for is finished. We have withdrawn our support." He wrapped his hand around Yusuf's. "We have become more."

"I am sick to work with infidels, with Russians. Hear me, Ali. I do not trust them." Yusuf buried his face in his hands. "I want go back to days in camp."

"We can never go back. Eastern Flame has a new vision, one that evolves." Ali ran his hand across Yusuf's head.

With a steady look, Yusuf gazed into Ali's eyes. "Who *are* we?"

"This mission will be our breakout. It diverts attention while we prepare for the West's collapse. Be patient." Yusuf's eyes locked on him as he paced around the coffee table. "This diversion must be precise, spectacular in its death toll and it must appear like a final assault. The other cells are in place, but ours has trouble again and again. Every phase had problems. Your work was most useful, but your return will risk the operation."

"I want complete my jihad. I wish to be martyr. Do this for me."

Ali shook his head as he circled back to Yusuf. "You have been in the West too many months. You now attract suspicion." Ali slapped Yusuf's belly. "And you have become soft."

"I cannot keep myself to be quiet. I have big thought to give you, my Brother, an easy way to pass instruction to anyone at any time, and no one will suspect." Yusuf sneered at three soldiers who lingered too close, and bade Ali to move to a private rear bedroom.

Ali instructed the foreign fighters to remain seated while Yusuf led him to the back. Ali cradled Yusuf's shoulder. "Tell me your idea."

"I met an American woman on the plane …."

TWENTY-THREE

Tuesday Night, 8:20 p.m.

RIOT POLICE from the Special Disciplinary Force blew open the apartment door and tossed in flashbang grenades. Sound and light exploded.

Hostiles in the front room grabbed and fired AKs, but officers shot them before the stunned men hit police.

One dead. Two injured.

Agents dragged the wounded to the hallway, hurled them down the stairs, and secured them in a transport truck at a dizzying speed.

The leader bellowed orders in Arabic before disappearing down a rear hallway.

Yusuf bolted into the front room, reached for a Kalashnikov rifle and aimed at an open laptop. While he struggled with the clumsy grip, Agent Banzik fired, nearly blowing off his arm.

SWAT police searched the rooms, pantries and closets.

"Is he down?" Banzik tore through the apartment. "Who's got Ali? Where the hell is he?"

Banzik expected to find five hostiles, but could only account for four.

"Dammit. God freaking damn it. Lock down the block. Lock down the whole damn country." He couldn't believe Ali had escaped; he searched the apartment himself, inspecting the rear service door and the back stairwell and courtyard where he saw a dozen agents searching neighboring properties. Nothing. He gripped his head grunting like a wild beast, and returned to the front room where agents had collected two laptops, about thirty CDs and a dozen thumb drives, a digital camera and eight mobile phones.

Injured hostiles were whisked away for interrogation. Seized evidence was removed and on its way to SIS Command Center in Stodulky in southwest Prague—and where the Warsaw agent had been delayed.

Great, Banzik thought. *The cavalry has arrived. Perfect timing.*

After watching and waiting for two days and nights, the final onslaught had begun and ended stunningly fast, with no injury to Czech forces or to Special Agent Marcus Banzik.

ALI HAD CLIMBED the fire steps to the roof and jumped to an adjacent building when police charged through the courtyard. He twisted over railings and leaped from landing to landing until he reached a footpath three blocks away.

Escape had injured his weak leg, an Afghan souvenir, with at least a sprain. The canopy of trees shielded the sidewalk from street lamps creating a lightless passage to Nerudova Street, where he blended with shop patrons at Malostranske Square. He limped from the area, hugging retaining walls and darting into shadows along the cobblestone lanes of the Little Quarter until he reached the river.

The flurry of police lights and sirens seemed a world away as Ali envisioned tens of officers cramming into the safehouse to examine his belongings and Yusuf's, and the martyrs left behind. He expected international agencies had also sent their best investigators in search of evidence—or glory.

Ali pulled a cell phone from his shirt pocket and dialed the local number that would detonate the C-4 packed in the safehouse walls.

At 9:00 p.m. the apartment … the building … the night … erupted with fire and smoke.

The blast thundered across the city and echoed against far hills. Structures rattled. Walls cracked. Windows blew out, shooting shards of glass showering onto courtyards, quietly pinging like little bells when they hit stone floors.

Then dead silence as if even God held his breath.

The air reeked of gunpowder, burning wood and charred flesh.

Chaos followed. Flames and ash. Debris rained down like a winter storm.

Like snow in September.

"SAHAR."

Agent Banzik stared into the man's eyes as he spoke his final word; his would be the last face Yusuf saw before he bled out.

He emptied Yusuf's pockets, seizing his passport and billfold, and stepped out of the apartment to examine them under the hallway light. Blood had stained the contents: more than $300 USD, a child's crayon drawing and a photo of a young girl. He pulled an evidence bag from his jacket pocket.

An explosion fired Banzik down the stairs with a blinding light and a deafening blast.

His body ricocheted against a wall and crashed onto a stairwell landing. Wreckage battered his body in a mound of shattered concrete, twisted metal and slivered wood. A splintered stair rail impaled his leg like an arrow. Broken tiles pummeled his torso with sheared razor edges that shred clothing and slashed skin.

Fine gray powder muddied his sight as he choked for air. A painless silence enveloped him like the cloud of dust, though Banzik couldn't distinguish genuine calm from impaired hearing.

Am I dead?

He lay stunned, trying to assess the damage to his flesh, but was unable to raise his head to see. A sharp pang pierced his thigh when he shifted his left leg.

Smoke and flames shot from the apartment.

The street facing façade collapsed and shattered on the road, crashing onto cars. Smashing onto people. Banzik winced when the sounds of crunching metal, screams and shrieks cut through his fog.

Flames flared with even more intensity fueled by the sudden rush of air. Smaller blasts popped in the rear of the apartment as fire reached a cache of ammunition and bottled fuels.

Banzik spit dirt from his mouth and coughed a distressed call for help. But even *he* could not hear his plea. He could barely hear emergency sirens.

Firefighters soon rushed the building. A cold spray from their hose blasted the stairwell like a broken dam. His arm piercing the rubble, must have looked like a dead man's limb reaching from a grave. A firm hand grasped it. Firefighters freed his body and clipped the rail impaling his leg. He bounced on a man's shoulders down to the street where a medical team waited.

"It's Banzik," Roman shouted.

"He's American FBI," Anna said.

They helped an attendant lay him on clean sheets and fasten him to a gurney.

The ambulance sped away, its wailing sirens synchronized with other emergency vehicles in a tragic opera. Banzik prayed for his life as fear pulsed with thoughts of his wife, Julie, raising their two girls alone. Even his damn cat came to mind.

An attendant with a broad smile leaned into his field of vision; both hands signaled with thumbs up. "You will live." Banzik's cell phone buzzed; the attendant answered and asked, "Can you hear?" His forefingers tapped his own ears.

Banzik nodded and the attendant pressed the phone against his ear; he barely heard the familiar voice demanding, "Find my agent. Is my agent safe? Where's my guy?"

"Boss?" Relief choked his throat as he struggled to speak. "Banzik here."

The attendant took the phone, "Banzik will be okay, Boss. ... Yes, we go now to hospital. No worry. Doctor will call. ... Okay. ... Okay, okay, Military Hospital, yes, we go there." The attendant's fist hammered the window separating the medical compartment from the driver as he shouted the new destination. *"Ustredni Vojenské nemocnice."* The driver veered west.

A few minutes later, the ambulance stopped at the emergency entrance where doctors, nurses and the FBI agent reassigned from Warsaw were waiting.

Attendants removed the stretcher.

The agent held his phone to his ear when he leaned over Banzik. "He's here, sir. Yeah, I'm lookin' right at 'im. ... Oh yeah, he's a mess. Minor cuts, dust, dirt .... Ouch, that's gotta hurt. One leg needs stitchin'. Looks like a wooden stake pierced his thigh, but bleeding seems controlled. No spurting."

Banzik blinked several times.

"His eyes are open and he's alert. He knows we're talkin' about 'im." The agent winked at Banzik. "Relax buddy. We're at the Military Hospital near the airport. Do you know what happened to you? Do you know where you are?"

Banzik struggled to swallow. "How many dead?"

"Numbers are still comin' in. You stand down, ya' hear. Let the docs fix ya'. I'm with ya' till we walk outta here. Boss's orders."

Every muscle in Banzik's body went limp.

As the gurney rolled inside, the agent walked beside it resting his left hand on Banzik's right shoulder. He leaned close to Banzik's ear and said in a gentle whisper, "I've got your back, buddy."

Banzik released a quiet sigh. A tear rolled down his face clearing a trail of pink human flesh through the mask of gray powder.

THE EXPLOSION was a diversion more spectacular than Ali had imagined. The usual tourist crowd strolled on the Charles Bridge, but their attention focused on flames that reached toward the sky—their fingers pointed, their camera phones aimed, their eyes riveted on the firestorm.

"What happened?"

"Did you see?"

"Oh my God. What was that?"

The voices of the crowd shrieked with horror in a half-dozen languages as eruptions popped like firecrackers. Nearby a young boy twitched with every blast. The man with him, likely the boy's father, lowered a hand to the child's shoulder to hold him in place.

A little girl's face puckered as she began to cry. She stomped for her mother's attention and raised her arms to be held, but the woman could not break her stare from the tranquil view that had devolved to destruction; a human scene repeated every few meters from the Little Quarter to Old Town.

Ali crossed the river unnoticed. *Perhaps no one had survived. Maybe proof of my presence had burned in the blast.*

Tomorrow he would have money wired to him. He knew where to go, but now, he needed to find supplies to get him through the night.

Activity in the Square appeared normal. He had outrun the storm.

He slid through the gates of a pavement café and moved behind a middle-aged woman, a Brit he guessed, to grab the purse strapped over the back of her chair. He hit on the next café and snatched a bag from a younger woman with a New York accent. Jew he suspected. He stashed the small purses under his jacket and on leaving the Square, he lifted a backpack from a Japanese teenager who wore expensive rings and an imitation military jacket.

The shops on Celetna Street were brightly lit with harsh fluorescent lights beamed on art crystal and amber jewelry, and he felt safer when he passed through the Powder Tower. Around the corner, he disappeared among vagrants gathered in a dark courtyard, a mere block from the Municipal House where theatergoers took little notice of the haggard group, as long as panhandling did not interrupt their path. Ali crouched among the tramps and waited over an hour for police to arrive, though none came.

With several Czech crowns and a few euros from the Brit's billfold, he entered a food market beside an Italian bistro to rob packaged meats, canned beans and a jar of ground cinnamon to sprinkle in tea. He stuffed provisions into the backpack, and paid at the checkout for four liters of water bottled in plastic.

By 2:00 a.m. Ali had found a grassy park not far from the Hotel Hilton. Six hours would pass before he could collect travel money from the Internet café, and by nightfall he would find a boat to steal and sail from Prague toward his mission—and to his destiny.

TWENTY-FOUR

Tuesday Night

THREE DAYS IN PRAGUE seemed more like three weeks with sightseeing and shopping, the opera and museums, and shooting photos of everything that didn't move. Kate and the teachers laughed so hard their sides ached. An early dinner cruise on the Vltava highlighted their last hours together. The moon cast a blue glow on spires of Gothic architecture, while a city guide spoke of history as they glided past landmarks. *Coop would have loved this.*

The evening ended at their favorite pavement café where they ordered coffee and dessert; and at nine o'clock, even through the crowd's chatter and even though the sky was clear, they thought they heard thunder.

"Perhaps it was a sonic boom," one of the teachers joked.

"The blast was too close. The ground shook and glasses rattled. More like a meteor fireball."

"That's funny, Kate. You must watch too many movies. Sure it wasn't a UFO crash?"

"There's an interesting idea." Kate tucked her purse into her lap and stretched to see the surrounding area. "I can't believe you'll soon be gone."

"I wouldn't mind a leisurely stroll to the Charles Bridge."

"I'm not crazy about that idea tonight," Kate said. "But it's up to you. You're leaving early, but if your purse gets snatched you'll lose your passport and they won't let you on the bus. You won't be able to exit the country."

"Where do you get those paranoid ideas?"

"Mostly, I travel alone and learned to be super cautious. I brace for every trouble and so far it's kept me safe. I'm trying to ease up, that's what vacations are for, right? Let's have a round of drinks before we decide what to do." *A good stall tactic.*

Murmurs crept from café to café and table to table until Kate overheard, "Bomb."

She twisted toward a nearby group of college-age men and women. "What happened?"

A young man leaned toward her. "The bridges are closed, even Karluv Most."

"Karluv Most! Impossible."

"What's wrong? What did he say?"

"Karluv Most. That's the Charles Bridge. He said the police closed it."

The teachers laughed. "Our last night and she suddenly speaks Czech."

"I can't speak, but I understand half of what they say. Three years of Spanish and all I can do is order enchiladas, but I learned Czech in a few days. Go figure."

Her back stiffened as she eavesdropped on conversations at nearby tables. Rumors of a bomb spread through the crowd like a bad flu. Someone said all roads leading to the river were closed and the Manesuv and Legii bridges were only open to police, ambulance and Fire Brigade traffic; some thought the measure too drastic to be true. There *had* been an unusual amount of police activity with officers running about and patrol cars speeding by. Emergency lights and sirens from all directions had skirted the Square, then faded as forces aimed away from the city center.

No one paid much attention.

"Something's happened." Kate pressed against her temple where it throbbed.

"Relax. Finish your drink," a teacher said.

The other asked, "Are you having a premonition?

"No, just common sense. Look around. Not an officer in sight. We've been here every night. They're *always* patrolling. At least a half dozen. I don't need a premonition. It's obvious something significant has happened."

The teachers scanned the area. "Maybe so, but no one's panicking; it seems like a normal night—and our last, so let's enjoy it."

The evening was pleasantly warm by New England standards though the Arizona teachers disagreed; the temperature hovered around sixty-five, but would quickly slip toward the forties if the forecast was correct. The crowd was vibrant and talkative. Kate sipped her drink while the teachers ordered refills and spoke of their travel plans through Slovakia into Poland to Zakopane, Krakow, Warsaw and home.

Kate would be on her own for another two days and everyone had a suggestion for the balance of her time. Her airport taxi driver had given her a flier about a ghost walking-tour originating at the Astronomical Clock. She aimed the candle centerpiece to illuminate the ad. "How can I host a paranormal website and *not* go on a ghost tour?"

"I feel them all around us." One of the teachers briskly rubbed her arms.

"I read Prague was built to a secret plan by mysterious brotherhoods," the other said. "Narrow passages and speaking stones."

"I'm certainly open to strange tales. I'd love to hear what those speaking stones have to say, and I must take photos; maybe I'll capture ghost pictures I can display on my site." Kate tucked the flier in her purse and shrugged. "Should be fun.

Other than that, I have no plans."

"You should come with us. I hear Krakow's haunted, too."

For a millisecond, Kate considered changing plans, but that wasn't how she lived. With enough stubborn signs she sometimes shifted off-plan, but in general she was more cautious and traditional than people thought, preferring to research, draw a plan and stick with it, though Jack would disagree. She wouldn't hear the end from him if she didn't return as scheduled. He'd call out the FBI to trail her and no one needs that—unless the agent was a hottie like Matt Chase.

"Kate, what's that sly smile? What are you thinking?"

"She's considering Poland."

"Are you?"

"No, but I appreciate the invitation. I was thinking about a guy I met at the airport." She shifted in her chair and ran her finger around her ear and down her neck. "It was one of those ships-in-the-night encounters. We live a hundred miles apart." She sighed. "We'll never find each other again. But my imagination …." Her voice trailed off as sudden sadness stole the moment and she stiffened. "Hey, I'm really going to miss you guys." She promised she'd visit Sedona in a year or two and they traded addresses, e-mail and phone numbers, and she gave them her Dreamwatch business cards.

A commotion broke out a few tables away when a woman screeched her purse had been stolen. Her accusation was followed by another and another, as others checked their belongings. An Oriental-looking man, maybe Japanese, seated at an adjacent café shouted his backpack was gone.

Everyone clutched their purses and packages, and held them close.

Kate's grip tightened around her bag. "I was worried about pickpockets on the Charles Bridge and it happened right here."

"Seems your premonitions are a bit distorted."

"Jet lag." But Kate knew the truth of it was nothing to joke about. She sucked in a deep breath. "We made it this far with no hassles. Let's return to the hotel and lock ourselves in our rooms." *For a year.* The teachers' bus to Zakopane would depart in less than eight hours. "I'll say goodbye tonight because I won't be up that early."

As they left the table, a crowd offering suggestions and advice about replacing passports, money, credit cards and the like, had formed a protective wall around the theft victims. Someone asked where the police were. Kate wondered too. Since the earlier commotion, no police had arrived to take the victims' reports.

No one would investigate the petty street crimes the State Department site had warned about. Not tonight. Probably not tomorrow. Possibly not ever.

Something bigger had happened. Of that much she was sure.

TWENTY-FIVE

Wednesday Morning

SIRENS WAILED ALL NIGHT and into morning waking Kate several times an hour until she gave up trying to sleep. The stunning views from her tenth floor room as well as her Prague experience could not have been better. She couldn't wait to tell Jack, not that his knowing would satisfy future concerns. She gazed over the city, her sense of timing keen, and it was time to go. A day less would have been too short, and a day more, too long.

What is *that?* A smoky cloud hovered across the river.

Her camera zoom didn't help much and she wished for her binoculars; she'd packed too lean for such useful extras. With the room's keycard tucked in her shirt pocket, she checked the clock and hurried to the lobby. *Maybe they didn't leave yet.*

The teachers and their tour group waited while porters loaded luggage into the bus storage bins. Kate shot group photos for her scrapbook and walked outside with them. They hugged and kissed and blotted tearing eyes until the teachers boarded. The doorman returned to the lobby and porters disappeared, leaving Kate alone on the pavement with her arms drooping at her sides and her camera swinging in her hand. The bus departed to her feeble wave.

She felt more alone than she had all week … really all month, even if she included the days at home immediately following Todd's exit.

A sudden yearning for male company confused her. *Keep yourself busy. Don't mess it up now. Mind your own business and go home.* Her self-scolding thoughts shifted to the FBI agent from the airport, the glint in his eyes when he glanced up from her passport and his touch on her shoulder. She'd felt his lips on her ear and the heat of his breath on her neck. Was it *him* she longed for? Or the fall into love—with anyone?

Missed opportunities in her life had been of her own making. How empty the past few days would have been had she not invited the teachers to walk to the Square, even though she was tired, her ankles swollen from the flight, her feet blistered from an earlier exploratory walk in shoes not meant for walking —but she had. After that first precise moment at the travel desk, their paths might not have crossed. *Good move.*

The English version of the newspaper had not yet been released, so Kate grabbed one with the most pictures, and entered the dining room where fine china and silver utensils laid on linen table cloths. She sat beside a window and studied the paper's front page photos of distressed crowds and emergency personnel; she pointed to the burning building and asked the waiter, "What happened here? Where is this?"

"Near Prague Castle." He read the headline and caption. "It says perhaps a bomb destroyed the apartment house. Many people die. Many Policie. They search for more feared covered under stone."

"Oh my God. I'm so sorry. When did this happen?"

"Night, passed." His hand waved backwards. "Nine o'clock."

"I thought I heard thunder, but the noise must have been the explosion." She spread the napkin across her lap. "I was at the Square with friends. No one knew what happened. We heard sirens and the police were running. They must have been rushing to the fires."

The waiter agreed.

This was exactly the kind of incident Jack would hear about and imagine her buried under debris. As news of the bomb spread and the death toll rose, he was bound to worry and would be expecting her call. She considered the time difference. "I passed a cyber café near the Marriott, do you know it?"

"You can go after eight o'clock."

She felt like a jerk for not carrying tip money.

After breakfast and back in her room, she showered and dressed. Fast. A lengthy set of tasks had suddenly developed with less than twenty-four hours to complete them: Ghosts and Legends Walking Tour; back to the Charles Bridge to shoot close-ups of the statues; shopping for souvenirs, and travel snacks at the little market with the courtyard and maybe a pizza lunch at the bistro next door. Tonight, an early bedtime. The sirens should be calm by then.

She thought she'd visit at least one church; she'd even light a votive candle. Coop loved old churches, though she would speak of them as "historically important architecture" to make them sound more interesting to Kate. *If she were here, we'd have visited a half dozen by now.*

Kate hit the power button on the TV remote and switched channels to BBC Europe in time to hear the news anchor announce, "Officials of the Czech government have confirmed last night's terrorist bomb destroyed an eight-story apartment building near Prague's prestigious section of Hradcany, home to popular tourist sites and several embassies. Unconfirmed sources report at least nine bodies have been recovered from the rubble including law enforcement and security officers. Identification has been hampered due to the condition of the bodies. More on this story next hour."

"Oh my God." She stared at the video footage. *That's the street! Another near miss to add to* the list.

The day *must* begin with an e-mail to Jack that would lie: "I wasn't close to the blast."

TWENTY-SIX

KATE WAITED OUTSIDE of the Internet café, the one she'd heard about from the guy on the plane. The manager, a short, dark haired man, probably in his mid-thirties, with a paunch greater than his years warranted, unlocked the door at 9:20. *So late. How rude. He didn't even acknowledge me.*

A handwritten sign taped at the service desk read: 1 Kc = 1 min. She handed over a 100 Crown note to pay for sixty minutes though she'd probably use only thirty, and held out her hand until he dropped 40 Kc in coins.

He seemed to watch her with special interest, which she assumed was due to her being his only customer. Still, his demeanor made her feel as if she were naked, even though she wore jeans and a baggy sweatshirt. *Now when I want privacy, he can't take his eyes off me.* Despite her warm clothing, a chill crawled down her spine. She settled at a computer station, tucked her canvas bag on her lap, and logged on to her e-mail account determined to do her business and get the hell out.

The manager worked on a laptop at the service counter, repeatedly tapping the same key as if advancing through a list of files or scrolling through images, a move with which she was too familiar. He abruptly stopped while his stare volleyed between her and his screen. He made a phone call.

She shivered, startled by the language shift to Arabic as he slipped into a back room.

Kate lifted her address book and camera from her bag before dropping it to the floor and squeezing it between her feet. She glanced over her shoulder even though the room was empty. When the manager returned, she sneaked a photo of him. A clue for Jack in case she disappeared. *Oh, stop.*

She typed a message to his personal e-mail. "Don't worry. I wasn't close to the blast. Only heard sirens. Saw photos in morning paper. Today, a walking tour, souvenirs and a historic church. Will call when I return on Thursday. Love, K."

Ten minutes had passed when a handsome stranger limped in, wearing charcoal slacks and a navy sport coat. Fine clothes were wrinkled as if he'd slept on a park bench. A shabby backpack, that hung as if he were unaccustomed to carrying it, didn't match his pricey attire. He and the manager greeted each other and kissed each other's cheeks. He pulled a thumb drive from his jacket pocket that the manager took into the back room. The stranger's eyes locked on her until the manager returned with his drive.

She craned to see his hands. He pulled out a money clip, but it looked less like he paid for computer time and more like the manager had passed a wad of U.S. hundred-dollar bills.

Though he could have sat anywhere in the empty café, the stranger took a seat at the station directly across from her. Setting his pack on an adjacent seat. His feet slid under the table until they nudged her foot. His trousers were soiled like a child's with grass stained knees and dirt ground into his seat. Facial hair appeared unshaved for days, but none of that distracted from his compelling smile and the piercing stare of his dark eyes.

Kate nodded, but didn't speak, preferring to hear his first language. Strangers abroad often greeted her in German; good guess, her ancestry being mostly Polish and Italian, with family rumors of German and Austrian descent, their assumptions weren't so wrong.

"Good morning." He spoke as if 'good' had a strong 'U' sound. "English?"

English. Not his first language. Her head bobbed. *I'll take a wild guess.* "*Laa.* American."

His face seemed to light when she said 'No' in his language. "You speak Arabic?"

She half smiled. "Only a few words." But now she knew *he* did.

"Coffee?" He pronounced the word as if it ended with a long *faye* sound.

Agent Chase's warning, *Don't talk to strangers*, came and went from her thoughts faster than last night's thief in the Square. She looked around. People walked the street, could easily see indoors and most did glance in. *Seems safe enough.* "Sure, why not."

"Why not." He repeated as if memorizing the expression, and introduced himself as Abdul, "But Ali is easier for you to remember."

I'll decide what I'm capable of remembering.

He called to the manager for two coffees, then said he was visiting friends and had been in Prague for three weeks. She told him about the sights she'd seen and that her friends had left earlier. Her itinerary spilled from her lips before she could stop it.

"What will you do today?" His stare captivated her.

She told him about the ghost tour and he confessed to several superstitious beliefs surrounding bad luck, like walking under ladders and breaking mirrors. She shared a few of hers, adding black cats and opening umbrellas indoors.

Kate logged onto her site where they read several ghost stories. His interest seemed sincere.

He said his mother had dreamed his aunt appeared at the foot of her bed the night she died. The fragrance of her jasmine perfume filled the house so strongly, he smelled it in the morning. "Though Muslims do not believe in ghosts."

"Get out. I've read your fables. Aren't the jinn the same as ghosts?"

"Jinn are spirits who tempt man, not spirits of dead people."

"May I post your mother's story? It's quite like others I've heard."

"Oh yes, how do you do that?" His lack of hesitation, or questions, surprised her.

"It's easy. Look here." She navigated to the Contact page and scrolled down. "Type in this text box titled: Tell Us Your Story! Then click this Submit button."

Ali dictated his mother's ghost sighting, adding more description, while she typed. "Good one. Very spooky."

"Spooky." He laughed as if he enjoyed how the word puckered his lips.

Their faces were close as they peered at the screen. Occasionally his arm would brush against hers and she'd recoil, more with surprise than anything, that he seemed to be flirting, though his technique obviously lacked the experience to come off smoothly. He was handsome, charming and intriguing; the kind of man she once found irresistible, yet he was cold enough to turn her skin to gooseflesh, even more than the manager and the creep on the plane.

She couldn't define what it was about him. The state of his clothes? Or his voice that said one thing while body language relayed another? She recalled a phrase Jack's friend Dante once used, crude but perceptive, like most of what escaped from Dante's lips even without the swear words: "Don't pee on me and tell me it's raining." That's how she felt about Ali.

If she had an umbrella, she'd open it. Bad luck be damned.

"Finished? Show my mother's story." He seemed pleased.

"The form will come to me by e-mail through a processing service. I read it and repair the language if needed, then I change the old page and upload the new one."

He studied the screen, waiting, hands clenching on the table beside the keyboard.

"Not now," she laughed. "When I get home." She had almost softened to his allure until he asked *When?* in a tone too sharp and too demanding. His eyes seemed to cut her. *I wasn't laughing* at *him.*

She told him she often updated the site, but he was relentless in asking, "Why not now?"

"I need editing software." The harder he pushed, the more she resisted. Women in his country might have found his attempt at dominance enticing, but he clearly didn't know how to act with independent Western women.

He waved to the manager and said something in Arabic. The manager snarled, shook his head and waved his arms, "*Laa. Laa. Laa.*" Ali rose to the service desk where they argued, hands and arms waving all over.

With one hand, Kate slipped her finger across her camera's On switch, tipped the lens upward to Ali's face while he was distracted by the manager, and snapped a photo—not a great shot, but good enough to stir future memory about who he was.

When he returned she asked, "What's wrong?"

"I asked for the password to use his software, but he does not share such things. I could not convince him." He shrugged his shoulders. "So we will wait."

"That's okay, I have to go, anyway." The computer's clock read 11:10. "I owe for extra time."

"I will settle because I distracted you. I beg your pardon."

"Oh, thanks." She collected and stashed her belongings in her bag. "I really must leave, now. Lots to do."

"Yes." He smirked. "Lots to do."

Outside the café, Kate shot its sign and the posted street marker to record the date. Months or even years would sometimes pass before she viewed travel photos, but not for this trip. She promised to share pictures with the teachers soon after their return home.

She estimated the teachers would not reach Zakopane until after lunch. She had their farewell photo dated—and the hotel staff, cellar pub bartenders, and the homeless men in the market courtyard.

And now she had a photo of the cyber café manager—and of the stranger named Ali.

She didn't resent the male attention, but his hubris made her feel insignificant. Ali told her he was traveling to the U.S. within the week, though his plans were not yet settled. She worried she'd revealed too much personal information. *If he boards my flight, I'll just die.*

ALI REMAINED at the café studying the stories and the language on Dreamwatch.com. He noted the variety of locations from which people wrote: states across the U.S. and countries as far as Australia and Southeast Asia, there must have been thirty or more nations represented.

He leaned back in the chair and folded his arms across his chest.

Yusuf's idea could *work.*

The safehouse raid had come too close to striking a death blow to his cell. His mission again thwarted by circumstance that could *not* have been coincidence. His cell should have been the most successful, yet they seemed like buffoons. *How did the Czechs learn of the Prague meeting and the safehouse location? From the Americans? I have not been there in years and they likely knew nothing of me. Who interferes? Yusuf? The Russian?*

Troubled by jinn? Or ghosts from my past?

For the rest of the morning and through the afternoon, he implemented a new strategy to communicate with his cell, confident at last, he would walk an easier road.

Tomorrow he would escape Prague, a step closer to America —and to his fate.

TWENTY-SEVEN

Wednesday, Late Afternoon

FIRES NO LONGER BURNED. Sirens wailed less frequently. A tragic assault on the people of Prague and all Kate could do was witness and tell what had happened.

One last chance for photos and she was done, ready to pack and get out of town. She heard they had reopened the Charles Bridge at four o'clock, even while rescue crews continued to search the rubble. One nearby bridge remained reserved for emergency vehicles.

The sun was about to set and warm light bathed the statues. *Could not have timed it better.* The river was a golden ribbon with diamonds flickering on the surface. She felt completely satisfied with her journey—except for the part with the bomb—and she couldn't imagine she'd considered canceling. An energy had shifted in her core, as if she'd been struggling to exit a congested stifling space and had finally reached the door to an outside garden. *Back on track.*

Prague will change everything.

She raised her lens to shoot each statue and the crowd on the bridge. She thought she saw Ali, but his face was shadowed and she was blinded by the low sun. A group of teenage boys jostled her. She fumbled, fearing they were a gang of thieves, and almost dropped her camera. She nearly collided with the man and when she regained composure, the stranger was gone, disappearing in the throng before they made contact—but it probably wasn't him anyway.

Oh my God. My bridge dream. She had just experienced: the familiar man who walked with a limp, his shadowed face. A golden glow on a crowd. Almost dropped her camera. *Wow, very accurate.* A satisfied grin crossed her face—followed by the unease of knowing her gift was returning flat out full.

Kate walked down Karlova and Celetna streets, shopping for souvenirs: fabrics, crystals and a book of Prague photos for herself, as if she didn't have enough of her own; black and white art prints for herself and Jack; a key chain for Dante to remind him to drive safely, a toy replica of a Czech Policie car for his son Bobo; and for Coop, a Byzantine icon of Jesus and Mary carved in relief.

Private security guards had established checkpoints at the Marriott and Hilton. Inside her hotel, a security table had been set up where two armed guards inspected guest packages, unwrapped her purchases, and verified her passport and keycard. She didn't know much about guns, but the guards' guns were the biggest she'd ever seen up close.

It was past seven when she reached her room. She dropped souvenirs on the bed and headed to the restaurant where she ate a light dinner, and tipped the breakfast waiter who had read the newspaper to her.

Kate packed everything except what she'd wear on the plane, while TV anchors reported news of the bomb, the injured and the dead. The death toll had risen to 18 including 11 police and security personnel. Another nine seriously injured and receiving treatment in area hospitals, including four firefighters injured while battling the blaze. Leaders and dignitaries from around the globe have "condemned this cowardly act of terrorism." Kate glanced up from packing when the anchor announced, "Together at an economic summit in London, the

U.S. President joined the British Prime Minister and French President, in a call to all nations to remain vigilant in resisting and fighting this plague of violent extremism."

It was a good time to be leaving Prague and returning to the U.S.

A good time to go home, where she would be safe.

~ *Part Three* ~

Northeast U.S.A.

Kathryn Orzech

TWENTY-EIGHT

NEW YORK
Thursday

THE BOMB HAD EXPLODED Tuesday evening at 8:56 p.m. Czech time, mid-afternoon in New York. Matt Chase had been alerted by 3:05 and within twenty minutes he'd established communications with foreign counterparts. The FBI's investigation began before fires had been extinguished and before bodies had been recovered. The death toll stood at 22 with 36 injured, of which several more were likely to die.

Fast acting Czech Security Forces had removed evidence before the explosion—the largest intelligence cache since SEALs had stormed bin Laden's final resting compound—phone data, computer files and a mountain of photos. Over one hundred interviews had been conducted, plus the ongoing interrogations of the two surviving hostiles. Chase's mind was in overdrive with new active leads and he might have felt like a five-year-old on Christmas morning if he wasn't in such a pissy mood.

There was no getting around the wake of his risky decision to release Yusuf when he could have detained him. The price had been too high. *How did I not see that coming?* He should have flown to Prague and followed Yusuf himself. He and Banzik could have pulled it off. Yusuf was dead and his trail to Ali … incinerated.

Agent Vargas tapped on the door frame and leaned into Chase's office. "Czech SIS recovered part of a UPS shipping label. It's scorched, but a partial tracking number was enough to find it in company records. You're gonna love this, Boss." He opened the JPEG on Chase's computer and turned the screen toward him.

"It's a beauty. What's the punch line?"

"The package shipped to Prague from one of their retail stores in Wallingford, Connecticut—*and* there were packing fees."

"Sweet." Chase leaned back, his hands cupped behind his head. "Wallingford's less than twenty minutes from the New Haven Field Office. Get one of their agents out there. See if the packer remembers what was shipped. I want confirmation of the contents and I want it in an hour."

Chase wasn't waiting for results from New Haven. The camera and CDs were loaded with photos that didn't leave the U.S. with Yusuf. They must have been shipped ahead. If anything *had* to get to Ali, *they* would have.

So what the hell was so urgent? And so worthy of protection?

Chase pored through the new images. Date stamps indicated they'd been shot when Yusuf was in the States, but with identifying landmarks and signage cropped out of frame, the photos seemed useless. *Peculiar reconnaissance.* Close-ups of stairwells and alleys, bridges and trains could have been shot anywhere in North America or even northern Europe. Their only value would be to someone who knew the location and needed to see details.

He forwarded the broadest landscapes to every East Coast field office and resident agency, hoping someone would recognize something. He consulted a geologist and a botanist, anything to narrow the search. Crazy idea, but hell, nothing to lose. More than once, the Director had decreed, above all:

"Know your domain." This was the reason and Chase was about to prove why.

Before the day got away from him, he grabbed a coffee, checked the time and closed his office door. He removed a folded paper from his suit pocket and punched the country code for the Czech Republic, the number of the Military Hospital, and the room of Special Agent Marcus Banzik.

The Warsaw agent answered and reported Banzik's medical condition. "The rail that impaled his leg hit muscle, but missed arteries and bone; infection remains a concern and he's on antibiotics." The agent sounded like he was reading from notes. "Hearing loss has improved and is close to normal. Concrete dust scratched his eyes; they've been irrigated and are healing. Vision was not damaged. Minor cuts were treated and closed with ninety-six stitches. Most scars will be minor. He's one lucky S.O.B. with a hell of an appetite for the local food."

Chase swiveled his chair to face outside and bent his elbows to his knees while he listened.

"With concern of infection and concussion, we might be here another two or three days."

"That's great news. Good job agent. Put him on the phone." Chase touched the coffee cup to his lips.

"Boss, Banzik here."

Chase set down his drink and sat straight. "Marcus, you sound better than the last time we spoke. Are the Czechs giving good care? Is my agent?"

Banzik's chuckle ended with a choking cough. "No complaints, sir."

"What do you need? What can I do for your family?"

"Call my wife. She doesn't believe I'll soon be home. She wants to fly here. But the girls just started a new school year and—"

"It's as good as done. I'll call immediately. Anything else?"

"This isn't over. There's more going on, Boss. Prague was their error. The blast wasn't supposed to happen. I watched them for three days and I'd bet my life they're planning a greater attack. We've got to stop the bastards."

"You get better, get rested and get back to work. We need you, buddy."

After he hung up, Chase called Julie Banzik and inquired about the kids. He told her Marcus was in good humor and that he'd arrange an afternoon video conference so she could see for herself. He insisted she call his personal cell phone if she or the girls needed anything. He told her he'd assigned an agent, who, he promised, would remain at her husband's side until he was back in her arms. He heard her release a deep sigh.

Chase felt a sudden emptiness after the call as he weighed Banzik's return home—wife, kids, cat—against what he faced each night, his empty apartment.

TWENTY-NINE

VERMONT
Thursday

AGENT JACK KASABIAN opened the file of his next assignment, insurance fraud involving a threat to the Burlington IRS office. The suspect was a known local with a history of mental illness. The case was practically solved before it reached him and the IRS investigators. Several more cases lay on his desk: bankruptcy, health care and mortgage fraud; a good variety, but not nearly as challenging as a missing person or a threat against a member of Congress.

The phone broke his boredom-induced stupor. Dante wanted to meet and he sounded serious so Jack agreed to meeting for lunch. An hour with Crash would at least introduce levity to the mundane cases he'd work for the rest of the week. At least that was the plan.

And Kate was due back later in the day, so there was that to look forward to.

JACK WAS SHOCKED to see Dante saunter into Scuffer's. His shirt was crudely tucked into poor fitting jeans; scraggly hair was more grey than brown. Worn loafers on bare feet was a leftover fashion statement from the eighties, like his black with gold trim TransAm that Jack thought he'd glimpsed moments ago, squeezing into an illegal parking spot. At six feet Dante Benard was 240 with burly limbs; and even with a midline paunch, he looked to be a force not to mess with. "Didn't that old muscle machine die yet?"

"Hey, hey. Don't insult my girl. She'll probably outlive me. I took out another fender on my last gig. Guy wouldn't stop so I rammed him." Dante greeted him with a slap on the back that threw him off balance. "But that baby runs like the day she rolled off the line."

Jack shook his head. "I hope the guy was a felon on the run and not some poor chump who accidentally cut you off." They took a table near the back. "I'll order for us; I'm treating."

Dante opened and closed a menu. "Felon, of course. What do you think I am?"

"Two cheeseburgers, one rings, a Diet Coke and a draft." Jack handed the menus back to the waiter and braced for Dante's rant of complaints. "So what's going on?"

"I'm not gettin' any work. Bounty hunting stinks. Too much competition. We're practically shootin' each other out there."

The waiter delivered drinks. "What happened to your application at ICE?"

"Rejected. U.S. Marshals, rejected. Local police, fired." Dante gulped a mouthful of beer. "Even freakin' Angie threw me out."

"Whoa. Where's this coming from?" *And where was it going?* "You can't blame Angie. She gave you more chances than anyone. Her hands are full with caring for Bobo, working full-time and—"

"Here, more ammo." Dante slid the salt shaker across the table. "Rub it in." He shifted in his seat. "You think I don't feel bad Angie has to work? I'm ticked. Immigration and Customs Enforcement on the New England-Canadian border. I was made for that job at ICE, so this is getting to be really crappy.

I'm a decent guy. All I need is one decent break."

Jack waited for the appeal.

"What do ya' think, Jack? Can ya' help me out?"

There it is. The waiter set rings and burgers between them. Dante ordered two more beers.

Jack shot a look at him. "Come on, you know better. I can't drink while I'm working."

"They're both for me," Dante said to the waiter. "Space 'em out."

Jack had prepared himself for a favor request; he didn't expect a plea for work. He was thinking more like: Can you lend a hundred till next week? But Dante was asking him to put his name on the line. And Dante's track record stunk. "Shit, Crash. I don't have magic answers. You brought this on yourself. What do you expect me to do?"

"Can't you get me into your place? Recommend me to someone?"

"Private security must have job openings. Even bodyguard. Why don't you look into it?"

Dante cut him off. "Not a rent-a-cop. The pay stinks and the work is crap."

"It's honest work until you find better. Show Angie you're serious."

"Nah. Can't do it. You're my last chance, man—the only friend I got. Don't you need some PI work? Give me a couple of junk jobs to get me in the door."

Jack threw down his fork. "We don't have junk jobs at the FBI. Besides, it doesn't work like that. If we need personnel we move people around field offices, that's how my team was temporarily transferred to Burlington, to a one-man Resident Agency in temporary office space. Remember?"

"I thought it was a one-woman agency."

"Sure, now you get literal." Jack shook his head. "I can't hire private investigators. What the hell are you thinking?"

Dante finished his burger. "I'm *not* thinking. I'm desperate. I got nowhere else to go. Come on, gimme somethin."

Not this time. He'd lost confidence in Dante so how could he recommend him to anyone. Jack's throat tightened as if it resisted his words. "Sorry pal, I can't help. You're on your own."

Dante chugged the third beer. Why not, he wasn't paying. He rose from his seat, leaned over the table and looked Jack square in the eye, "Sorry. That's all you got? Sorry? I thought we were like brothers." He walked out and into the crowd of pedestrians in Market Square where he paused.

Jack threw two twenties on the table and ran after him. He didn't want to forsake his friend and didn't feel he had, but Dante clearly had a different opinion. Before Jack could stop himself he said, "Maybe I can come up with something. Let me sleep on it, then we'll talk."

Their hands glided in a smooth handshake and they went separate ways. The more Jack thought, the more angry with himself he became. Dante would probably get drunk and still be drunk tomorrow. As if once wasn't bad enough, Jack would have to repeat the whole ugly refusal. He should have kept his big damned mouth shut.

THIRTY

CONNECTICUT
Thursday

RETURNING TO THE SAME AIRPORT, and same terminal where she had met Agent Matt Chase, felt hollow. Kate couldn't help wondering how often he'd probed the same passages or how often he'd boarded a plane—she wondered everything about him. She had hoped he'd be there to meet her, and in her fantasy she envisioned him carrying her off to a cozy Manhattan love nest—if he remembered her at all. She'd have to call Jack to say she was taking a few extra days in New York, and he'd believe her. She laughed. *Great imagination, kiddo. Doesn't happen in real life.*

By late morning she was home, just over three hours after landing. Her guard, that veil of caution she wore when traveling, fell away and disappointment about her fantasy lover faded when she stepped into familiar surroundings. *Reality.* She stacked her bags beside the front door and called Jack. Voicemail. Eleven-thirty. *Must be out to lunch.* She hung up without leaving a message and wouldn't call his cell. He hated to be bothered and she tried not to annoy him any more than she had to—she really did try.

Kate had emptied perishables from her refrigerator before she left; only condiments and three bottles of Bud Light from an early summer picnic remained; a few cans of soup, a jar of tomato sauce and a box of Minute Rice were stacked in the cabinets. She drove to Sal's Pizza in a strip mall around the corner, three miles from Summary Road. An extra large cheese and mushroom pie would last for six or eight meals if she limited her portion size. She'd soon restock groceries, but not today, probably not tomorrow, and she might skate through a third day. *Not true.* In a couple of days she'd recover from jet lag, replenish kitchen supplies and prepare her favorite comfort foods: shepherd's pie, lasagna, New England boiled dinner.

Sal's face seemed to light when she entered. "Where you been, Kate?"

"A week in Prague. I landed only hours ago. You're my first stop."

He winked. "Good girl. I give extra cheese. No charge."

"You're a funny guy. While you're feeling generous, throw some sausage on half." She moved a bar stool to the counter, flipped through the local paper and called to Sal in the rear kitchen. "Did I miss anything?"

"No. Very quiet. Very good." Sal peeked through the service window. "Where your nature boy been? Long time I no see him."

"Old news, Sal." She skimmed the paper's international section, but there was nothing about the bomb in Prague. "Todd and I are sooo over."

She readied to pay for the pizza, sorting through souvenir banknotes of Czech koruna, euros and U.S. dollars. "See you next week."

At home, Kate opened the pizza box. Mmmm ... nothing like a hot home cooked meal, even if Sal had cooked it. *Ouch.* A bite too eager and too robust blistered the roof of her mouth.

She dumped the contents of her luggage in the laundry room beside the washer, threw in dark clothes, and separated lights from whites while the first cycle ran. She rummaged through receipts and ticket stubs, fliers and maps. She spotted her map notes about the cyber café recommended by the stranger on the plane, wondering if he'd reunited with his little sister. She felt guilty for her bad attitude, after all, his most serious fault was that he sat in Todd's seat—and he wasn't Todd.

She dropped the street map and other papers into a plastic storage box she labeled Prague, and stashed it with her empty luggage in the basement; gathered souvenirs and spread them on the dining table. Unwrapping them would someday be like receiving gifts. *I should have bought more.* Mementos always looked more special at home where they were out of context and unique.

The subtle paint colors of Coop's religious icon were prettier than she remembered. Her gaze darted from room to room as she considered where to place it. Presenting the carving to Coop wasn't at the top of her list, but it *was* easing upward. She propped it on a table beside the front door where it would serve as a scolding each time she left the house. *Oh Coop. I'm doing the best I can.*

Kate skimmed through the mail her neighbor had collected when he checked on her house. No note from Todd—no message on the answering machine. He didn't care enough to see she'd safely returned. She could have been killed in the bomb blast for all he knew. *OH SO OVER!*—a realization she'd embraced the moment her gaze fell on Matt Chase. Now that she knew how it felt to be smitten, she knew not to settle.

She put the last load of travel clothes into the washer, regretting she had begun. It was already late evening by Czech time. She yawned and fell asleep on the sofa, lights and TV on, windows cracked open; laundry half done and standing damp in the Maytag washer.

It was past four in the afternoon when she awoke. And the room was freezing cold. *Oops. Jack expected my call hours ago.*

He must be pacing by now. She secured the windows before hitting his speed dial button.

He sounded irritated, but she countered with a cheerful, "Hey. Miss me, big guy?" He didn't respond. "I'm back ..." No response. "In my house ..."

"I get it. You're home. It's not a good time."

She had anticipated more of a greeting, at least from her own brother. Not a bouquet of flowers at the airport, but something. She could have stayed abroad another month for all anyone cared. *At least the pizza guy missed me.* "Tough day?"

A deep sigh preceded, "I had lunch with Dante. He's spiraling down. I feel for the guy, but I can't get caught in his drama."

This was to be one of Jack's less-is-more conversations. "You'll figure it out. Anyway, I wanted you to know I was safe at home. I'll call tomorrow."

Jack paused. "Or next week would be okay."

Hey. No need for attitude. That did it. She reached her tipping point. "Forget you Jack. Forget that I could have been exploded in a million pieces. Or that I was interrogated at the airport by the FBI. Or that a rude creep sat next to me on the plane all the way to Prague, or that another scary stranger stalked me at an Internet café, where I wouldn't have been if I wasn't e-mailing *you*, like you insisted. You don't want to hear about it. Fine. So screw you." Kate slammed down the phone. "Geez." She took a breath, shook her shoulders and grinned. "Rats, I overreacted."

Kate spent the rest of the day trying to recover from jet lag; eating when hungry, napping when tired, but nothing improved her gloomy mood. *Friendless. Boyfriend-less. Brother-less.* Post vacation blues could be the cause. *Can you run away from home if you live by yourself?* If she could afford to walk out the door and leave on vacation, she'd repack the laundry, head back to the airport and board the first flight out.

With her workspace arranged with pizza, Pepsi and a few music CDs, she turned on the computer and escaped to Dreamwatch.

New site submissions included the story from Ali, Abdul, whatever his name was, about his mother's ghost sighting that they wrote at the Internet café. She wondered if he would write again and hoped he would not, though her sixth sense grumbled she'd not seen the last of him. And how ironic, the guy who made her skin crawl was destined to reappear, and the one man she yearned for was gone forever.

She logged on to the site stats, stunned to see that while she was away, traffic had bumped so dramatically she verified she had accessed the correct report. The graph confirmed it: little, little, little, lots. Even in a week with a full moon, a time that typically spawned an increase in all things weird, this amount of traffic was over the moon. She checked the previous eight days of hit reports from her tracking service and confirmed a four hundred per cent surge during the past two days. No links. No site referrals. No search strings. Visits resulted from direct addressing to the URL. *Too strange. Suddenly everyone knows Dreamwatch?* The anomaly was peculiar enough to post, but she didn't.

More traffic *was* what she wanted, but she hadn't done anything yet … didn't know where to begin. Search Engine Optimization was a process she'd just begun to study. Thinking in algorithms was contrary to her nature. So what happened on her site? She paced to the rear sunroom and stared out the back windows. Her face puckered, puzzled. *How can it be? Maybe the new stories will explain. Maybe they're friends and friends of friends.*

She stretched her arms high above her head, bent to reach the floor and returned to a standing position. Squirrels scooted up tree trunks. *Fall is near.* In another month, branches would be bare and grass would turn brown. Cold, snow and ice would soon follow. She wouldn't go out much, but would hunker down for three or four long months to hibernate like the animals.

Time is running out. Don't squander it.

Okay. Okay. She printed all site submissions from the past two weeks.

It was after six o'clock when she poured another cola and microwaved a slice, but caffeine wasn't clearing the fuzziness in her head, and the earlier nap hadn't helped. Jet lag? No, this was new terrain. When she walked, she felt she was backwards sliding on ice. *Too weird.*

She turned on a lamp and bundled herself in an alpaca blanket on the back porch lounge, with her reading glasses and the stack of printouts on her lap.

The state trooper's story about being yanked from the path of an oncoming truck, and the ghost sighting by Ali's mother, were the last two stories she could account for. She set them aside, along with the few that predated them. Stories submitted afterwards deserved scrutiny.

After Ali's story, some forty messages had come in—all with one thing in common. They seemed *off.* Nothing specific to cause alarm, yet they disturbed her. Most were premonitions about small incidents like losing electronic items: cameras, cell phones, CDs and thumb drives. *Been there. Never dreamed about it.* Several visitors dreamed of fire in a palace. A few stated they had accurately predicted their friends would travel to Paradise. *Nice, sounds like the name of a resort. Saw their commercial on TV.*

She wondered if the senders could be traced, or if server locations were identified in the code. Jack would know, but she couldn't ask him. Not today. When digital tasks stumped her, she'd construct a software workaround relying on common sense to save her, but that only worked when her senses were sharp and operating in logic, not split between home and Prague.

Her feet still walked cobblestone paths. Gothic towers and linden trees loomed above. Church bells rang and sirens wailed.

Her technical skills frustrated her on a good day. Despite her muddled state, the pattern of premonitions was so unsettling, it could not be ignored. General themes seemed similar. A cluster of people dreamed of lost items, but several wrote they had lost themselves and found their way across an open sea.

Eight reported visions of "a broken arm" had come true.

Eight. Seriously? So specific. Chance beyond coincidence.

Kate had been reading dreams from around the globe for over ten years and they'd come to resonate like familiar melodies. These were different—the change too extreme and too abrupt.

Danger is near.

She shuddered with a sudden chill and retreated to the living room, grabbing a yellow legal-size pad and a fistful of colored markers from her office taboret. She reread and studied each story, separating those that most bothered her and highlighting comparable terms with thick markers. She spread her notes on the coffee table. A mass of color coded words lay before her. "What the heck is going on?"

Related words repeated: team, group and brothers referred to social groups; arm, brain and cells described body parts; bridge, rail and tunnel related to transportation; spray and spread were dispersal techniques.

A reference to two police cruisers screamed for attention.

Body parts and infrastructure, dispersal methods and the cops. *This is bad.*

Words and phrases were too similar to be random, and

there were lots. Too many. *Crap. I confused myself. Take a break. Walk away.*

Talk to Coop.

She chewed on pizza crust the same way she nibbled her fingernails before she broke the habit. If only she could decipher a few key details, she could present them to Jack to investigate. *I still believe in Santa Claus, too.* She listed the circled words in tidy columns on the yellow pad. Even though the lists made no sense, the categories seemed menacing. *Am I reading into something that isn't here? Could I be wrong?*

Or were new Dreamwatch visitors from around the world predicting the same catastrophic attack?

A migraine didn't smolder, it fired into her head like when she was seven and a line drive smashed into her skull during Jack's Little League game. She collapsed into a half sleep with her lists resting on her chest, but after an hour she crawled upstairs to bed—her tangled thoughts bumping against visions of death and destruction.

THIRTY-ONE

NEW YORK
Thursday Night

AT EIGHT O'CLOCK a bright moon, a few days past full, lit low clouds speeding across the sky. Brisk winds funneled through Manhattan's canyons as Chase walked alone for an hour or more, hoping to air out and stimulate his brain. He buttoned his top coat, pulled up the collar and slipped his hands into the pockets. He stared upward at the sky show like a tourist awed by skyscrapers.

New leads had recharged him, but the fuel made him wired. His thoughts scattered. If he had planned and carried sportswear, he'd shoot hoops at Chelsea Piers or lock himself in a batting cage for an hour—a good fist fight would help. He couldn't go home. His empty apartment was the last place he wanted to be.

A neighborhood tavern appeared misplaced from an Irish village. Chase pulled a money clip from an inside coat pocket and laid a twenty on the bar. He ordered a Vodka Gimlet and slid onto a stool. A dozen patrons chattered in small groups, their conversations bouncing off paneled walls with hard, clipped sounds. No one watched one man interviewing another on a flat screen mounted on the wall. News of the Prague bombing barely received thirty seconds of coverage. Chase suspected if Banzik hadn't been injured, it wouldn't have been broadcast at all. He sipped his drink, holding it in his mouth before he swallowed. He shook his head, squelching an urge to berate the screen.

Attention from a lovely woman at the end of the bar seemed to invite advances before he finished his first drink. A quick hookup would have been easy and bound to be effortless as the evening passed. He yearned for soothing conversation, longed for a tender touch, needed wild sex to release the raw energy restrained in him for far too long. But he didn't trust the man he was now—frustrated, angry and tense enough to snap. He would never hurt a woman, but it was in him. He'd come close a time or two when he'd returned from war and not yet suppressed his killing side. It had surprised him that rage stirred so close to his surface. Perhaps it was his strength. But with the frustration he felt tonight, there was no telling what he might do.

He sensed change coming in the seasons, in the city and in himself. Whatever he needed at this moment, he wouldn't find in a neighborhood pub. And he was proud of himself and relieved that he still recognized the nuances of his needs. He nodded at the woman across the bar, paid his tab and wandered south.

Chase soon stood at the corner of Christopher and 7th, the very place where his wife had been killed in a pedestrian accident—the intersection he had avoided for two years. He'd been dreading this moment for as long as he could recall, even while he knew his mind could not clear until he found conclusion. Tonight's aimless meandering had delivered him to the spot where he now stood, the very spot where *she* had stood —*where her secret lover had stood.*

He imagined them laughing, debating whether to eat cannoli from the bakery or burgers at the steakhouse grille. It was a sunny afternoon. An ordinary day. No reason for caution, just stand at the damn curb and wait for traffic lights to change. Her lover saw the van speeding toward them. Tried to push her from its path. Even put his life at risk. But he couldn't react fast enough to save her.

So he'd been told.

Her lover survived with injury. The driver ... never caught.

Lights had changed to red and cars had stopped, but Chase remained where he stood as light foot traffic skirted around him to cross the street. The wind eased, blowing a gentle coolness across his face. He thought he smelled her perfume.

He didn't suspect she was cheating. To him, their marriage was solid. *What kind of half-assed investigator am I?* He blamed his frequent absence and singular focus on work for her affair, and faulted himself for the accident.

What must her lover have felt when she was crushed before his eyes?

He could have asked the guy, face to face. Man to man. But he'd refused medical attention and walked from the scene before anyone could stop him.

Chase never met him, never saw his face.

Just as well. He would have pummeled it.

Chase had searched his name, but found no records. When a credible threat crossed his desk, his personal search fizzled.

Guilt had cloaked Chase like a cold blanket and became his comfort. What could he have done better? *He'd* not been unfaithful, never considered it. He lived where she wanted to live, even waited to have children at her insistence. *Dammit, I was a* great *husband.* He laughed at himself, the perfect man. Not at all hampered by lover's guilt—but emotionally paralyzed by grief guilt—denial, anger and pain. *Textbook.* The revelation was stunning, as if the canyon winds had blown away a hill of shame to reveal forgiveness.

His recent interests in life and love: closed feelings turned on, attraction to a woman like the one at the airport, the lust for sex—real desires—marked his return to normalcy. At the corner of Christopher and 7th, Chase knew exactly what he wanted and what he must do to get it. He said goodbye to his wife, mentally walked away from her grave—and he forgave himself.

He hailed a taxi and returned to his apartment, stopping at a Subway sandwich shop near his building. He changed into Nautica flannel pants and a Henley shirt, and hauled out his wife's clothes packed in cartons on the closet floor. He stacked them near the front door to drop at the women's shelter down the street from his office.

The hospital's patient bag containing his wife's belongings remained. The plastic bag probably held jewelry and rings, his gifts to her—maybe her bloodied clothes. He'd done enough for one night, so he slid the bag back in the corner where he wouldn't see it everyday.

He burned his wife's photos onto a CD and tucked it in the desk drawer before removing the images from his hard drive. He pulled off the wall the paintings she loved and pictures of family affairs. Any bauble or travel souvenir that wasn't his— gone. He rearranged furniture until nothing remained where it had been. By three o'clock early Friday morning, the apartment was so changed, it appeared some other man lived there.

And he probably did.

THIRTY-TWO

CONNECTICUT
Friday

WHERE AM I? After a week of hotel rooms and plane seats, last night was the first time Kate had slept in her bed. Sleep should have been heavenly, but displaced pillows and twisted sheets indicated otherwise. The clock read 3:08 and she felt as restless as the moment her head touched the pillow. Off balance like sliding backwards on ice and only half awake, she wondered if her spirit remained elsewhere.

Each cautious step downstairs sparked a vision of another reality in a chaotic slideshow: a sportsman's cabin; a traffic clogged bridge; an Irish pub, set amid skyscrapers. *Crazy.*

Pay attention. Look deeper. It's your life.

The direction was loud and clear. She froze where she stood beside the dining table. Her gaze circled the space as if seeking the speaker, a spirit or a sign, but no one was there. No photos fell to the floor, no red scarves blocked her path. *My life?*

She chugged a tall glass of water … *river, river, Charles, Charles* … names echoed in her mind. *But I've already been to Prague.*

Kate. Kate.

An erratic hum signaled a shift in her vibration followed by a sudden, quiet peace impossibly silent. She opened the front door to listen. No wind carried highway sounds and no train whistles blew. But from nowhere—and everywhere—church bells rang. *In the middle of the night? Coop? Is that you?*

She eased the door closed and shuffled to the TV looking for news, anything to drown the bells. As fast as the earlier visions flashed on the stairs, she flipped through channels of sitcom reruns, talk shows and classic movies—all fading to hazy visions of emergency vehicles, vapors rising from auto tailpipes, and a hotel lobby with polished marble floors. The faces of news anchors morphed into Todd's face and Jack's, Agent Chase's and Ali's, the face of a woman with cropped hair she didn't know; and lastly, Dante's ….

Where was Kate when ya' need 'er?

The room filled with an unusual odor she had smelled only once while crawling through a tunnel robbers had dug in a collapsed pyramid in Egypt. Not totally unpleasant with a hint of ammonia, she had emerged covered with, and smelling of, bat droppings. Funny now, but at the time it wasn't as amusing.

Danger is near. Get out, now.

She hit the remote's power button and the screen blinked like it did when lightening struck too close. Between her eyes and the darkened television, a transparent version of Coop's face appeared; lips moved with no sound until a few clear words broke through. "Don't be afraid."

Coop? What's happening to me?

Kate awoke from a nap with the remote encased in her hand. She tossed it like a hot ember and bolted up the stairs. After a long shower she felt more grounded. The bathroom was so filled with steam, condensation dripped down the tiles. She pressed a towel onto her face, but it didn't feel like it had touched her skin. If she looked in the mirror, she didn't know what would look back. *This craziness has to stop.*

Stop it now.

Later that morning, the walk across the parking lot of Westwoods Senior Care seemed too brief, even though Kate had parked at the farthest edge. She scanned the lot as if looking for ghosts of gunmen lurking behind cars—like the day Coop was shot.

The courthouse scene and dramatic animations had been broadcast so often on the evening news, Kate felt she'd been there—more than in spirit. The cold damp bite of winter had gripped the edge of spring as if clutching to life. A layer of sand from snowplows edged curbs as a March soaker threatened to make mud of it.

A simple divorce case had degraded to the nastiest on record and would have been challenging for a veteran attorney, but Coop's law firm had assigned it to her and she wouldn't abandon her client when the case became complicated. Since that first look at her client's broken face, evidence of her last beating and those that had come before, Coop had become emotionally involved. *Big mistake.*

The crack of a single shot had awoken Kate from a dream and she scrambled to record its details while she remained in a clairvoyant state. The courthouse steps. The blast. The client appeared mesmerized by the red spot on her white coat, spreading across her chest like a rosebud unfolding to full bloom—the blood. The collapse. The cameras.

Coop wasn't supposed to be in court that day; an associate was to file a simple motion. Kate weighed what to do with the omen. *Was the client destined to die? Then why was I warned?* The premonition was too vivid and too specific to disregard.

She told Coop, never expecting her to change plans. Coop could have easily rescheduled the appearance or requested security. She should have parked at the curb where police managed the crowd. *How did she think she could stop it, alone and unarmed?*

Coop and her client had pulled into the underground levels to avoid press at the courthouse entrance, parked the car and headed toward the elevators. A witness, a juror assigned to another case, had said Coop was clutching her client's arm while scoping the area; that a man, the same man the witness had seen in earlier news coverage of the case, had emerged from between parked cars—that he fired four shots. The first shot missed. The next hit the client near the collar of her white coat. Coop had pushed her aside as they tried to run, but the client fell, taking Coop with her. The third shot hit Coop's head. The fourth, it turned out, grazed the arm of a state trooper in the stairwell and seconds later, the whole thing ended in a volley of gunfire and the gunman's escape.

And here we are. Coop in a coma. Her client dead. *Way to go, Kate.*

She shifted her purse and canvas tote, and tapped lightly on the door of Coop's room before easing it open. She caught her breath. *Be brave.*

The room's painted walls were a buttery yellow with white trim molding. Light oak flooring and furniture was accented with pale blue fabrics on chair cushions, the plaid bedspread and the drapes framing a window that overlooked a garden Coop had not seen. A bouquet of fresh daisies sat on the desk Coop had not used; and a pink summer dress Coop had not worn, hung in the closet. An optimistic gesture by someone.

An aide entered the room.

"I'm a close friend. Kate Kasabian. I'll just sit a while."

"Yes, Elizabeth's mother included your name on her visitor's list." She closed the closet door and pointed to the vase. "Miss Cooper's law firm sent the dress and arranged for weekly bouquets of fresh flowers."

"It's a nice room." Kate pulled an arm chair beside the bed. "She'd like it. The colors suit her."

The aide nodded. "Stay as long as you want."

Kate closed the door and pulled the religious icon from her tote; she held it in front of Coop's eyes as if they were open—as if they could see. She propped it on the nightstand and repeated the pointless action with the framed photo of her and Coop on vacation in Darjeeling.

Coop's still body was thinner now and smelled of lotion. Her hair was no longer sandy blonde, but had grown out to its natural brown color, and her skin appeared healthy, though indoor pale.

Kate rubbed her hands to warm them before sandwiching Coop's cool hand between them. "I love you and I miss you. Sometimes I feel you near so I know you're in there. I *know* it, Coop. I often hear you and talk to you. Today, I saw your face." She laid Coop's hand on the blanket, placed one of her hands on Coop's solar plexus, and the other on her forehead with fingertips touching her third eye; the same spot where the Indian holy man had blessed them with oils and grains of rice. "Part of you is free and wandering spirit planes so let's try something."

Kate closed her eyes, her mind's eye visualizing around them a shield of white light. She lowered her voice to sound firm and definitive. "We're going to a safe place. The schoolyard steps at the playground. Remember? Meet me there. The schoolyard steps. Go now."

Their two-story grade school was red brick with concrete steps and iron handrails painted gloss black. The steps at the edge of the playground were least used and afforded privacy, yet were near enough to classmates and teachers to be safe. Numerous plans, dreams and confessions had passed between them on those steps.

In an instant, Kate's spirit appeared in a bodily form. She grounded herself by focusing on the songs of birds and the squeals of children at play. All her senses attached to the setting. A white mist hovered nearby. "This way, Coop. Can you hear me?" Kate rose and extended her arms. "I'm here."

"I'm lost."

"I've been lost, too. I can't move past what happened."

"Where are you?" Coop's garbled voice seemed to change direction and fade with sound waves stretching and reverberating as if she spoke underwater.

"Can you hear me? Try harder. See it happen in your mind. Stand with me on the steps. Claim them. We can find our way back if we help each other. Come this way. Take my hand."

The mist seemed to shimmer as Coop materialized, wearing her new pink dress and beads of rice-shaped pearls on her forehead. "How did I get here?"

"I don't know. Where have you been?"

"I think I've been to school in an ancient Greek temple. I wasn't alone. There were others, yet we were one." She seemed to look around. "I know this place. Am I coming back? Is it time?"

"I think that's up to you. I want you to. Everyone does."

"I can't find my way."

"I know. Follow me. I'll take you there. I need you. My guilt is eating me."

"You didn't shoot me."

"I put you in front of the bullet and I've resisted my gift since then."

"No. No, no. Gifts are meant to be given. Knowing isn't enough."

Kate's burden lifted and she felt the greater lightness and brightness of her being. A pulling in her stomach drew her away from Coop as she fell toward gravity and back into her physical body. Her arms stretched toward Coop. *Come with me. Take my hand.* "Take it!"

Kate was back at Coop's bedside nudging her hand, now hot.

But it didn't move.

She remained at her side for another hour before returning home. Their connection seemed intact, though through a delicate bond. Her expectations for Coop's recovery were stronger than before her visit; not today or tomorrow, but someday it would come.

She entered the back sunroom, away from most of her home's electrical fields and closer to nature. Her feng shui consultant would be proud.

Sadness eased and lonely space filled with hope for more. She felt capable of levitating if she let go of disbelief. She laughed. *This feels so good.* Maybe she'd float back to the schoolyard steps. Maybe something bound her to the other side or maybe her business there wasn't finished.

It's never finished.

"I'm ready. Speak to me."

An ethereal mist formed around her in a fragile layer at eye level. A wave of warmth and love enveloped her, unconditional and all consuming, as she saw her connection to all living things. Outside, the animals and trees shimmered with colorful auras like her outstretched arms that radiated blue, purple and green. Energy jutted from her body like the sun's coronal ejections she'd seen on the Space Weather site.

She knew this was coming, had felt it for weeks. *I understand.*

"I accept my gift with all its responsibility. Show me what I need to see."

THIRTY-THREE

FRIDAY'S NEWEST DREAMWATCH premonition stories inflamed Kate's sense of dread. A dozen more and the day wasn't over.

Dreams submitted overnight wrote of travel and heat. Eastern. East. *What the heck are they dreaming about?* The tone of the new submissions was similar to those she'd read yesterday. Were they related? Dreams of a trip? A vacation to a warm destination?

A tropical resort called Paradise?

Too bad they lost their cameras.

Too bad they broke their arms.

Were they heading to, or coming from, the east? East of where? She had to figure out the source of the messages.

References to body parts didn't fit with anything else, nor did the two police cruisers. And definitely not the dispersal tools. Her head throbbed as knots tightened at the base of her skull. A tensing stress, like when you leave home wondering if you locked the door, could no longer be ignored.

Something horrible is about to happen. Knowing isn't enough.

Kate needed Jack's help regardless of his Jekyll or Hyde frame of mind. Time to make the call.

He answered, "Welcome home."

Her head jerked with surprise. "You sound better." She almost called him Dr. Jekyll.

"I'm having a fairly decent day. And you? Hang up on anyone today?"

"Not yet, but you're my first call." She paced the back porch.

"Your voice sounds funny. Still jet lagged? That's why I didn't call."

"I had a crazy night." She was sure the idea to call her had not occurred to him. "So what's going on at work today? Hunting bad guys?" She half hoped he'd admit investigations of new terror threats; it would have made her task a lot easier.

"I'm not looking for anyone until tonight's Giants game. What are you up to?"

"Lying low." She paused. "Jack, I need your help with something. It's important." Her body cringed. "My psychic vision has been returning and it's stronger than ever."

"Well, it is what it is. You should go with it."

"That sounds like something I would say." She wandered to the laundry area where vacation clothes remained half cleaned. "You won't like the messages I've been getting. We can talk about them tonight if you'd rather."

"I'll be watching the game. Tell me now. The short version."

How do I shorten this extraordinary idea? "My site's getting much more traffic and a disturbing pattern of symbols has emerged. People are submitting stories to Dreamwatch that predict the same deadly attack."

"I don't follow."

His tone suggested she was losing the benevolent big brother and would soon hear from Mr. Hyde. *Spit it out.* "Some group is planning an attack on a major U.S. city and time is running out." She leaned against the clothes dryer during a long silence until she finally banged the phone three times against the appliance. "Jack! Did you hear me?"

"Yeah, I'm still here. With a torn eardrum. How did you come to that conclusion?"

She heard his snicker, yet he didn't say her idea was crazy, absurd or stupid. "From stories coming to my site describing the same events I'm seeing in visions."

"An intriguing theory, but it sounds nuts."

There it is. And he was doing so good. "You think I'm delusional? I'm not. I'm worried. Can I read a few stories to you? Or you can read them yourself? Tonight?" She pulled a fistful of clothes from the dryer and piled them on the washer for folding.

"I'll be watching—"

"I know, I know, the game. But you have to do something. I've narrowed the target to the East Coast."

"What do you want me to do?"

Isn't it obvious? "Investigate. You're in the FBI. Don't you eavesdrop on chatter, phone calls or e-mails, or something? You know. Patriot Act." Jack sounded like he'd swallowed a belly laugh. She gritted her teeth while folding tee-shirts and jeans. "Watch for alerts in an East Coast city. In the fall. Can you at least do that much? And someone of high-rank is arriving soon. Watch for the name Ali. That's all I know so far."

"Big city. Fall. Ali. Maybe I'll look into it."

"You say you will, but you won't. You're not going to help me any more than you helped Dante." She gripped more laundry, imagining her hands around Jack's neck and shaking his stubborn head.

"Where did you hear that? Did *he* call you? What did he ask for?"

"He e-mailed last night. I just read his message. Your lunch conversation discouraged him and he wants to visit for a few days. I wrote the job market wasn't any better here. Maybe he needs a change of scenery to clear his head."

"From alcohol. Don't give him anything you can't afford to lose. Have him help with maintenance chores then send him back to me. I'll talk to him. He won't bother you again."

"It's no bother."

"I mean it, Kate. Don't get in the middle of his problems. You can't save every stray."

"Okay, I won't. So what about my Dreamwatch stories? You don't have to sugarcoat it because I'm your sister. Say what you're thinking."

"This is one of your conspiracy theories. You don't *drift* toward the fringe, you charge full speed aimed at it. I love your imagination. I wish I had some of it, but I can't risk looking like a damned fool."

"I'm telling you as sure as I breathe, if we don't stop it, something horrible will happen. And a lot of people are going to die."

VERMONT
Friday Afternoon

THE PERSISTENT APPEALS of Kate and Dante weighed on Jack like an underwater mortgage. He slipped off his suit jacket and hung it behind the door of his closet-size workspace. If he stood in the right spot beside his credenza, he could catch a glimpse of Lake Champlain tempting him to blow off the rest of the day and go for a run.

Part of him wanted to help Kate; she *was* his sister. She hadn't called back, nor did he call her. Why look for trouble when he couldn't act anything short of sensible anyway. He had to go with fact over fantasy and was determined he would *not* coddle her supernatural silliness—not this time.

When he was a boy, a premonition of his own had saved his life, making him dive into a snow bank to avoid his school bus skidding on ice; it came to rest at the very spot where he'd been waiting to board. He had no doubt it would have broken bones.

Paranormal culture had no place in his belief system, yet the experience *did* happen. *The incident,* as he referred to it, had ambushed his principles and he'd not yet come to terms with it. Only Kate believed his story. If he had told her the sun would rise in the west, she would have believed that, too. But this forewarning of an attack was too preposterous, far more so than *the incident.* He owed Kate—but she often asked too much. Between her and his troubled friend Dante asking for work, he was fed up. Just once, he wanted to be the one to catch a break. He pulled his chair to his desk, his attention back to his fraud case when the phone rang.

Kate calling. Again. *She must have another angle.*

No hello, no how are ya big guy, she blurted, "I know you think these stories are coincidental, but what if they're not?"

"They *can't* be true so they *must* be coincidence."

"You don't believe in coincidence."

Jack took his seat and powered up his computer. "I don't, but I'm trying to be reasonable."

"I am too. Can you trace the stories to see where they came from? Just one. See if it came from … I don't know, where terrorists come from."

"No." For the first time in a long while he didn't fudge his reply. He wasn't going to think about it or look into it or sleep on it.

"Jack, I'm scared. We're running out of time. My nerves are bristling. My head's pounding. You know how I get when I'm tuned in. So much internal noise. I get so full of energy, I feel I'll explode."

He didn't doubt her passion and he understood her persistence. If she had one tangible piece of evidence he might consider minimal follow-up; she had nothing but anonymous stories on a paranormal website. *Case closed.*

"A new story came in a few minutes ago. Someone called the Head or the Brain is arriving soon. I don't know where, but that reference belongs with earlier submissions about a Broken Arm."

"What's a broken arm got to do with anything?"

"If I knew that, you wouldn't be yelling at me. The Broken Arm was in a story that also referred to Boston, so it must be connected to The Brain, and Boston fits with the other East Coast clues. I can't figure it out. It's not like they sent their mission statement and contact information. They write in symbols. I need help to decipher what's going on."

"Kate. Stop. You're not making sense. If you could hear what you just said, you'd agree. Important work is going on here. Don't bother me with this crap."

"*This* is important. Stories are coming in faster. We're almost out of time."

Jack hung up the phone, folded his arms across his desk and bobbed his head against them. Thump, thump, thump. He imagined she did the same, and if Dante were here, they'd be a head thumping trio.

The agent in the workspace next to Jack's leaned in. "Sorry Jack, I couldn't help but overhear. Girlfriend trouble?"

Jack pulled a small photo of Kate and Todd from his wallet and flashed it to the agent. "If only it were that simple." He sighed and tossed the print on top of his credenza. "It's my sister. Can't trade her in for a new model."

"I hear ya." The agent laughed as he glanced at the picture. "Nice couple. So what are you working on?"

"Mortgage fraud with identity theft. I'm reviewing background."

"The crazy old dude who lives in the mountains? Taught college math years ago?"

"Bingo. That's the one."

"Every newbie gets his latest case. He once tried to squeeze health insurance claims out of Ben and Jerry's even though he didn't work there. You're lucky you can stroll to the bank and the Federal Building. I had to chase the asshole through a pasture of cow pies in an August heat wave."

"I'll never look at you the same way." Jack laughed. "I feel better already."

"Seriously, if you go to his farm, use mosquito repellent. Wear your body vest. Load your firearm and carry extra clips."

Jack raised his brow. "Thanks for the tip."

From then on he wouldn't leave the office without a vest and a loaded weapon.

THIRTY-FOUR

CONNECTICUT
Saturday

KATE HAD ACCESSED HER SITE so frequently over the past thirty-six hours, she knew the login procedure by memory for the first time in ten years. She scanned and made PDFs of her handwritten lists, and e-mailed her notes and story links to Jack. He didn't reply. She didn't know if he'd even read her message. She could forget the whole thing, put aside memories of Prague and bombs and premonition stories, store them in some dark place like she'd stored her souvenirs and her luggage, but she couldn't live with herself if the worst happened because she quit trying too soon.

Clock's ticking.

"I know the damn clock's ticking." She'd dumped responsibility on Jack until she thought of one more thing to do. Impulsive and extreme.

She'd plead her case in person.

She'd bring her files and drive to Burlington for a showdown. Ten thirty. If she left within the hour, she'd be there before dinner. Surprise attack.

Summer and fall clothes stuffed her overnight bag. Shoes, snow boots and a heavy jacket spilled into the trunk of her Ford Focus. An ice pack, water and Pepsi, Fritos and DoubleStuff Oreos, that she'd picked up at the gas station market late last night, filled a cooler within reach on the passenger floor. Enough road food to last a week. Flashlight, bug repellent, first aid kit, blanket and flares. *Cash and gas and away we go.*

"Rats." She turned off the ignition, ran back inside and grabbed the Prague souvenirs for Jack, Dante and Bobo. On the way out the door, she glanced at the empty spot where the holy icon once stood. "When I get back, Coop. I promise I'll visit again."

Driving past her neighbor trimming his holly bush, she lowered the window, told him she'd be in Vermont for a few days and asked him to watch the house.

"Going to see Jack?"

"Yup, I don't drive north in the snow. It could be April before I get to Burlington and you know how he hates to drive down here."

He nodded and waved. "I'll grab the mail, too. Don't worry about a thing."

Kate threw him a kiss and headed toward the I-691 connector to I-91N.

By the time Kate crossed into Vermont, she was on schedule to arrive at Jack's by five. It had taken ninety minutes to drive from her house to the first Vermont Tourist Rest Area. The only turn was a merge onto I-89N, then a quick stop at McDonald's in Randolf. But maybe she'd use the drive-thru and eat on the road.

Maybe she'd skip the lunch stop altogether.

The long drive seemed more lonely than usual with Agent Chase seeping into her thoughts. Everywhere she looked, every song she heard, forged a path to him. She'd even seen him in a vision on the TV. Why her heart and mind yearned for someone she wouldn't see again, she could only guess. Maybe their encounter was an example of what *not* to do the next time an opportunity presents itself. Should she have said something when they met … something like, I'll be back in six days … then …. Then what? Coffee? Dinner? Happily ever after? She glanced at the passenger seat littered with cookies and chips; it would be nice to have someone, anyone, sitting there.

Kate exited in Burlington at four thirty and drove to Jack's condominium in the city's center; parked in the underground lot, slung her bag and laptop over her shoulder, and grabbed the cooler. The elevator rose to the eighth floor of the twelve-story building where Jack had lived for the past year and a half. She rang the doorbell and braced for a smack of housekeeping inadequacy, attributing his meticulously clean home to the fact that he was seldom there, and that he splurged on a biweekly cleaning service—but still.

VERMONT
Saturday Evening

JACK HAD NIXED A DINNER DATE with a woman he'd met last weekend at the Pub & Brewery and hoped to spend a quiet night at home. The doorbell rang. "What the hell." If that was his canceled date, he'd have her pinched for stalking. He lowered the television volume and tiptoed to the door. The only thing worse than a female stalker would be a drunken Dante reminiscing about their college years. He didn't see anyone through the peephole and put his ear against the wood. He whispered, "Who is it?"

A fist struck the door. He jolted backwards, rubbing the side of his head.

"It's Kate. Let me in."

Whoa. Didn't see that coming. He opened the door. "Why didn't you say you were driving up? I'd have baked a cake."

"You might have said, no."

"Never," he lied. He grabbed her overnight bag. "What's in the case?"

"My laptop. I brought my files."

"Oh geezus, Kate." He should have guessed, if she was here, she wanted something, and this time he knew what he was in for. He once thought of setting her up with one of his Navy, Marshal Service or FBI buddies—to share his burden. The opportunity didn't present itself, yet, but he held hope. He'd bailed out his quirky sister often enough. His obligation was born long ago when their parents supported him, but not her; acknowledged his intellect, but not hers; paid for his education, but not hers. Now was *not* the time for payback. Better to be prudent. Try to care about what was eating Kate, and demonstrate more caution with Crash, who also needed something impossible from him.

Tomorrow afternoon he planned to hang out with Dante. Her timely visit meant he could now kill both birds with one picnic, and send them packing until spring.

KATE FOLLOWED JACK toward the guest room where he stashed her overnight bag. "This bland room looks so much like a nunnery, I'm tempted to hang a crucifix and light a candle." *I should have brought Coop's icon.*

"It's clean and uncluttered. You should try it. Free some space for new energy to enter your life."

She shot an incredulous look and planted her hands on her hips. *What has he been reading?* "Are you dating someone new? A holistic organizer, maybe?" She stashed her cooler's ice pack in the freezer.

He laughed. "I have leftover meatloaf. Mashed potatoes and steamed asparagus. You hungry? We can walk along the waterfront after dinner or go out for coffee and dessert."

They returned to the living room. "Perfect. Either way." She knew they would do neither. To flatter his ego she'd compliment his cooking by eating too much. They'd watch TV and talk during commercials until one of them fell asleep.

"I thought you'd visit in a week or two."

"This can't wait. Come here you big lug." She kissed his cheek and squeezed him in a tight hug, but not as tight as his. "You look good." She slapped her hands against his chest until she remembered seeing gorillas performing the same gesture on a Discovery Channel program.

"You look good, too. You cut your hair."

She circled the living room, checking new decor. "Your place looks great." Contemporary with a hint of traditional; leather furniture, the newest electronics and DVDs sorted by genre in a glass cabinet; and silk greenery because he'd kill live plants in a month.

Kate arranged place mats and plates on the dining table, which she suspected he used only when she came to call.

He pointed to the drawer near the microwave. "How was Prague?"

She removed flatware for two. "Excellent, and I had fun, too. Fascinating ghost legends. Lovely architecture. I think it's the only European city that wasn't destroyed in World War II. I met two schoolteachers at my hotel and we hung out for a few days."

"History teachers?"

"How did you know?"

"The World War II reference."

"See, Jack, this is why I need your help. You're so clever." She winked. "I might visit them next year in Sedona."

"Cool. Heard from Todd?"

"No." She rattled the knives in her hand. "And you can stop asking."

"Where is he anyway?"

She stood behind a chair, her hands braced on its back. "No idea."

"Has he called since your split?"

"No," she snapped. "I mean it. Stop asking." She plopped onto the chair, pushed the plate toward the table's center and folded her arms across the place mat.

Jack joined her with two beer bottles and one glass; he dished out meat and vegetables while glancing at her laptop. "What brings you here?"

Now our dance begins. It was a twitchy balance to tell him just enough without stepping onto the ballroom floor where he'd feel obliged to lead. "You know what. I promise, between the two of us, we can get this done in an hour."

"Those premonitions of a terrorist attack? Your brain is in the clouds."

"Maybe dad dropped me on my head." She slapped his arm. "Maybe *you* did. So help me out. I drove five hours to get here. That's got to count for something."

"Okay. Okay. I'll look at your damn notes. Let's eat first." He passed the butter.

Kate filled her fork with meatloaf, blowing it cool before biting. Grinning inside. "Mmmm. This is really good. More please."

THIRTY-FIVE

Sunday Afternoon

JACK PACKED KATE'S COOLER with sirloin patties, fresh tomatoes, four ears of shucked corn, a jar of Hellmann's Mayonnaise and Vlasic Bread & Butter Chips because he won't eat any other brands.

As fussy as when he was a kid. "I pity your wife."

"I want what I want. Save your pity for when I actually have a wife. But don't hold your breath."

"Where are we meeting Dante?"

"His house."

She laughed and tucked paper napkins beside the pickles. "But we're bringing the food?"

They loaded Jack's Fusion and drove twenty minutes to Milton. "I've never seen him lower so go easy. Don't pry. He has no good news." He paused. "I could be the only friend he has."

"*We* could be."

They arrived at Dante's, a 1980s Cape with mountain views like the fifty or so others in the same development. They pulled into the driveway and parked beside the battered TransAm— the inspiration for his nickname, Crash, along with a half dozen wrecked Milton police cruisers.

Dante bounced out the front door in wrinkled khaki shorts, and a blue Hawaiian shirt with red and orange flowers. "Hi little sis, give me a big wet kiss on the lips."

Kate shuddered.

"Come on, plant one on me." He lifted and twirled her until she giggled, then set her down with a peck on her forehead.

Jack opened his arms as if soliciting a hug and Dante swung a light punch to his gut. "Not when I have your better half here." He swung his arm around her and led her around the garage to the back yard. "How ya doin' Kate? Heard you were away."

"I'm good. And you? Angela? Bobo? Jack e-mailed photos. He's too cute. Where is he?"

Jack shot a pained look at Kate then turned toward the house with the cooler.

"I'm hangin' by my fingernails like always." He reached for a beer when Jack stepped from the kitchen onto the back deck.

"Sure, you guys go ahead. I can manage." Jack placed a tray of condiments on the picnic table beneath a silver maple, laid out barbecue tools and fired up the grill.

Kate asked Dante, "So what have you been doing?"

"Bounty hunter."

"I can see that." She patted his forearm. "I'll bet you're the best in the East."

"I am." Dante winked and gulped his beer. "I applied to ICE, but it doesn't look good."

Jack glanced at Kate. "Immigration and Customs Enforcement. They're staffing up at the border."

"Don't they consider your Marine record? Afghanistan? Iraq? Haven't you been vetted enough? Would poor hearing stop them from hiring you?"

Dante scratched his damaged left ear, half shot off by a Taliban sniper. "I hear as good as anyone. They saw how I was wounded. Then they found my screw-ups."

"How bad is it?"

Dante looked to Jack who said, "Tell her. She already knows ..." He counted on his fingers. "About your drinking, risk taking, rage issues, and despite all that, we're both here."

"I don't know what to do. Hunting bounty won't support Bobo when he gets to be expensive."

Kate didn't hesitate. "Stop screwing up and get a job with steady pay and benefits."

Jack pointed the spatula at Dante. "No punching civilians, no beating down prisoners. That's what you do."

"I know. I know. I only walloped guys who deserved it. But I'm tryin' to keep control 'cause Bobo's six and soon he'll figure out his old man ain't the superhero he thinks he is."

Dante opened another beer and poured half into Kate's glass. "Did Jack tell ya' Angie and I are takin' a break? I visit my kid a few times a week and she can get her nagging in, so she's happy. She took Bobo to visit her mom in Bennington for a few days, so I'm watchin' the house this weekend. Didn't Jack tell ya' I don't live here anymore?"

"No." She glared at Jack. "He didn't. I'm sorry to hear that."

"Meanwhile, Crash is renting an apartment in town."

"Yup, she gave me the boot. Said to come home when I sobered up. Can't say I blame 'er. If I could leave me, I would."

"I feel like that sometimes. What are you going to do?"

"Stop drinking I guess."

"You guess! Of course you have to stop. Do you have any *good* news?"

"Sure I do. I sleep in a clean warm bed. I'm well-fed. I'm here with my best buddy and his pretty sister." He pointed to the mountainous horizon. "And no one out there is shootin' at my head."

They all laughed. Kate almost spit up her beer.

"It doesn't get better than that." Jack shifted patties and corn on the grill. "When his landlady complains something is broken, Crash waits for her to sleep then sneaks around the house repairing everything."

"So sweet. Come to my house any time."

"Sometimes I sleep late 'cause I've been up all night and she grabs her broom and bangs on the ceiling under my bed."

Kate laughed so hard her eyes teared.

"Bobo used to wake up crying, scared that a witch lived under his bed. I shrugged him off, but I'll tell ya', I hear that broom bangin' and the landlady screechin' and I get it now. So I kick the floor to get 'er to stop pounding. Now she knows I'm awake." He thrust his hands in the air. "Then the nagging starts."

Kate pressed the stitch in her side. "Stop. Stop."

Dante's impersonation continued. "'Get up you lazy bastard.' I lie in bed pushing pillows against my ears, slapping my head against the mattress." He demonstrated on the picnic table. Thump. Thump. Thump. "I swear when she nags like that, she sounds like Angie." Dante wasn't laughing when his voice dropped to a whisper, "Makes me miss 'er even more."

Kate wiped her eyes. "Oh baby, I'm so sorry. It's not too late to work it out. Do your best and know Jack and I love you like a brother."

"Thanks Kate, you're a good kid. So how's your house, your work? How's your website? Still online?"

"Don't encourage her." Jack topped the burgers with thick slices of American cheese.

"You're so thoughtful to ask about my site." She shot an icy look at Jack.

Dante patted her hand. "I think Dreamwatch is kinda fun."

"It was *supposed* to be fun. And mostly it is. But sometimes I read those stories and shiver. I don't have answers. I'm not sure what I believe myself, but there's something more out there than we can explain. I want an open forum so people can know they're not alone. One story touched me in a way I can't explain; maybe it stays with me because I've had similar visions."

Dante leaned closer.

"A woman in South Carolina, my friend Evelyn, wrote about a dream where she saw hundreds of people staggering up concrete steps from underground. They're drooling and foaming at the mouth. Then they drop to the street twitching and screaming they are blind. They lie on the ground unable to breathe while police in gas masks run by."

Dante's brow furrowed. "What do you think it means?"

"I don't know. Do you? Evelyn's details … they sound like a real event, don't they? Like I've heard it all before. But it could have been familiar from a dream. I sometimes get confused about what I saw in a vision and what is real life."

"Maybe you heard it on the news. Sounds like a chemical weapon, like the attack in Japan by that religious sect. Jack, what am I thinking of?"

"Tokyo Subway. Sarin attack. Ninety-five I think. Or Saddam gassing his own people."

"Yeah, yeah, that's it."

"Evelyn worries the same thing will happen here. I don't know what to tell her because I worry too. I've had similar visions that I'm not confused about."

"She sounds wacky to me," Jack said.

"We know," Dante and Kate said in unison.

"But the people who write to my site tell me about themselves, personal information I would never post online, but they tell me. They're as normal as you and me."

"And me," Crash added.

"Before I left for Prague, a state trooper wrote about an invisible force that prevented her from stepping in front of a speeding pickup. Not an idiot, Jack, a state trooper. And a few weeks earlier, there was a story from—"

"Who's hungry?" Jack set down a platter of burgers, buns and corn. Grilled, toasted and roasted to perfection.

"Are you kidding me!" Dante said, "If I had to pick a last meal, this would be it."

Jack popped a corn kernel into his mouth. "Make mine prime rib. Kate?"

"Lobster, scallops, rare prime rib or rib eye. Make that both. Baked potato with butter *and* sour cream. Snickers, Butterfinger and Baby Ruth bars, followed by a Sombrero or two." Kate ran her hands down her sides and hips. "All that I limit to maintain my youthful figure."

"Oh, poor thing." Dante patted her knee. "He was a jerk. Jack told me. Walked out one night, huh? Forget him. You'll find the right guy."

"Remember house shopping?" Jack said. "That first time we drove up Summary Road and walked inside your house?"

Kate nodded. "I stood on the back porch, looked to the forest and knew I wanted to live there. I saw myself safe and happy. I saw a vision of a man chopping wood. In *my* forest. My future husband, I thought at the time. Now I'm afraid I'm headed toward a house full of cats and clutter. I was never like that and I don't know when I changed."

"You don't have a cat," Jack said. "My point is, you'll find someone and you'll know him when you see him. It wasn't Todd the tree-hugger. He would never chop wood, even if it was lying dead on the ground."

"You're right. He wouldn't want the log's family to witness the violence." They laughed until Kate added, "He's a great guy, just maybe not for me. I hope he finds someone whose love matches his. I'll keep you guys posted on my love life."

Bobo's pet cat, Fancy, clawed down the tree trunk, rubbed against Jack's and Dante's legs, then jumped onto Kate's lap and snuggled into a comfortable curl. Her eyes shot open. "Did you see that?"

"A cat prophecy unfolds." Jack laughed. "Eat before the food gets cold."

SUNSET DELIVERED AN EVENING CHILL. "Kate, tell us a ghost story." Dante wrung his hands.

Jack rose and loaded the tray with dirty plates, glancing at her. "We should get going?"

She rubbed her arms. "I wish we could stay. It's too long between visits."

"Get over here." Dante hugged her as they walked to the front driveway. He kissed the top of her head. "I love ya, kiddo. All kidding aside, take care of yourself."

"*You* take care. Don't give up on yourself." She remembered yesterday's vision of Dante's face and hearing the words: *Danger is near. Get out, now.* Her heart nearly stopped as she considered warning him. What if the same thing happened that happened to Coop? How could she *not* tell? *Knowing isn't enough.* "You be careful, too. I mean it." She held his face between her hands and aimed her eyes at his. "When your inner voice speaks, you listen."

"I will." He tilted his head and bent down to her eye level. "Look, she's so serious."

Kate forced a smile. "I worry about you guys."

"I'll come visit for a couple of days. Check job opportunities where they don't know me, and help you cat-proof your house."

"That'd be great. I'll hold you to it. In a week or two. Promise? And don't drive like a maniac." She ran to the car for his souvenir key chain. "Here's a little something for Bobo, too."

Dante laughed when he saw the toy car marked Policie. "That's funny, Kate. You and your brother have a subtle way of rubbing my faults in my face."

Kate winked. "We know you can take it."

They lingered in the driveway where Kate and Jack peeked inside Dante's car to see dented cardboard boxes, clothing, papers and receipts, sports equipment and beer cans. Jack shook his head. "Oh yeah, Crash will supervise cleaning your house. Good plan."

"This beauty's dressed down for hard work."

Jack turned right and out of the driveway.

"I'm worried about him."

"Don't. He brings it on himself. But he lands on his feet."

"It breaks my heart to see him like this. All he's been through and the guy doesn't even curse for his kid's sake."

"Look, I love Dante too, but he has to get his shit together. We can't do it for him."

"Maybe we can help."

Back at Jack's, Kate gazed out the window toward the lake.

"It's pretty, huh?" Jack said, "Get yourself a drink. And grab that meatball sub from the fridge, would you, please." He turned on her laptop and logged onto her site, releasing an exasperated sigh. "Let's see what you have."

She heated the grinder and cut it in two.

They read several stories. "The whole thing about chemicals and dispersal, and the visions of people dropping in the street, I can see where the idea of an attack came from, but it's a stretch."

Kate pointed to words on the screen. "See that last story tells me Boston is the target. And the sequence indicates an accelerating momentum. Don't you think?"

"I can't impress how much the next few weeks mean to me. I can't help you now."

She picked up half of the grinder. "I understand. I'll leave these printouts with you while I get started in Boston."

"What are you going to do? Drive around until you *feeel* something?" He shook his hands in a spooky way.

"Unless a better idea comes to mind, that's exactly what I'll do. It'll be better than reading about the attacks in *The Boston Globe*." Kate threw the printouts on the coffee table, said goodnight, and disappeared into the guest room.

THIRTY-SIX

Monday

ON MONDAY MORNING Jack straightened his tie at the door of the guest room. "Look, I have to get to work. Stay another day or two. Pretend you're still on vacation. Take a walk in the park or ride the ferry around the lake. I have a big day and can't meet for lunch, but we'll have dinner. I'll pick up something on the way home, then we'll talk."

Kate waved and rolled over in bed. "Did you look at my notes?"

He closed the apartment door.

Jack arrived at his office about twenty minutes before the others. He opened the e-mail and PDF attachments Kate had sent Saturday morning before she left home, browsed her list of leads and notes and logged out.

Counterterrorism SSA Matt Chase had distributed images seized in a recent raid. Jack dashed to the briefing to set up Chase's PowerPoint presentation.

Two other agents entered. "This must be from the raid in Prague that went bad, the site of the blast. I heard we had a man at the scene."

"I trained with him," an agent said. "Marcus Banzik. Good agent. Hell of a nice guy."

The Agent-in-Charge launched the slideshow, skipping the introduction and background sections. "The images were downloaded from an insurgent's laptop and might've been shot over several weeks, months or years. Regardless of the timing, we're asked to identify landmarks, anything to narrow the location."

Photos flashed on the screen.

An agent said, "If they were shot around here … see, these trees have buds … happens in April. These purple shrubs bloom in August. Unfortunately they're common in the northeast. Could be anywhere in the country's northern tier."

"Didn't know you were a botanical savant." An agent laughed. "Stop the slideshow. Is that what I think it is?" He rose and pointed to a small blur. "Here in the background. Jack, can we zoom in?"

"Geezus, that's the Citgo sign."

"Not unlike thousands. So what?"

"No. No, it's outside Fenway Park. I was there for a Red Sox game."

"Are you sure?"

"Positively, it also marks the final quarter mile of the Boston Marathon, any runner can tell you. Search online for Marathon photos and we'll confirm it. This is Boston."

Jack's throat tightened. *Boston, a major East Coast city. It's now September.* His neck hair bristled.

Add Prague to that, and … oh crap.

"He's right. Go back two slides. There. Those are the painted tanks on the Southeast Expressway coming into Boston."

"The park scenes could be Boston Common. Try Google Images for that monument."

Jack's supervisor punched numbers on the phone. "This is Burlington, Vermont's Special Agent-in-Charge. I need SSA Matt Chase."

In a moment, Chase was on. "Sir, about the raid photos you sent last night. My agents have identified at least three locations and we're confirming several others. We're looking at Boston. … Yes, sir, no doubt about it."

Jack's heart sank. He should have listened. What more did Kate say? Brains and broken arms. The name Ali.

The agent said, "He'll be here tomorrow at nine."

A briefing by none less than Matthew Christian Chase. *Holy freakin' crap!*

"Let's add captions to these photos. Jack you're on this too. You're my tech guy today. Play it back. Anyone ever live in Boston?" No one spoke. "What, no Harvard grads? MIT? Who's online? Search these addresses, get contact names, phone numbers and more descriptive information. Let's put meat on these bones."

Jack said, "We can capture GIS satellite images for wider views of adjacent landscape. Context. I'll search for live Web cams." *Now we're cookin'.*

All Kate's warnings suddenly pushed to the forefront of his thoughts. A possible attack in Boston? Damn. She could have been right all along. But how can he pass her vague suspicions up the command chain without sounding like an idiot? Suspicions were bad enough, but supernatural? Premonitions? Not a chance he would expose himself to that. Similarities seemed legitimate, but the connection to Prague was probably coincidence. The raid photos of Boston landmarks were not as easily explained. As much as he wanted to dismiss her intuition, history proved she was seldom wrong. He hoped she was wrong about this.

THIRTY-SEVEN

Monday, Late Afternoon

DANTE SAT WITH BOBO who was running his new Czech Policie car back and forth on the picnic table.

Angie called from the kitchen window. "Thanks for picking him up at daycare. Why don't you stay for an early dinner? You can grill burgers and dogs."

"What do you think of that, little buddy?" He rubbed the top of Bobo's head.

After the picnic, he put Bobo to bed while Angie cleaned in the kitchen. "He's down." Dante leaned against the door jam.

"He needs you. We both need you." She didn't look up from the sink.

Dante walked behind her, held her close and nuzzled her neck. "Let me come home."

"We need *all* of you, not your drunken shell." A nudge of her hip pushed him away.

"I'm tryin' Ange. I haven't had a drink in a week. Not even beer."

She poked with her elbow. "Even if I believed you, that's not long enough. Are you working?"

"There aren't a lot of openings. A guy like me is only good at sneaking into villages and blowing stuff up. Seen that in the Help Wanted ads?"

Angie wiped her hands and tossed the dish towel on the counter. "Don't use that excuse. You can do more than blow stuff up."

"I applied for a job as sheriff."

"Where? Did you get it?"

"Yeah they offered, but it's in Kentucky. I thought about it, but turned it down."

She threw the towel at his face.

"I told them, I didn't want to move my family. I was afraid you wouldn't come."

"Good goddamn guess."

"I'm gonna try Jack again. Not so much for work. Don't want to tick him off … but for ideas. He's a smart guy."

"You're a smart guy, dammit. When you're sober. By all means talk to Jack."

"I'll even apologize for putting him on the spot. I'll call tomorrow." He kissed her forehead. "Tell Bobo I'll see 'im in a couple of days. Love ya' babe."

He left the house and drove off.

When he walked into his apartment, the phone was ringing. "Hey, Jack. I was thinkin' about you."

"I have a little job for you, but I need to see you at seven."

"In the morning?"

"Yes, in the morning. Get some sleep, buddy, pack a bag and gas up the car. I'll know more tomorrow, but plan on going to Boston."

THIRTY-EIGHT

Tuesday Morning

WHEN JACK RETURNED from his morning run at six fifteen, Kate was dressed, sitting at the dining table and sipping coffee; her hair still damp from a shower. He glanced at her and wiped his brow sweat with a hand towel. "Did you meet anyone there?"

"What are you talking about?"

"In Prague. Did you meet anyone? Tell me everything. Every place you met, or went with any stranger."

"Jack, please check out my site stories."

He spotted her overnight bag at her feet. "Where are you going?"

"We went through this last night. I'm scared. This ends in Boston and if you won't help, I'll go alone."

"I can't help. And other than the obvious, I can't tell you why." He paused. "But I'll get Crash to go with you. Can you wait a few hours so I can get him up to speed?"

"In a few hours you'll say, wait till after work, and you'll get out of work and say, let's talk about it tonight, then you'll say, wait till tomorrow. Do what you want. I'm leaving. I'll let you know when I find something to investigate that won't embarrass you."

Kate slung her bag and laptop over her shoulder, grabbed her cooler and walked away.

She was barely out the door when he called Dante. "You're meeting me, right? It can't wait. The bagel shop at the Marketplace."

"Yeah, I know it."

"Thirty minutes. Don't be late."

Jack rushed his shower and dressed. He gathered three hundred dollars from a dresser drawer and stopped at an ATM for another three. He ordered two coffees and omelet sandwiches, and grabbed the first vacant table. He was relieved to see Dante saunter in a few minutes later; sober, well groomed and wearing fresh clothes. He waved him over. "You look good."

"Thanks, man. I've been cleaning up my act."

"I can see. Listen, I need a favor. Here. Sit. Eat."

"What's goin' on?"

"Something's come up." Jack slid a coffee and sandwich across the table.

"Anything, say the word."

"My sister has this notion something dangerous is in the works. She's trying to figure it out, but she's not a detective, and you know how these things work."

Dante didn't ask a single question. Jack knew why. His mind had to be reeling, but if Jack needed a favor, Dante was in. No question. The only thing he probably did wonder was: Would his expenses be covered?

"What's up?"

"Catch up with her in Boston. Help her out for a couple of days. She'll likely get discouraged and head home. She left my place less than an hour ago. She's constructed this crazy theory that terrorists will attack Boston—premonitions on her website. Just, ah … keep her out of trouble."

"Sure. I'll watch Kate for you. I'm a little short of cash. You'll cover expenses?"

Jack laughed. "Of course I will."

"I'd go myself, but we have a Supervisor in from New York." Jack pulled his billfold from his inside jacket pocket. "Here's six hundred bucks to get you started. Kate will be staying at the Renaissance Waterfront Hotel."

"Yup, I know it. I'll find her."

"She'll take I-89 to I-93 into Boston. She rarely travels that route so she'll be driving slow. She might stop a couple of times to confirm she's on the right highway. You know Kate."

Dante laughed. "She worries about everything."

"Will your clunker get you there?"

"Baby runs better than new. Just like her daddy."

"Anyway, Kate's at the Renaissance—"

"Yeah, yeah, you said. Chill out Jack. I'm not gonna try to catch her on the road. Might spook her. I'll find 'er at the hotel. Don't worry."

"In case this is for real, are you carrying … ah …" Jack peeked over his shoulder.

"A gun? I don't go grocery shopping without a gun." Dante stuffed the wad of hundreds in his pants back pocket. "Relax, I'm there."

"Better get going, she has an hour head start."

"Thanks a lot buddy. For trusting me. I won't forget it."

"Remember, you don't have to call every half hour. Get it done however you think." As Dante rose from his seat, Jack said, "Crash. If you spot trouble, keep her safe. Don't scare her. And take care of yourself."

Dante was on his way to protect Kate, likely hoping for an inroad to government work, and perhaps to redeem himself. Jack felt better already. Both Dante and Kate were out of his hair for a few days and it only cost him six hundred bucks.

THIRTY-NINE

WHILE JACK REVIEWED a threat briefing his internal voice was beginning to nag. Not as mercilessly as Kate had, but enough to divert attention from his assigned cases. Normal chatter had all but stopped since the bust of the Prague cell. Nothing much else to cause alarm. He joined others grouped at the entrance.

"Matt Chase got this done," an agent said. "Again."

Another said, "He had Yusuf tracked from New York. They came close to nailing The Brain, I heard."

"The whole cell network must be pissing their pants wondering what intel we grabbed off their computers."

"Listening for drones."

Jack returned to his workspace, attentive to the conversation down the hall. *The Brain?* Kate had also used that term.

An agent said, "I heard Chase personally follows up on the smallest threat report. He must hunt those two guys 24/7."

"He was Naval Intelligence, right?"

"So I hear. Obsessed with Eastern Flame since Afghanistan."

"Been on those two assholes like a Rottweiler."

A new voice interjected, one Jack had only heard during podcasts and video conferences; it said, "But I rarely bite and I've had my shots. SSA Matt Chase. Good to meet you."

"Welcome to Burlington, sir." The agents introduced themselves.

A few minutes later, Chase appeared at Jack's door. "I hear you're my tech guy."

Jack's guts flipped worse than the time he intercepted a final second pass at the Rose Bowl, his senior year at Boston College. He thought he was done with Kate's preposterous terrorist notion, until the legendary Matt Chase stood before him. He barely got words out as he rose from his chair. "Jack Kasabian. It's an honor to meet you, sir."

"Kasabian?" Chase's head tilted. "I know that name." He glanced at the files stacked on Jack's desk. "Have we met? Maybe at the academy?"

"No, sir. If I studied with you I would have remembered."

Chase shrugged. "What are you working on?"

"Fraud and identity theft. Cleaning up a backlog."

"That's important work. But we need everyone on this new threat so step in as soon as you can break away. We're in the conference room in five."

"I've set up the computer as you requested."

CHASE TURNED TO EXIT, but stopped short when he spotted a photo on Jack's credenza.

"What is it, sir? Can I get you anything?"

In an instant, Chase was back at JFK airport almost two weeks ago, reviewing the day's events and the people he'd seen: the loving couple at passenger drop-off, TSA's Reyes, Yusuf's interrogation. And the woman—then she was gone. Someone he thought had been lost forever was now in sight. That special woman had consumed his quiet thoughts, his private thoughts, and dare he admit, his most intimate thoughts.

He pointed. "Who …" He looked at Jack then back to the photo. "Who is this woman?"

"That's Kate." Jack smiled. "My kid sister."

"Kate Kasabian." Chase's heartbeat accelerated as he stared at the picture, reliving the moments he'd spent with her like he had a thousand times since. Her easy manner and playful smile, the fragrance of gardenias when she moved. He recalled her first words when he'd identified himself as FBI, and she, boldly standing with her hand on her hip, mirroring his stance. He had barely contained his laughter when *she* questioned *him*: Did *my brother* put you up to this?

Her reaction wasn't the typical civilian response to an agent demanding their passport. They normally stammered. Blood drained from their cheeks and moisture dampened their foreheads. With all that was going on that day, he didn't pick up on the brother reference. *Did my brother put you up to this?* Sloppy investigative work. He laughed.

"Does she live with you? Here in Vermont?"

"Connecticut." Jack tilted his head with a puzzled look.

"I may have met her at a New York airport. Possible?"

"Likely. She recently traveled to and from Prague through New York."

"Did she tell you I questioned her?"

Jack fidgeted worse than a civilian during a security screening. "I'm sure she did. The day she returned."

Chase's smile stretched to a grin. He hoped Jack didn't see beyond it. "Interesting."

"Sir?"

"It's nothing … the whole Prague thing … quite a coincidence." Chase rattled his head.

"Yes, I guess it is."

But Chase assumed Jack didn't believe in coincidence any more than he did. "Join us in the conference room." He extended his hand for a firm handshake. "Good to meet you."

His stomach fluttered when he thought of her. She'd turned and thrown a kiss, innocent and free, acting how she felt for one outrageous moment. He'd feared he'd lost her like the tens of thousands of faces he'd observed in his career, but now that there was a chance for more, he felt giddy and adolescent.

But who was the man in the photo? And why was he hugging her?

JACK LED THE WAY to a small conference room where Chase relayed an abbreviated version of his hunt for Ali and Yusuf.

Did he say Ali? Prague. September. Boston. *Dammit.* He should have listened to Kate.

"Yusuf also called 'The Arm' was a muscle soldier known to have operated on the East Coast. He was searched and interviewed in New York prior to departure on an Air France flight to Prague by way of Paris."

Geezus, that was Kate's carrier—and her same itinerary.

"These photos document his arrival in the Czech Republic, processing through Customs and Immigration, his airport exit and private car pickup.

Jack thought he spotted Kate in the background of several images shot outside the terminal at ground transportation. *No way. It couldn't be. Could it?*

He tried to recall the day she returned. Her last words before she hung up on him were something like, "Screw you Jack." But she started with, "Interrogated at the airport … a creep sitting next to me on the plane … lured me to an Internet café." He should call her to verify the facts, but he couldn't leave the briefing—not *this* briefing. As soon as possible, he'd get the whole story from Kate, knowing she'd demand humility for his dismissive attitude. He'd start with begging and wouldn't even mind, because he had it coming.

Chase's presentation included city maps, photos of several foreign embassies located in adjacent neighborhoods, and finally the apartment safehouse agents had monitored and ultimately raided.

It wasn't a stretch for Jack to see Kate walking the same streets. He *did* see her in a photo. Even with her back to the camera he recognized her distinctive blouse she bought in Vermont last spring. She *was* there, with two women on the sidewalk talking to two workmen that Chase identified as Czech agents. Like she said, she could easily have been at the blast site.

Chase paused at a split screen with two photos. "Yusuf alive in JFK's interview room. Yusuf dead on the bathroom floor, a blood trail showing he'd crawled from another room.

"Yusuf had been in the U.S. for six months. Arriving in Boston. Departing from New York. We don't know where he was, what he did, or with whom he met. It's not been determined if other cell members preceded him, are resident sleepers, or if they're on their way. New York and Albany are investigating. New York is also tracing identities of several men associated with the vehicle that dropped him at the airport, registered to a Russian national living in Bayonne, New Jersey."

Jack said, "Where's Ali's photo?"

"We don't have a photo of Ali. His full name is Abdul Wahab al-Khalifah; we're unaware of aliases. He escaped the Prague safehouse and we presume it was he who triggered the bomb with a mobile device." Chase advanced to shots of the explosion's aftermath. "We lifted Yusuf's prints and an unidentified set from this computer." He pointed to a laptop. "We believe Ali is now in the northeast and close to executing an attack in Boston."

The agents looked at each other and muttered. "Boston? What the hell!"

Jack said, "The photos we identified yesterday?"

"That's right. Shipped from Connecticut to Prague. We downloaded them from Ali's laptop and found duplicates on other media, so we assume they're crucial to the cell's plan, and that Yusuf had time before the raid to brief Ali on logistics."

Jack stared at the screen image of the charred laptop and furniture, the building's shattered facade and crushed vehicles—the scorched bodies.

Prague. Boston. September. The Brain. Ali. The arrival of a high-ranking member.

Every detail in Chase's briefing was identical to Kate's warning.

He wondered if she and Dante had arrived in Boston, but didn't dare check his watch.

Chase paced in front of him. "This won't be easy. They've been planning for more than three years and will have contingencies for every obstacle. You disarm a bomb, a blast explodes elsewhere. That's what happened here." He knocked his knuckle against the screen. "They're ruthless barbaric killers willing to die—wanting to die."

While Jack learned first hand about the raid and possible U.S. threat, he knew he had to tell Chase about Kate's suspicions —no matter how preposterous. Chase seemed like a guy open to fresh ideas.

Wow, do I have a story for him.

After the briefing, he approached Chase. "I need to show you something related to this case." He led Chase to his workspace, rolled in an extra chair and signed onto his computer.

"This is going to sound ludicrous. I thought so, too. But please hear me out." Chase nudged the chair beside him. "When my sister returned from Prague, she noticed an uptick in traffic on her Web site. It's a silly thing, a hobby really, but it's been online for years and she gets a kick out of it." Jack typed the URL: Dreamwatch.com. "See, anyone can write about their paranormal experience. Ghost sightings, psychic dreams, premonitions, like that." He scrolled to show the variety of stories. Chase seemed to remain with him though his expression twisted. Nothing scared him off, yet.

Chase leaned closer. "And people write in?"

"They do. I guess when something spooks you—"

"Okay, I get it. What's this got to do with our threat?"

"Well, since she returned, traffic has more than quadrupled and 'a disturbing pattern of symbols and warnings has emerged' … her words. When she put the pieces together, she suspected new premonitions warned of a terrorist attack in Boston."

"She deduced Boston, specifically? On her own?"

Jack nodded. "*Before* you sent the photos. It's a gift. She sees connections others miss. Always been like that. She thinks it's a supernatural sixth sense type of thing. I think she's just sharper than anyone gives her credit for … including me."

"I usually get called in for my baseless presumptions." Chase squirmed in the chair. "It sounds farfetched."

"Hey, I agree. It totally *does*. I've been telling her all along."

Chase turned toward him. "But?"

"But compare her warnings to what we now know as fact." Jack ticked a count on his fingers. "Prague. Boston. September. A high-ranking arrival. The Brain. Ali."

"Too much to be coincidence."

"And another thing … she met someone in Prague and shared information about her site, then suddenly, there's this miraculous change in traffic stats."

"Are you suggesting she met Ali?"

"I'm not suggesting. I'm *sure* she did. Here, look at these." He pulled a stack of paper from his briefcase and handed the Dreamwatch e-mails to Chase. The printouts had both the key words Kate had circled with their connecting lines and her handwritten notes.

"She presents a compelling argument." Chase pointed to several highlighted words. "These could be targets. They've used a code like this before."

"I didn't think of it earlier, but now that you told us Yusuf The Arm is dead, I wonder if this often repeated statement about a 'broken arm' alerted the group he's out of service?"

"Interesting interpretation. The timing matches." Chase's head bobbed up and down. "I agree. That's exactly what it means."

"She gave me her password in case a technical issue stumped her. I have full access to the site." Jack logged onto the Dreamwatch host server and linked to: Manage Site. "Look at this." He turned the screen toward Chase, pointing to the login record. "See, these messages didn't come from the US like they indicate on the surface. Over the past week, beginning before Kate's return and continuing to the present, they've been routed through proxy servers. Look at the IP countries: YE, SO, PK, MT, EG, CZ, CI."

Chase agreed. "Messages received before Prague did indeed originate in the U.S., Canada and the U.K., even a few from Australia." Chase shifted and leaned his arm on the back of Jack's chair. "All English-speaking countries. But the messages from her last days in Prague bounced off servers in Yemen, Somalia, Pakistan, Malta, Egypt, Czech Republic. What the hell is CI?"

"Yeah, I had to look up that one. Ivory Coast. Coast Ivory? CI. Go figure."

"Your sister doesn't use a firewall or security encryption?"

Jack laughed. "Kate doesn't know how to do that. Someone logged on her last day in Prague, and I'm telling you there's no circumstance where she would manage her site from a foreign computer. She barely knows how to use her keyboard."

"Your sister may be in danger. Contact the New Haven Field Office. Ask them to arrange for state police protection." Jack didn't move. "Now, Jack."

"She's not in Connecticut. She stayed at my place last night, but left early for Boston."

Chase shook his head.

Jack's face burned. "It was such a crazy idea. She asked for my help and I thought—"

"Yeah … well, who wouldn't."

He had to tell Chase about Dante even if it risked trouble— even if it cost his job. "I've got a man on her, too, a former cop, a friend with military training who works as a bounty hunter. He left here more than an hour after Kate. I wanted to help him out, throw some work his way so giving him money wouldn't feel like charity, and frankly, I wanted Kate off my back about her paranormal theories."

Chase patted Jack on the shoulder. "We'll review procedures another time, but right now, your sister needs protection, and your friend needs backup. I have to talk to her about Prague. What's your friend's name? Where are they?"

Jack checked his watch. "Probably en route, maybe near … ah … I have no idea."

"Try to reach them."

"His name is Dante Benard. He won't hear his phone and Kate doesn't turn hers on. We shouldn't waste time trying. She always stays at the same hotel, so they'll be meeting there." He checked his watch again. "They should arrive by noon."

"Alert the manager and hotel security we want to warn them the second they walk through the door. I mean it Jack, if the cell believes Kate and Dante are on to them, they won't hesitate to kill. If we had more time, I'd phrase the danger more delicately, but we don't. Do you have a photo of your friend?"

"No." Jack shook his head.

Chase grabbed Kate's picture from the shelf and handed it to Jack. "Forward this to the Boston Field Office and have a JTTF team set up at the hotel. I'll have someone get Benard's photo from Vermont motor vehicles."

"What team?"

"Joint Terrorism Task Force. I want an agent with Kate every second. Give them my cell number and yours, Kate's and Benard's; I'll need them, too." He tossed his phone to Jack who keyed in the data and tossed it back.

Just as Chase caught it, it buzzed with a call. He listened for a minute, closed the phone and pointed. "Conference room. Now. We caught a stunning break."

They rushed back to the raid photos. "I've just been notified fingerprints recently added to the IAFIS database are an exact match to prints lifted in Prague." He pointed, tapping, to a blood spattered Kalashnikov rifle pictured on the screen. "Prints matching those on a camera and CDs seized in the raid matched Yusuf's prints taken at JFK. The same prints were lifted two weeks ago at a crime scene outside of Worcester where two men were murdered."

Chase paced toward a wall where a world map hung and traced a trail. "I've been tracking this cell's leaders since they met at an al-Qaeda training camp; from Afghanistan through Iran to Germany. Recently from Worcester to Wallingford and Bayonne, New York City to Prague. Everything tells us they're back ..." He pushed in a flag pin to punctuate, "In Boston.

"One Massachusetts victim, white male, Ryan Calumet, had recently purchased land and a cabin in a remote area near Worcester. Found in the woods. Buried in a shallow grave. The body of the second victim, a John Doe, was inside the cabin apparently killed days later."

"Prints of John Doe?" Jack said.

"Nothing in the system."

Chase ordered one of the agents, "Get the Mass. state police to locate the investigating officer and the technician who processed the crime scene. I don't care who they are or what they're doing. We need them in the Boston Field Office …" He checked his watch. "By two o'clock with all their notes, photos and files—anything related to that double murder."

"Sir, what can I tell them?"

"Nothing except that it's an FBI priority investigation. Do not call it a credible threat. Don't even think the words 'terrorist attack.' I'll tell them myself."

Chase pulled his cell and hit a number that beeped as it speed dialed. He paced while he spoke, running his fingers through his hair, small indications that made Jack wonder if he was nervous or worried.

"Vargas. Chase here. I need someone to vet a civilian Web site. Run an audit trail." He motioned Jack to follow.

Back at Jack's computer, Chase tapped the keyboard to wake the screen from sleep mode while continuing with Vargas. "Look for recently added pages, any page that doesn't appear on the original site map or in the directory. They should not have been updated later than, say, August 31. I want to know every damn thing about this site." Chase glanced at him. "Yes, the owner is the webmaster. You'll be working with her tech guy. We have her full cooperation."

Jack nodded in agreement.

"Hold on." He pressed the phone against his chest. "You're going to make this right with your sister."

It wasn't a question. "I will."

"Agent Jack Kasabian will give you directory location settings and login info. ... No there's no firewall and no encryption. She doesn't even use a robust password. Leave the site unchanged as if only the webmaster had logged on. You know what to do. Keep me posted."

Chase passed him the phone suggesting he wrap up quickly. He said, "Grab your bag, you're with me."

"We're going to Boston?"

"Damn straight."

Kathryn Orzech

~ *Part Four* ~

Boston

Kathryn Orzech

FORTY

BOSTON
Tuesday Noon

KATE CHECKED INTO THE RENAISSANCE, set her overnight bag at her feet, and pulled her driver's license and VISA from her card case. The registration clerk assigned a single room on the eleventh floor with a view of the harbor. She was returning her card and ID to her purse when Dante bolted into the lobby, catching the attention of hotel guests who lounged in various seating groups.

"Hi there, Kate."

Oh geez. Her stunned expression eased into a sly grin when she turned.

"Hey, little sis. What brings you to Boston?" He grabbed a street map from a stack on the front desk.

"Oh stop." She slapped his arm. "He's not my brother," she said to the clerk. "But he *is* a good friend, so far." She signed the registration and took her room keycard. "Jack sent you?" She glanced across the counter. "My *real* brother."

"He wants you to keep me out of trouble, no wait, I'm to keep *you* out of trouble." Dante lifted her overnight bag and followed her to the bank of elevators and to her room.

"You must have flown down the highway to catch up with me. What did I tell you? You'll never lose the name Crash if you drive like you're going to cause one."

He set her bag on the luggage rack and excused himself to the washroom. She wondered if he was checking for intruders or marking territory. "You didn't make a rest stop, did you?" She unpacked her laptop and logged onto her site.

"So what's got Jack in a huff?"

She pointed to the screen. "This is what I tried to tell him, but he wouldn't listen."

"I'm listening. Whatcha' got?"

"These premonitions predict an attack right here in Boston. This story is new. Just since this morning."

"Come on, Kate. It doesn't exactly say that."

"Read between the lines. It's all there." She explained the details she'd put together, and spread on the bed the stories where she had circled relevant word clues. "These could be targets. But these refer to a meeting place or living quarters or a storage hold." She handed him a set of printouts.

"How many copies do you have?"

"A few. I expected Jack to toss a couple."

The hotel phone rang. Kate jumped and shot a look at Dante. "No one knows I'm here, except for Jack, but he'd call my cell." She checked to confirm her phone was turned on and that there were no missed calls.

Dante motioned her to answer. She held the handset between them.

"Miss Kasabian, this is the front desk. You're needed in the lobby. Please come immediately."

"Ah … I'll be right down."

"Go. They already cleared your credit card, must be FBI. I don't know why Jack sent them, but …" Dante folded the printouts and stuffed them inside his jacket. "I'll check the locations you marked. Do *not* leave the hotel."

"I can't just sit here."

"If they know you're here, they won't be looking for me. I can get more done."

She paced and pressed her fingers against her temples.

"Don't worry, kiddo. I know what to look for. We're gonna figure it out and do what we have to do. You'll see. Everyone will go home happy. In a couple of weeks I'll come down to Connecticut and we'll be laughing about this over a couple o' beers on your back porch."

"If you say so. But it'll be over coffee."

"Go on, get outta here." Dante kissed her forehead. "Use the elevator. I'll take the stairs to the parking lot."

"Be careful." As soon as she wrapped her arms around him, she sensed danger, danger she'd felt before. "Dante, I mean it. Don't mess with this. Pay attention to your hunches."

KATE STEPPED INTO THE LOBBY to see an attractive young man dressed in a dark blue suit, white shirt and gray tie, leaning on the reception desk; he was using a smart phone or palm device until the clerk pointed to her.

"Miss Kasabian. I'm FBI Special Agent Alex Fendi. I've been charged with your protection until Agent Jack Kasabian arrives."

"Jack's coming here?"

"Yes, ma'am. He should be here in an hour or so."

He called me ma'am. Ouch. "An hour! What's he doing? Flying?"

"That's right. Would you mind if we wait here." He gestured to a chair grouping against the lobby wall. "I've ordered snacks and beverages. Your brother should be here in no time."

"Do you know Jack?"

"No ma'am, I'm assigned to the Boston Field Office."

"Why is *he* coming? I saw him this morning in Burlington. He didn't say anything about Boston except that he wasn't coming."

The agent's phone buzzed. He listened, glancing at Kate. "Yes. I understand. Yes, sir." He put the phone away. "Jack will be delayed at my field office."

"Good. Can we meet him there?"

"Best to wait here. He'll join us as soon as he can."

"I don't understand. What's happening?"

"I can't say. I'm sure it's nothing to worry about."

"Then we might as well wait over lunch and the bureau should pay. There's an excellent restaurant right here. Their fresh seafood is the best. This way."

Kate crossed the lobby and Agent Fendi followed, requesting a table against the back wall near an exit. Strategic seating allowed a view of everyone entering the room. She asked Fendi, "Considering a quick getaway?"

"Keeping options open, ma'am."

After ordering seared scallops, Kate folded her hands on the table. "What shall we talk about? And don't call me ma'am." The longer she sat patiently with her guardian agent, the better for Dante's investigation, but patience didn't come easy. By the time Jack arrived, she hoped to have evidence, but as minutes ticked by and pressure built in her head, she grew more sure the day would not go as smoothly as she wanted. She wished Jack was with her, or better still, Matt Chase. If he assured her everyone was safe, she would believe.

"Everything all right, Miss Kasabian?"

Kate snapped back and managed to force a feeble smile. "I hope so."

FORTY-ONE

DANTE SAT IN HIS CAR studying Kate's notes and marking the street map from the hotel. He was more interested in scouting living quarters or a weapons cache, where he had practical experience, than of guessing suspected targets. He narrowed his search to a half dozen abandoned factories and warehouses in South Boston. The geography was ideal. Rundown commercial areas with privacy and easy access to rail, highways and the harbor. That's where *he* would stage an operation.

By 5:00 p.m. he'd eliminated four possibilities from Kate's lists and searched for the fifth. He screeched to a stop on Dorchester near 4th, when he spotted a handmade sign taped on the window of Southie's Texas Burgers that read, Semper Fi. He perched at the counter and checked the chalkboard menu, ordered chili, a well-done sirloin burger and a draft.

The cook, an older dude, was visible through an opening to the kitchen and sported the Marine Corps eagle, globe and anchor emblem on his left forearm.

"Where'd ya serve?" Dante asked.

"Kuwait. The 1/6 in Desert Storm. You?"

"Two tours in Afghanistan. One in Iraq."

The cook washed his hands, tossed the hand towel over his shoulder and set a spoon, napkin and a bowl of chili on the counter.

"Damn long tours, I hear. Name's Billy Barnes." He extended his hand. "Ain't seen you around."

"Dante Benard. Livin' in Vermont." He shook the man's hand. "You train up there?"

"Nah, Texas. Vermont ain't nothin' like Kuwait."

Dante laughed from deep in his belly. "That's for sure."

"What brings you to Boston?"

"Helpin' a friend. He's lookin' for a couple o' ragheads might be holed up 'round here. Seen anyone like that?"

Billy pointed south. "Down the road on the right, maybe two klicks, near B Street. They come 'bout three times a week for soup and meatloaf specials."

"How many in their group?"

The guy shrugged. "Can't say for sure. They come in two at a time. There's at least four, maybe six I'd know by sight. They speak Arabic, but get by with English." A kitchen timer beeped. Billy returned to the grill and assembled a burger.

"This is great, man." Dante devoured it in six bites. "Whaddo I owe ya?"

"First one's on the house."

"Thanks man, but I can expense it." He slapped a twenty on the counter.

"'Preciate it. Say, if you need an extra hand, I'll take you there."

"Thanks, but I'll check it out first. Maybe I'll be back."

Dante waved as he walked out the door. His manhunt had begun.

FORTY-TWO

MASSACHUSETTS TROOPER LEIGH DANNER from Crime Scene Services felt self-assured when she and State Police Detective Lieutenant Mike Riley first entered the FBI's Boston Field Office, but as she waited alone in an interview room, time eroded her confidence. The call-out seemed more secretive than most: Drop everything and get to Boston with files, photos and notes related to the cabin murders. *Why the hell not?* It was a strange case from the beginning so nothing about it surprised her.

Even the pulse in the building seemed different with agents scrambling, neatening, organizing—waiting. *They'd slap a fresh coat of paint on the walls if they had more time.* Danni had been to the field office many times, trained with Task Force agents and knew most by first name, but the energy was never this prickly. It felt electric, much like the spirit hand that had yanked her from the path of a speeding truck. Her shoulder still buzzed as if it had left something inside her.

From time to time Danni would visit the Dreamwatch site to study the account she had posted on that creepy morning, and she stood by it. She'd read others' paranormal experiences, too, but no matter how often her mind revisited her ghostly encounter, she couldn't make sense of it. She had hoped the memory of it would fade, but the opposite had happened.

Danni had been instructed to post her crime scene photos on the display board. *What was the FBI looking for?* She now wished she'd written her notes neater. Had she known they'd likely be scanned into their files, she would have printed box letters, precisely punctuated and accurately spellchecked. *What was it about this damn case?*

Riley mingled with agents in a briefing room, glancing occasionally at her in the room where she'd been directed. He didn't seem to know any more than she did.

She reviewed the day in her head. Tuesday, early morning, two weeks ago; so foggy she hadn't seen the cabin until she was twenty yards from the front deck. A fit young male lay dead on the floor of the main living area. She'd returned around eight when Riley had the search warrant. A second body, killed days earlier, had been identified as the property owner and his vehicle was found at the scene. John Doe in the cabin remains unidentified.

That about summed it up. A double murder at a remote location. Not an everyday crime scene, but hardly FBI noteworthy. She'd done everything right. There was nothing outstanding about the incident, except for the ghost hand, but she left that part out of her report.

Danni didn't seek help from the Employee Assistance Unit for fear they'd order a psych evaluation. She knew of others who had admitted bizarre incidents and saw they had been judged. *She* had judged them. Pretending it didn't happen the way it did seemed to be the best way to deal with it. Her police experience had taught her a half dozen witnesses to an accident will report as many different versions, so how could she distinguish between what really happened to her, from what was colored by the night and the fog?

"Trooper Danner." An agent tapped on the door. "They just set down at Logan Airport and should be here within thirty minutes."

"Who set down? Do you know why I was called here?"

The agent approached. "They didn't tell you?"

"No. They requested my files on this double murder near Worcester."

He stepped to the display board. "You shot these?"

"Who are you?"

"Special Agent Jamie Herrera. These are very good, and we see a lot." He moved from one photo to the next. "Great detail. Excellent context."

"Agent Herrera, why am I here?"

He didn't hesitate before he said, "All your questions will be answered. They'll be here shortly. Can I get you anything? Our coffee room is—"

"I know where it is. You don't have to escort me."

"Actually I do." Herrera accompanied her to the vending machines where he bought her a fruity tea Snapple. As they returned to the interview room, she noticed most agents' eyes on her. Most looked as confused by the day as she was. Two agents waved; she recognized them from last summer's training.

"That's my desk if you need anything." Herrera pointed nearby.

Danni raised the bottle. "Thanks for the tea."

All that was left to do, was wait.

FORTY-THREE

JACK AND CHASE ARRIVED at the Boston Field Office at two thirty. Jack stood in the room's rear while Chase began his briefing about the incidents leading to the Prague raid; introducing "Agent Jack Kasabian who will focus on an unorthodox perspective that has just come to light."

Movement across the hall caught Jack's eye. His attention shifted to an attractive young woman in a smaller meeting room, conservatively dressed in a navy colored pantsuit not unlike the female agents at Chase's briefing. She stood at near attention while reviewing a collection of 8 x 10s taped on a whiteboard. *Could be the trooper who lifted Yusuf's prints.* If he imagined her fully suited in the uniform of a state trooper, petite and doll-like, he might be amused, but she would be insulted, he had no doubt. If he'd learned anything from sparring with Kate, it was not to patronize a woman or trivialize her work. He eased into the hallway then entered the room, glancing at her face as he passed.

She stated her name and title. "But everyone calls me Danni."

Jack's eyes riveted on the board. His head pitched forward with squinting eyes and a furrowed brow. He couldn't stop facial muscles from contorting. His mouth twisted into a freakish gaping cavity. "What the hell!"

His gaze snapped toward her then back to the photos.

Danni moved beside him. "What is it? What's wrong?"

He walked along the board as if in slow motion, with a sense of floating over solid surroundings. Everything around him froze. Sight and sound. Even Danni faded into the background. His own steps disappeared. All meaningless.

Except for the photos on the board.

Was it possible?

He might have repeated, "Danni," as he inched nearer. He couldn't believe what he was seeing. He could barely choke out the words, "Were you the investigating officer?"

"Part of the team, but yes, first on scene. It's Detective Riley's case. That's him in the front row, listening to that guy you came in with." She pointed to Chase. "The callout came in around 1:00 a.m. on the night of—"

Jack raised his hand, signaling silence, as he studied the array that drew him the way a gruesome highway accident mesmerizes passing motorists. "You shot the photos?"

"I was the only CSS Tech at the scene for most of the day." Her arms flailed. "Look, what's this about?"

Jack didn't reply. He glared at the morgue photo, his eyes mere inches away. His heart pounded faster than if he'd sprinted a mile. *It can't be.* His lips parted. Mute. He pointed to the slain victim and backed away from the board.

"Yeah, him. Sorry, we haven't identified him yet. I ran his prints, but there was nothing." Danni moved to the board, her left forearm turned behind her back; her thumb hooked into a thin leather belt as she pointed with her right hand. "I sent his picture to local departments, missing persons. No response. DNA isn't back, but I doubt he's in that database either." She stretched, adding nearly two inches to her height. "I'll find him."

Jack looked straight in her eyes. He hesitated to make it real, afraid that if he opened his mouth, he'd vomit.

"Todd. His name is Todd Avery."

There, he said it.

Danni grabbed his arm and turned him toward her. "You *know* him?"

"Twenty-eight year old single male. Lives ... lived ... at 7 Summary Road in Shefford, Connecticut."

"Hold up." She pulled a notepad and pen from her purse and scribbled.

"He has two sisters. Caroline lives in Hartford. Beth in Mystic. Parents ..." Jack shook his head. "I don't know ... I can find out."

Danni wrote faster than he'd ever seen. "I'll take care of that."

Jack planted his hands on his hips, a stance that mimicked Chase. He stared across the hall and waved for him to come.

He swiped his chin. "Geezus! How am I going to tell Kate?"

"I beg your pardon."

"My sister. How do I tell her her fiancé is dead? Damn." He turned away from the image of the sweet guy who loved his sister, the slit throat, the brutal horror. "God damn it!" He wanted to put his fist through the photo ... through the board ... through the wall.

He turned from Danni and wiped an eye with the back of his wrist before Chase stepped in.

"What's going on, Jack?" Chase reviewed the photos; his jacket open and swept back, hands on his hips. "Good work trooper."

Danni nodded and introduced herself.

Chase turned to Jack and back to the board. "The photo in your office ... Jack? Isn't this the guy—"

"It is. Kate's not-quite fiancé. The one who didn't go to

Prague with her—the one who took off then disappeared."

"Apparently, this trooper found him. He was dead all the while?" Chase's hands gripped his head. "I'm sorry, Jack. So, what the hell do we have here?"

Danni flapped her arms. "Is someone going to tell me what this whole thing is about?"

Jack paced the room in circles around the conference table, agitated like a beast in a cage. Danni jumped a step back to clear his way. His lips mumbled an occasional audible phrase while he talked himself through the process.

Chase did the same, shifting weight from one leg to the other, pointing to various photos. At the same moment they stopped as if inspiration had struck them with the same idea. They faced each other.

Chase slapped the board with the back of his hand. "This could have been part of their plan."

"They set up Kate from the start? But why?"

"Did they target Kate, then kill Todd? Or did they kill Todd, thereby finding the plane ticket—or the website—that led to Kate?"

Danni looked from one to the other. "If I may …"

"Jump right in," Jack said.

"The evidence indicated the suspect … what's his name?"

"Call him Yusuf." Chase folded his arms across his chest.

"The evidence, along with statements of townspeople, indicated Yusuf had been squatting at the cabin until the new owner Ryan Calumet arrived. Yusuf killed him straight off and buried him in the woods. Fine for Yusuf. Plan disrupted but back on track.

"Couple days later, Avery shows up. Prints on carpentry tools dropped at the front door matched the vic, sorry, matched Mr. Avery, so I figured he'd come to help his friend. Yusuf attacked before he reached the center of the room.

"We found Calumet's pickup on the property and assume Yusuf left in Avery's car. We haven't located that second vehicle, but can match tire tracks when we do. And now, with an ID, I can find his car. If a couple of hunters hadn't reported the body, the murders might have gone undetected until spring."

"Maybe that was the plan," Chase said. "Yusuf made no effort to sanitize the scene, right? Whatever they have planned will be long over by spring."

"That's right, he was sloppy about leaving evidence."

Jack said, "You're looking for a Toyota Rav4, dark green with Connecticut 'Save The Sound' plates beginning with LI 5 …"

Chase called in Agent Herrera. "Get a BOLO out on this vehicle, the Northeast then expand. Connecticut DMV will have its full registration. Secure the vehicle, but do not approach. It may contain explosives, chemical- or bio-weapons. Go on Danni."

Danni's jaw dropped.

Jack said, "Trooper, please continue."

"Yusuf had rifled through Avery's belongings, took his wallet, keys—"

"Shit. He had Kate's keys."

Danni's eyes widened. "Wait, back up. You said explosives?"

Jack nodded. "He did. Please go on."

"If Yusuf took credit cards, we don't know if he used them. There was nothing on Avery to identify him … no way to know what was missing."

"Right. Anything more you want to add?"

"Ah … yeah. If you put my statement in a report, I'm sure the prosecutor would want me to add all the 'allegedlies' they need."

"Don't worry," Chase said, "I've got your back on that. Jack, is there anything Todd might have carried that would lead them to Kate?"

"Who is 'them'?"

"Kate didn't find his plane ticket to Prague, so he might have packed it, and his passport, too. Maybe he planned to meet her at the airport after all."

"That still doesn't lead to Kate. Think Jack. Danni?"

"It would help if I knew what the hell was going on!"

Chase twisted abruptly toward her. "No one told you?"

"They said to wait for you."

Chase shuddered. "The fingerprints you found at this cabin belonged to a known terrorist, member of the multi-national extremist group, Brothers of the Eastern Flame. One of their cells is planning an attack on Boston. That's why you're here."

"Whoa!" Danni took three steps backward until she bumped into a conference table. "And we're trying to find him?"

"No, and there isn't going to be any trial. He was killed last week in the apartment bombing in Prague, the one that made international news. We're looking for the mastermind and the rest of the cell, so it's important we learn all he did when he was here."

Danni's head snapped toward Jack.

"Let's get to Kate, too," he said, "and figure out how and why she's connected."

"Yusuf had Avery's home address. We can assume he also took his phone ..."

Jack rubbed his face with a downward swipe. "Kate's photo was Todd's screensaver. Her number was programmed in."

Danni raised her finger. "Does she work on websites?"

"She designs them and manages her own site. Why?"

"Avery had several purple business cards ..."

"Like this?" Jack pulled one from his wallet. "Cards with the site's URL. Her low-tech promotion campaign. She must have printed a thousand and gives them to everyone."

"Don't minimize that; Eastern Flame is most effective when they go low-tech on us." Chase moved to the window. "Kate may have become an unwitting component of a terrorist plot. Finding her site could have inspired the hijacking of a hide-in-plain-sight communication venue to replace the network we busted—busted by me."

Danni said, "I don't follow."

"They can't use phones because we're listening. We've compromised their Internet communications. They were using couriers to hand deliver messages until one of them led us to bin Laden in Pakistan, and recently, their couriers have a higher mortality rate than suicide bombers. Used once and killed."

"How does that figure in? And what's it got to do with Kate?"

"Think about it. They need to talk to each other, but what's left?"

"Well," Jack shrugged. "I can't think of anything."

"Exactly. They've been assassinating their own couriers to protect themselves before something big. Even if their mission was set, they still need to coordinate logistics."

Danni said, "So they're using Dreamwatch.com?"

"It wouldn't surprise me if they had eyes on Kate, especially if the attack was imminent and she was closing in on their location." Chase said to Jack, "I need to talk to her about these website messages; she's been piecing this together longer than we have. And she'll have to tell us what the hell happened in Prague. No holding back. I want to know what she suspects and what she told Dante Benard; he's out there alone tracking a credible threat."

Jack stared out the window across the cityscape. "He has no idea what he's up against."

"How can I help?"

Chase replied without looking up. "Danni, you're with us."

"Where is Kate now?" she asked. "Am I the only one who thinks she could be in danger?"

"An agent is with her at the Renaissance," Jack said.

"Agent Herrera will drive me and Jack to the hotel, you follow in your car. We might need to split up. Jack, wrap it up here."

Danni waited in the hall.

Chase asked, "What is it with Kate and Renaissance hotels, anyway?"

"I don't follow."

"She stayed in Prague at a Hilton, formerly a Renaissance."

Jack shrugged. "Really?" Chase seemed to have retained an awful lot of detail about Kate's itinerary.

"Forget it. Just something I remembered when I interviewed her at JFK."

There might be more to Kate's meeting Chase than they had let on. Jack also had to consider at some time over the past six hours, he had become the right hand man to an FBI supervisor. But until this threat was resolved, he wasn't considering how recent events impacted his future in the bureau. Kate's safety was all that mattered—and he was terrified he'd dragged his best buddy into a bigger pile of crap than he knew about— bigger than he could handle.

Jack checked his service revolver and secured it into his shoulder holster. It was clear to him as it must have been to Danni, they had become the fighting front of an event more momentous than they could have imagined.

FORTY-FOUR

KATE WAS WAITING at the hotel with Agent Fendi when Jack ran into the lobby followed by—Oh my God. She couldn't take her eyes off Matt Chase. His magnetism was as powerful as she remembered. Seeing him again, two hundred miles from where they'd first met, was either miraculous coincidence, or it was fate—and she leaned toward fate. *What brought them to this moment? How did he get to be with Jack?* She was eager to greet him and be near him again, but wondered if he even remembered her.

Fendi spoke with Chase, waved to Kate and exited to the drive-up area under the portico.

She turned to Jack. "Thank goodness you're here. Dante's in town, oh, you would know, you sent him, and he said he'd keep in touch, but I haven't heard from him since Agent Fendi arrived. He took off with my notes almost three hours ago, but he hasn't called and I'm worried. We have to find him. Has he called you?"

Jack said nothing as he took hold of Kate's arm.

"What's wrong? You're scaring me. You look like you've seen a ghost."

He led her to a conversation area in the corner of the lobby. "Sit down. I have bad news."

She glanced over her shoulder to Chase while Jack tugged at her.

"It's about Todd."

"Todd? What is it?"

He eased her onto a chair. "I'm so sorry to tell you. Todd is dead."

She bolted up, pacing in circles, jerking her arms to push away his words or the space she didn't want to be in. "No. Are you sure?"

"I am."

"How? When? I don't understand." She fell back onto the chair while Jack divulged general circumstances. "He's been dead since the day after he left home."

She cupped her hands over her mouth. "All this time. How could I not have known?"

Didn't you? You saw the signs. He came to you the night he died.

You ran your fingers through his hair.

She glanced at Chase.

"He was murdered at a friend's cabin in Massachusetts."

"Was his throat cut?"

Jack ran his hand across his face. "You don't want to hear about—"

"Was it?"

He nodded, staring at his shoes. "How did you know that?"

"A red scarf told me."

His eyes fired at her. "Geezus, Kate. Don't talk about that crap with—"

She gazed across the lobby, blinking away tears as Chase and a woman neared.

"With them." Jack rose. "This is Danni. State Trooper Leigh Danner. She's helping with this case."

Danni sat perpendicular to Jack, facing Kate. "I'm sorry for your loss."

"Have we met?" Jack shot a look at Kate as she continued. "I'm sure I've seen your face. I feel I know you."

Danni shook her head. "I'm sure we haven't."

Chase stooped beside Kate. "I'm—"

Words escaped before she could stop herself. "I know who you are. Agent Chase, right? Matt Chase. From the airport. What's going on? What are you doing in Boston? Are *you* investigating Todd's murder?"

"I remember you too and we'll have time enough later to talk. I realize timing is bad." He laid his hand on her hands that were crossed on her lap. "I'm so sorry about your fiancé, but I must ask about Prague so you'll have to put aside your feelings until later; it's the only way."

"I understand."

"Did you meet anyone in Prague?"

"Todd and I weren't engaged, but we were very close. We planned to go to Prague, but he didn't show up, like I said at the airport. I thought he was impressing that ... that we were over, you know." She glanced at Jack then back to Chase. "What's Prague got to do with anything?"

"Kate, please. Just answer his questions."

Chase pulled his cell phone and called up two photos of Yusuf, one from the training camp video and a not-so-ragged version taken at JFK. "Do you recognize this man?"

She took hold of Chase's hand, tilting the phone to see. "Sure. He sat next to me on the flight to Prague. Is that why you were at the airport? Searching for him? Did you catch him?"

"He was killed by security forces in Prague."

"During the safehouse raid? I saw it on the news. I was there." She twisted toward Jack then back to Chase. "Really. I was on-the-spot there. I walked down the same street hours before the blast. I asked workmen for directions in front of the building."

"We know. We have you on tape. They weren't workmen."

"Your people? I heard the explosion later in the evening. Were they hurt?" Kate picked through her purse for a tissue. "Oh my God, he sat next to me—in Todd's seat."

Chase nodded. "He was killed during the raid. Did he speak to you during the flight?"

"Not much … but some during dinner. He was creepy, you know. I didn't encourage—"

"Tell me everything."

"Mostly, we talked about tourist sights."

"So nothing specific?"

"He told me about a cyber café near my hotel." She turned toward Jack. "He also said they paid a good black market exchange rate on dollars, but I didn't think they did." She told Chase, "He tore a city map from the airline magazine and marked it up for me."

"Do you have the map?"

"Not with me. It's at home. In Connecticut." She glanced at Jack. "A souvenir."

Jack said, "Anything else we should know?"

She tried to recall. "Oh … he said he'd soon be joining his little sister. Not his exact words. His English was sloppy; I remember that."

"Don't worry about it, she died years ago during a civil demonstration in Cairo." Chase continued, "Did you go to the café Yusuf suggested? Did he meet you there? Was anyone else hanging around? Acting suspiciously?"

"I didn't see him after we disembarked, but I stopped at the café several days later."

"Did you speak to anyone?"

She nodded. "The manager. He'd just opened and I was the

only customer. Hey, it was the morning after the bomb. I remember because I knew Jack would worry so I wanted to send an e-mail saying I was okay, but there was some technical problem at the hotel business center so I went there. Then some guy came in. The manager talked to him, and I did, too. He was foreign, not Czech. I shouldn't presume, but if I had to guess, I'd guess Saudi."

"I reviewed your passport history. You frequently travel to the Middle East."

Kate sighed. "Is that why TSA searches my bags?"

"Kate, not now," Jack snapped.

"So this guy ... he helped me get an Internet connection. I was having trouble because the keyboard had ... it was different. My typing ... I have to look at the keys; I got confused."

Jack was fidgeting. Chase was wringing his hands. "It was frustrating for you. I understand."

"I'm rambling because I'm nervous. Todd murdered." She shook her head. "It's very upsetting and I'm worried about Dante."

"I appreciate that," Chase said. "But we're running against the clock. Tell me about the manager and the other guy who might be Saudi."

"The manager seemed to be watching me while he talked on a cell phone."

"Did you hear his conversation?"

"I could hear, but didn't understand. He spoke Arabic or Farsi or something, one of those, I'm sure." Kate let out a deep breath. "Oh my God, how stupid! He kept looking back and forth from his screen to me. He must have somehow had my picture on his laptop and called the guy to come because he walked in shortly after."

Chase pressed, "So this foreign guy shows up. Handsome?

Charming? Flawless English? Willing to help with your connection or anything you need?"

"Yes, all of that." She blew out a sharp breath. "What an idiot I was. They set me up. Who was he? Do you have a photo of him on your phone?"

"No. I wish I did."

"Wait … wait a minute. I didn't get around to downloading my vacation pictures. They're still in my camera." She rummaged through her oversized bag and pulled out her Nikon. "I managed to snap his picture on the sly. It's not perfect, but …." She called up the photo and handed the camera to Chase, who flashed the image to Jack and Danni. "He said his name was Ali, but the manager called him Abdul."

"This is the same guy we captured on tape when he arrived at the Prague safehouse. I wasn't sure he was Ali until now." He glanced at Jack. "Upload this to our server for distribution to the Task Force and Boston PD. Do it now."

"Yes, sir." Jack took the camera and bolted to the front desk.

Chase said, "His name is Abdul Wahab al-Khalifah, the head of a U.S. based extremist cell. I've been after him for years."

"The one they call The Brain? Did *he* kill Todd?"

Chase leaned toward her. "Who's *they*? Where did you hear about The Brain?"

"Whoever is sending messages to my Web site. I don't know who they are."

"Ali didn't kill him. He was off our radar until he surfaced in Prague. It's likely Yusuf murdered him and his friend."

"What friend?"

"Ryan Calumet, the man who owned the cabin. Yusuf searched Avery's belongings, that's probably how they learned about your site." He pointed to Danni. "Trooper Danner worked the crime scene. She believes he died instantly."

Kate covered her gaping mouth. "It's too much. I don't want to fall apart," she leaned close to Chase, "but I am slipping."

"I'm sure Danni and her team were respectful of the bodies." Danni nodded as Chase continued. "It *is* a lot to process. But it's not too much." His hands enveloped hers. "You can keep yourself together and you will, because we need you. A lot of innocent people might be in danger, and we can't stop the attack without your help. That's what you want, isn't it?"

"Todd always carried my cards. Do you think Ali heard about Dreamwatch from Yusuf? That he came to the cyber café to meet me and learn about my site?"

"We don't know enough yet, but it's likely. A tech team in Virginia is working on back tracing everyone who's logged onto your site during the past two weeks. Jack assured your cooperation."

Kate glanced toward the front desk looking for Jack. "Yes, of course I'll cooperate. Whatever you need." She flapped her arms; they dropped to the chair's armrests. "Take the whole damn thing."

"Tell me what you know about Ali. Everything. No detail is too small."

She told him about Ali's business with the manager, and that he seemed too interested in her site. "He walked with a limp. Twisted ankle or something like that."

Jack returned. "Probably caused by jumping to escape the raid."

"I might have seen him later in the day on the Charles Bridge. I was distracted and he disappeared into the Little Quarter. I flew home the following morning."

Jack handed the camera to Chase who passed it to Kate. "His photo is out."

"He smelled like spice. Cinnamon or cloves. I think it was in his hair. That's all I remember." She took a deep breath. "I can't believe how stupid I was. I'm usually alert, and overly suspicious."

"I noticed at the airport," Chase said. "The alert part, anyway. You've done everything right. We're here aren't we? And we're listening. No one is hurt, and we're all going to prevent that from happening."

FORTY-FIVE

DANTE DROVE DOWN THE ROAD from the burger joint, parked his car a block away and around the corner. He checked that his pistol was loaded and stashed a box of ammo in his pocket. He grabbed a backpack of tools from the trunk and cased the warehouse perimeter for signs of activity and to scout entry points, like so many reconnaissance patrols in rebel villages. Adrenaline surged as he crept down a dank asphalt alleyway that ran the length of the red brick building. Railroad tracks with I-93 beyond them bordered the building's rear parking lot. A loading dock at tailboard height centered on the building's back wall, and chains secured rear steel doors.

Bat guano layered the floor of a rickety wooden freight chute, marking the exit tunnel for the creatures likely living in warehouse peaks. Dante climbed to the chute's opening and wiggled inside, his middle-age gut barely squeezing through the passage. *Where was Kate when ya' need 'er?* She wouldn't hesitate to crawl through such a tunnel, especially if it led inside an ancient tomb. He tried not to stir the dust, but he could feel it in his eyes and nose, and taste it in his throat.

Once inside, he slithered out of the opening, hopped onto a shipping ramp four feet below, and dropped his pack. *Not bad so far. Looks like no one's home.*

He estimated the inside space to be 25,000 square feet with good clear height. He hugged the walls like a rodent as he explored the boundary for alternate exits. The warehouse might have been an assembly plant; it held the smell of motor oil. Faint footprints marked the concrete floor where machines once stood.

Air mattresses, blankets, basic foods on shelving, and a dorm-size refrigerator defined a makeshift living area without walls. A set of steel utility shelves, like those sold at home improvement box stores, stored clothing in different sizes, all smaller than he; backpacks, cameras, and two dozen prepaid cell phones in various states of disassembly. Next to the street side cargo doors, four Kawasaki motorcycles lined up beside two Boston police cruisers layered with dust. Two bathrooms, one with a small window painted shut, housed only sinks and seatless toilets. A separate room that might have been a foreman's office now held a heap of construction trash bags that reeked of rotting household garbage. From the hoard of supplies and refuse, Dante reckoned five or six men with modest needs could have been living in the warehouse for thirty days or more.

Heavy duty lines ran the width and length of the building, likely wired to the power supply of a neighboring storage facility. Someone with electronics know-how had to do that, though he'd be a fool to try.

Dante turned on one of several laptops where the browser history confirmed frequent visits to Kate's Web site. "Holy crap." His skin crawled like it did in Afghanistan, senses on fire like when he kicked in doors of insurgent strongholds. *This* was *an insurgent stronghold.*

"Kate nailed it." She suspected an extremist group would reign terror on multiple targets in Boston in September. *Looks about right.*

He knew he should split. Every nerve in his body screamed for him to flee. The information he discovered was more valuable than his urge to confront these guys. *Call Jack and get the heck outta Dodge.* He could leave now and be a hero, but he couldn't resist poking around to learn what weapons they'd collected and what they were planning.

Leave now.

He couldn't help himself—it *was* who he was. Seek and destroy.

His flashlight beam swept across the warehouse. Along a wall, a black plastic tarp covered a mountainous stash. He pulled up the corner edge revealing a cache of firearms, grenades and explosives; its size rivaled those his unit had found in Iraq. "What the heck?" He moved the tarp, saw a case each of aerosol dispensers and gas masks. He lifted more of the cover until he spotted crates of canisters he didn't recognize, labeled with words he couldn't read.

Go now.

He had to call Jack, but first he aimed to identify the contents of the cylinders and memorize the labels. Diiso ... propyl ..., Methyl ... phos .... *Forget this.* He checked other containers until he found a name he could pronounce: SARIN. "Holy freakin' crap."

The only good news was if munitions were here, they weren't scattered around Boston. *They're not ready. They got what they need to pull off the big nasty, but they're not ready.*

Run.

Dante grabbed his phone, hit Jack's speed dial number.

The cargo doors roared open and a van entered.

"Shit!" He hung up before Jack answered and switched the phone to silent.

Run. Run. Run.

Bathroom window or freight chute? The bathroom was closer, but its window was painted shut and it exited to a side of the building he hadn't surveyed. "Freaking goddam hell." *Stick with what you know.* He scrambled toward the freight chute. The hostiles entered before he reached it. He braced against the wall and hid behind a stack of slatted pallets. The men unpacked and stored boxes on the food shelves. Dante understood only a few words of what they were saying, words that meant: dinner, Ali, paradise.

This was the base of their operation and he'd seen enough. He plotted his exit, risky, but he had to tell Jack and get back to the hotel to keep an eye on Kate like he promised.

Someone called out when a car drove into the warehouse, "Ali. Ali." Headlights caught Dante and the driver squealed when he spotted him.

He bolted to the loading platform and dove into the freight chute before the others knew what happened. Their numbers were too great, their weapons overpowering, and he feared their determination was unbreakable.

He should have left when he had the chance. He screwed up and was as good as dead.

And he knew it.

He wiggled down the chute. Loud chatter broke out as the five hostiles fired commands at each other. One hostile followed him through the chute while other voices faded, circling around the building.

Dante fell onto the outside loading dock and scrambled for a place to hide. But they were everywhere.

His life depended on escape—thousands of lives did.

Run. Run for your life. He ran, wildly shooting his pistol until his last bullet was gone. No chance to reload.

They cornered him in the alley, firing small caliber handguns until the leader ordered them to stop the noise.

Dante froze, assessing his chances. His heart jumped against his chest as if it, too, attempted escape.

Two hostiles in front. Two behind. Another crawling down the chute. No way up the warehouse wall, or down to sewers. They closed in on him. Punched. Kicked. Stabbed him.

He dropped to the asphalt in a bloody mess, gasping for air, feeling his life drain and pressing wounds to hold it in.

The leader shouted; he must have ordered them to move his body. They carried him to the van, drove a short distance, and tossed him off a pier into Boston harbor. He landed on hard sand, not water nor a beach, but sand bags stacked on top of a concrete sea wall. *Lucky SOB.*

Dante was close to dead … if he could hold on till they drove off, he might squeak outta this. He *had* to hold on.

He had to warn Jack.

Lying still. Holding breath. Feeling colder as blood pulsed and soaked into the sand. He barely moved air wondering if maybe he was already dead, but stubbornly refusing to depart.

The van pulled away, lights out, almost silent but for tires crunching sand against road.

Dante woke to the sound of water lapping against moss covered pilings, smelling seaweed, salt and fish. He struggled to reach his phone, labored to hit Jack's number, and he did.

With all the breath he could muster, he whispered, "The threat is real …."

FORTY-SIX

OVER FOUR HOURS had passed since Dante left the hotel. Kate quietly sat pressing her temples, her attention seemed to bounce from Chase to Danni to outside police activity and back to Jack. He tried to hold a poker face but his sadness for her was too strong. He worried about Dante and it was clear Kate did too. After what happened to Coop, if anything happened to Dante because of her intervention, she might lose herself in dark guilt, forever.

"He's been in situations far more dangerous than this." His assurance didn't sound convincing, even to himself.

"Has he? If I'm right, he could be facing more danger than we know."

Jack thought though didn't say, We know.

Chase added, "We'll find him."

Jack's personal cell phone rang. Kate flew to his side and they glanced at the caller's name. "It's him."

"Answer it," Chase said.

Dante's voice was weak and slow and broken by erratic wheezing. Jack could barely make out the words when Dante said, "The threat is real …."

"Dante. Are you there? Crash! Hang on buddy." No response. "Should I call him back?"

Danni was already contacting her headquarters for a phone trace of the signal.

Chase said, "Don't hang up. Keep the connection open. Work with Danni. Contact the state police and Boston PD. I'll update the JTTF and they'll—"

"We also have SERT on standby," Danni said.

"What's that?" Jack asked.

"Special Emergency Response Team." She looked briefly at Kate. "They find people. As soon as we identify the general location, they'll cover the area."

Jack moved to a quiet corner with his phone pressed to his right ear, his other hand blocking his left ear. "Dante! Stay with me. I love you, buddy. Hang on. We're coming."

He strained to listen, eyes squinting. "I hear a boat horn and background noise like water lapping against something solid, but not hard.

"I don't hear him breathing."

FBI AGENTS AND STATE TROOPERS back traced the signal, narrowing to an area in South Boston, Dorchester, East 1st, the channel. Troopers, canines, SERT and Boston police swarmed the area with more on the way. Searchlights cut through a murky mist. The nearby fish market reeked of leftovers from the day's catch. Rescue helicopters lit access roads, parking lots and piers; boats and Whalers aimed spotlights on pilings and underneath docks. Divers prepared to plunge. The dark and quiet location reeled in a buzz of activity that rivaled a fully staffed war game.

A single clear voice pierced the clamor. "Over here."

A trooper stood tall, waving his light to signal. Police radio frequencies relayed the word, and air and marine spotlights aimed like lasers to guide rescuers.

A cop hopped down to the sea wall, knelt beside the body, gloved his hand and felt for signs of life. He shook his head and everyone knew the victim was dead. The officer lit the misshapen face and scowled at the brutality of the attack. He couldn't identify the body with the FBI's photo—he didn't even try.

He handed a wallet up to a supervisor who stooped on the pier above him.

The supervisor pulled the Vermont driver's license of Dante Benard. 42-year-old white male, six feet, 240 pounds, brown hair and eyes. He called headquarters and notified the supervisor on the scene. "We've got Benard. He's dead."

FORTY-SEVEN

DANNI WAS FIRST TO HEAR from her headquarters and Chase immediately read bad news on her face. He followed her outside to where state and city police cruisers had assembled, and where they could talk in private. He stood facing her; his back toward the lobby window. "Tell me."

"We're on the scene in South Boston." She looked past him into the hotel. "My people have tentatively identified the body of Dante Benard."

Chase leaned against the glass, glancing over his shoulder toward Kate. His eyes met Jack's. Seconds seemed impossibly long as he considered how to tell him … tell *them*. He stared at Jack and shook his head, No.

Jack rushed toward him and they met at the door. "I'm so sorry about Dante."

Danni turned away as if to grant privacy as they spoke.

"I appreciate the sentiment." Jack nodded in the direction of the lobby. "We can't tell her. Not yet."

"I agree. We need her full attention." He gently squeezed Jack's shoulder. "Tough day for you, too. We need *your* wits. Can you handle this? I wouldn't hold it against you if you preferred to remain here with your sister."

"I can handle it. I want to see Dante and where he died … to see for myself. No one else can get up to speed fast enough.

Besides, I know Dante like a brother, he needs us to succeed even if he'll miss the victory … for his kid. I need to help. I'll tell Kate later in my own way."

"Good. Tell Fendi we're ready. We'll go to the pier and identify your friend. He must have found something that led him to the cell, and he might have left a clue to their location only you can understand."

Danni expressed condolences. Chase pointed to Fendi leaning against a car. "Jack and I are going to the scene with him. I need you to stay with Kate. You heard? No discussion of Benard. Review her notes. Check out possible targets. Tell me what you find. That's it. Do you understand what we're up against?"

Danni nodded. "Yes, sir. What can I do?"

"Kate has clear and specific thoughts about the targets. It's a long shot, but you know Boston's landmarks better than we do. What would make a global statement? Take her to scout those locations. Try to think like they do. You know what to look for?"

"Yes, sir. I trained last summer with the Task Force. I know what to do."

"I don't want you to *do* anything. Locate the targets and call me or Jack."

"But—"

"Don't dismiss her because she's a civilian. I've been hunting Ali day and night for years, but she's the only one here who's actually met the guy. The only photo we have of him is because of her. And she's the only one without a gun." He pointed to Kate. "Get a vest on her. And Danni, she put this together on her own with no training. Were it not for her imagination and persistence, you'd be reading the body count in the *Globe*."

Danni glanced at Kate and nodded. "I understand."

"Let's go. Keep in touch. As we close in, they won't blink before they kill, so stay alert and for heaven's sake be careful."

Red and blue lights on police and emergency vehicles lit the outside entrance of the hotel and the surrounding area. The JTTF coordinator spread a map of the city across the hood of a cruiser, consulting with a SWAT commander. Chase and Jack reviewed plans with agents and police before they dispersed.

Jack ran to Kate and hugged her. "Stay out of trouble."

"I love you, too."

Danni led Kate to her CSS van and Jack headed toward Fendi.

Before Kate walked away, Chase held her arms in a firm grip, protective and serious. "I meant what I said about catching up later. If we didn't need you, I'd order you to stay here with one of my guys. Promise you'll be careful." She nodded. "If you and Danni separate or something happens, call for help on her radio. Channel One." Kate seemed bewildered. "Special TacOps is using Channel One's frequency."

"Oh, okay. Got it. Channel One. Call for help."

Chase ran toward Jack, Fendi and his waiting car.

"Hey," she called out. "You be careful, too. And bring my brother back in one piece."

Chase gave a thumbs up sign and he and Jack raced away, tires squealing, because they knew exactly where they were going.

FORTY-EIGHT

POLICE HAD CORDONED OFF a broad area at the channel, much more than needed. As Jack, Chase and Fendi approached the line, a cop raised the yellow tape and pointed ahead.

A trooper, a 40-ish muscular guy and member of the Task Force, was on-site to meet them. Chase asked, "Have you been briefed?"

"Yes, sir. This way." He led them toward the water. "Rumors say this is a drill gone bad." Chase glared, but the trooper didn't stop. "Is this for real?"

"It doesn't get more real than it is tonight."

"Trust him on that." Jack extended his hand. "Agent Jack Kasabian. He's Fendi."

Fendi waved.

The trooper escorted them to the edge of the wharf where an officer pointed below. Several police Whalers bobbed in the channel. Jack and Fendi leaned over.

Chase knelt on one knee, gripping a piling as he peered over the dock. He seemed skittish about the height, each move seemed surprisingly cautious. "Is this your friend?"

"Hard to tell." Jack pointed down, asking permission to jump.

The trooper extended his arm. "Grab my hand."

He hopped down to the sea wall, rocking on sandbags until he found his footing and dropped beside the body.

The trooper directed one of the boats to aim its spotlight.

Jack rubbed his hand across his mouth and chin as he studied wounds.

The face was swollen, discolored and bloody. The skin torn, exposing bone in several areas, clear shoe prints marked the tissue. Eye sockets crushed. Nose flattened and dislodged. Lips split. Front teeth gone.

Despite the damage, he knew. "This is Dante Benard."

The trooper stared below as the boats lit the body. "How can you be so sure?"

"He served in Afghanistan. Half his ear was shot off." He pointed. "Old wound. It's him." Jack placed his hand on Dante's chest. "Sorry buddy, I didn't know." He turned away and stared across the channel. "I'll do my best for your kid. Brothers, right? I love you, man." Jack wiped his eyes. "Get me the hell out of here." He grabbed the trooper's hand and climbed to the pier.

Chase asked for Dante's personal effects and the CSS tech passed him several evidence bags. Jack struggled to keep a professional focus while examining the wallet and note pad. "Dante rarely wrote notes and his wallet looks like it always does; the few hundred in bills I gave him this morning for expenses, but otherwise empty. We got nothing."

"We have his phone." The tech handed it to Jack; he requested TacOps to backtrace signals from the Vermont border to Boston Harbor.

The technician held out an evidence bag. "We found an unusual residue on the victim's clothes and shoes, but accurate analysis will take hours."

"We don't have hours."

"If I had to guess, I'd say bird turd. It's ground deep into his pants at the knees like he crawled in it. We see a lot of pigeon crap under bridges so that'd be my first idea. I don't have a second guess, but when you find it, figure you're in the right place."

Chase opened the bag, pinched a few pellets to rub between his fingers. "Odor's not too bad. Hint of ammonia." He raised his hand.

Jack caught a whiff and winced. "Got it, Boss."

Dante's phone rang, startling Jack with a jerk. He took the call from TacOps and reported to the others. "He called three numbers in Massachusetts. Kate's hotel and my cell; it disconnected before I answered. The third call came from here at the pier."

"The tower location of that second call?"

"Dorchester Avenue near B Street."

"Old factories and vacant warehouses." The trooper pointed down the road. "A few miles from here. How do you want to handle it?"

"We don't know what they have stockpiled and the place could be booby-trapped like the safehouse in Prague. Put the Task Force bomb squad and hazard team on alert and position them at least a mile out. Tell them to come in dark and remain hidden until they get new intel. Close off the roads behind your teams at least another mile out."

He asked Chase, "We're providing the intel?"

"It's you, Fendi and me, but we'll take backup from Task Force SWAT."

Jack sighed. "Yeah. I'm all for that."

FORTY-NINE

KATE AND DANNI PULLED AWAY from the hotel lot as she strained to read her printouts by the glow of passing street lamps. "Is there a light in this thing?"

"It's new. I haven't mastered all the features, though I've played with the electronics for Web access, database interface and screaming GPS. There must be a switch somewhere."

Kate ran her hand over the console, the dashboard and around the front window frame.

"Careful."

The siren suddenly bellowed, WHOOP-WHOOP. An airport shuttle in front of them pulled to the side of the road. "Oops." A passenger map light turned on with the next lever. "Found it."

Danni choked back a laugh. "Next time, try it without fanfare."

"I can see." Kate was oblivious to the traffic she'd diverted, or to Danni, as she focused on her notes and the critical clues she had circled.

"You know this is impossible, don't you? We've been delegated to a goose chase. The FBI wanted us out of the way."

"You get that a lot, do you?"

"I did until I proved myself. Now, my teams treat me like one of the guys."

Kate glanced at her facial features. She was pretty. "Too bad."

"Yeah."

"Well, whatever trials they put you through, you're here now. Your work grabbed their attention. Pretty impressive, I'd say."

"Yusuf's fingerprint got their attention, but I appreciate the vote of confidence. You're the one who poked a stick in their eye. There must be something useful in those stories."

"There must be, but being a stranger to Boston, I'm not seeing the connection."

Danni pulled into the vacant parking lot of a middle school, shut the engine and turned on the overhead dome light. "Let's have a look."

For the first time Kate didn't feel patronized; she heard real interest in Danni's voice. "I imagine all this paranormal talk conflicts with your beliefs."

"What do you think my beliefs are?"

"I assume you trust evidence to prove facts. I know your type." Kate chuckled. "My brother is like you."

"You're right. I don't see where you're coming from."

As Danni reviewed the story notes, Kate studied her face. She'd swear they had met before. "Do you ever get a gut feeling? Ever follow a hunch?"

"Sure. Why?"

"That's all I'm doing. Maybe to a greater degree, but it's the same."

"When you say it like that, I understand what you mean."

I saw her face in a vision. She was the woman I didn't know when I saw Dante, Chase and Jack. She immediately connected Danni to the Dreamwatch story from the anonymous state trooper, and her own premonition about their linked fate. *It's you.* A warm empathetic smile broadened and her spirit eased with a sense of satisfaction. No resistance to fortune surrounded them. Kate was sure they were exactly where they were meant to be, doing what they were meant to do. Order seemed stable.

Continuity or doom. Whatever happened next, must happen.

"What? You're too quiet." Danni turned toward her. "What is it?"

"Did something miraculous happen to you? Was your life saved in a strange way? Did you ever write to Dreamwatch?"

Danni shot a look.

"It's my site. There's no need to be embarrassed. You're not the only one. Most people feel the same. They're skeptics until it happens to them. I wanted you to know."

"I wrote to a paranormal website and now we're in the same car. This is too freaky. And that doesn't mean I believe any of it."

"That we're here at this moment has been mapped out by providence."

Danni shook her head. "Yeah, whatever you say, Kate. So show me what you've got?"

They eliminated several messages, made a list of those most likely and sent it to Chase.

"The FBI traced this pile to foreign servers." Kate handed the stack to Danni. "I know they're using a simple code like they've used in the past. Chase told me. Instead of the target, cell members and weapons, communications might describe a celebration, guests and gifts, but this is different and I didn't figure out the code words."

"If it were me, I'd submit something that would go unnoticed. What do most people write about besides getting grabbed off the road?"

"Most ghost sightings are of dead grandparents or husbands and wives, more husbands."

"Wives don't come back?"

"I can't say for sure. I think it's because more women than men view my site."

"You trust that people write the truth?"

"I do." Kate thought a moment. "Premonitions of auto accidents. Dreams of death. It's rare for people to write about a specific place or a celebrity. But I did get a warning once about danger to a British royal. I didn't post it. Didn't want to give anyone an idea. I told Jack about it, but didn't ask how far it reached up his chain of command."

"So most are about personal experiences? These stories are all over the place. I don't see a pattern either." Danni winced. "Hard to believe your suspicions got you this far."

"Bridges are a recurring theme, here and in my visions. And look at this, a repeated reference to something flowing could represent a river. Or it could be interpreted as a transit route of any kind."

Danni chuckled. "I'm trying to work with you, but how do you get transit route out of 'something flowing'?"

"When a person has a premonition, the location is rarely spelled out. It's more about the symbolism: a thing flowing through confined space could be water in a river bed, or it could be people moving in one direction like on a train, or filing through a tunnel at a sports complex."

"I see, but none of that is helpful. Keep talking."

"I had a vivid dream with snowflakes falling in September. I'm sure the vision belongs with this attack, somehow, but I'm clueless to what it means."

Danni looked to the sky. "No snow."

"I'll get back to stories, but before I forget, there was one thing that sticks with me. I'm a little obsessive and can get hung up with even numbers. I tried to store this in the back of my mind, but it bounces back. Early visions duplicated symbols and names like Charles-Charles."

Danni's brow furrowed.

"I was recently on the Charles Bridge in Prague and that same day I met Ali at an Internet café. I was on the bridge more than twice, so I don't think the doubling refers exclusively to *that* bridge. Is there a Charles Bridge here in Boston?"

"Are you kidding? Boston has at least a half dozen bridges crossing the Charles River. Does that count?"

"Sure it does." Kate twisted in the seat. "It tells me targets are at or near the river."

"Near the Charles? Define 'near' because I'm thinking that's all of Boston."

Kate checked her hard copies and asked for Danni's iPhone. "Can I get online with this thing? I need to see my Web site."

"Here, try this." Danni turned on a monitor built into the dashboard and punched a few keys. "There you go, surf away."

"Wow, this is so cool." Kate typed her site's URL.

"What are you looking for?"

"Checking something … I got it … See this newest posting?" She compared yesterday's printed copy to the current online version. "They're different. A few words have changed. Now the story predicts multiple auto accidents, but it doesn't say if anyone is injured." She glared at Danni. "So who the hell changed it if I'm in the car with you. They updated this story minutes ago. Chase was right, those bastards are using my site. They hack in and change the damn postings." She tossed the old printouts onto the back seat. "Useless. Not even this original is the original."

"Don't get flustered. That's good news. We don't need all these papers. We only have to read the newest postings." Danni tossed her stack on the back floor.

"Can you tell where the last story originated, the one with the auto accidents?"

"It's not my strongest talent, but I'll try to figure it out." She navigated to Manage Site and pointed to the login history. "See, these messages came from the U.S. like they indicate on the surface, but look, they routed through a proxy server in Malta, that's what MT means ... wait, is that right? I can't see from this angle."

Danni interrupted, "I think you need glasses. You're looking at the e-mail address and it's not MT. It's MIT, Massachusetts Institute of Technology. Across the river I think. In Cambridge?"

"You're asking me?"

"I don't live in Boston either, but I have a fair sense of direction. We'll head toward the Charles." Danni turned on the engine and they left the lot. "What does the new message read?"

"It warns about a skating accident. Tracks on water. And multiple auto accidents. I'm seeing pieces come together. MIT. The Brain. "The Brain. Ali. He's here."

Kate hit the refresh icon and stared as a story appeared. "This one just came in from someone new in Canada who writes proficient English. It specifically names the Charlestown Bridge with today's date and a precise time." She checked the computer's clock. "Oh no. Danni, it's happening now."

Danni repeated the message to herself, slightly moving her lips. She cocked her head and repeated the words, then yelled, "Hang on!" She slammed the brakes to the floor and spun a U-turn. The rear wheels squealed as they fishtailed. Rubber burned. Kate was thrown forward in her seat. Danni turned on lights and siren.

"What is it?"

"We are so screwed."

"I don't understand. What happened?"

"MIT. And on the way is Boston Garden, a dam, Harvard, bio-science and bio-med labs, energy research, and the main hub for the trains. Every desirable target is in that area."

"For someone who doesn't live here, you seem to know the city pretty well."

"Boston's soft targets were part of my Task Force training. Know the area, that's what they taught us."

Kate studied the GPS map as they drove north. "Here's the Charlestown Bridge."

"Where?" Danni asked.

"Next to Zakim."

"I know *that* one. We can't miss it."

"Charlestown Bridge. Charles River. Doubled names and the newest site message. I'm sure that's our destination." Kate called Jack then Chase, but her messages went directly to voicemail. "Why aren't they answering?"

"Whatever they're doing, we'll hear about it soon enough."

"That's supposed to make me feel better?" Kate squirmed in her seat. *Hurry.* "Hurry. I have bad feeling." She yanked her seatbelt tighter.

Traffic slowed as they neared the bridge. Too late, they were boxed in like everyone else. "Look. Vehicles in both directions are stopped."

"This can't be coincidence." Danni signaled with the siren's WHOOP-WHOOP to no avail. Cars had nowhere to go. Vehicle tail lights cast an eerie red glow on their faces. Vapors drifted from exhaust pipes as hundreds of auto engines hummed. The ramp shook with a slight vibration. "This isn't good. I get so frustrated. And all I want is to get through the day." Danni pounded the steering wheel with both fists and screeched, "Move it!"

"I've seen this in a vision, the tail lights and the vapors." Kate gripped the arm rest. "The other bridge is backed up, too." They looked at each other.

"Definitely not coincidence. Someone did this."

"Oh my God, multiple accidents with no one hurt. Why would someone want to clog traffic? Why direct us to this particular location?" She turned to Danni. "What advice did Chase give you at the hotel?"

"To think like they do."

"Maybe they're studying traffic patterns. To create this mess, all they needed was a few fender benders, or a couple of abandoned cars at strategic locations."

"Maybe. Thousands of people are stuck and it's not even a sports event night. Maybe they wanted to trap the people. Scare us. Panic is a dangerous weapon."

"That's why we call it terror."

Kate quietly stared out the side window while Danni ranted and ran her thoughts. The night was warm, the air at the river was a misty light fog. Foliage glowed orange from tail lights. "Something is going to happen." She bolted upright.

"Not for hours. Not in this mess."

Kate straightened her shoulders, pressed them into the seat back. Scanned the surroundings. "My head's throbbing. I can't breathe. It's getting closer."

Danni glanced at her as she depressed buttons to lower the front windows. "Better?"

Kate stared out. "It can't be." She pressed the pain in her temple. "Oh … My … God …." Her heart sank as she recalled her bridge dream. *A dark stranger on the Charles.* The familiar figure still walked with a limp. His face was in shadow, but she recognized him as the man in her dream, the man she'd crossed paths with on the Charles Bridge. Here he was on a Boston bridge that crossed the Charles River … the Charlestown Bridge. Charles Bridge, Charles River. "It's him! It *is* Ali. Danni, kill the lights." She excitedly flapped her left hand for Danni to hurry.

"What is it?"

"That man. Crossing on foot. Past the ramp … see him? It's Ali. I'm sure of it."

"How *can* you be? He's a shadow. So far away, he could be anyone."

"Listen. I've seen that next bridge, it's silver and its support wires are the lines in my vision. Leaves were orange. Look out my window at the trees in the park. The red tail lights colored them. I thought my vision indicated fall foliage, but it's the lights.

"The Charles Bridge where I last saw Ali. The Charles River —we're on it and I see Ali."

Danni paused, then nodded. She turned her head to see traffic on her right. "I can't cut off the car beside us. No one is moving. I can't get to the right lane. Dammit." Danni spoke clearly and firmly into the radio mic, "Officer needs assistance on Charlestown Bridge approach. In pursuit of Abdul Wahab al-Khalifah, extremely dangerous and wanted by the FBI. Request SWAT, canine, bomb squad and snipers. Will advise of suspect's movements."

Kate gawked at Danni with a nervous smile. "I guess that covers it. What do we do till they get here?"

"Call Chase and Jack, tell them we got 'im and give our location." She pointed and tapped on the GPS display. "Give these coordinates."

"Yes, yes. I got it. But what are *you* going to do?"

Danni shoved the gear shift into Park and exited the car.

"Where are you going?" Kate tried to unlatch her seat belt, frustrated with the difficulty. The mess of papers. The unfamiliar vehicle. "Wait. Chase said not to do anything on our own."

Danni grabbed her vest from the back seat, pulled it over her head, and slapped the Velcro tabs closed. "Yeah, but this

SOB is going to set off a bomb or worse." She unsnapped her holster to free and check her weapon. "There's another vest in back. Find it and put it on."

"Danni, wait!"

"Look around Kate, bumper-to-bumper in every lane of every road, on every bridge. Really, look. No one's getting through this mess. We're on our own."

"We already called for backup."

"But they're not here, are they? Go on, call again. Call every minute. Backup won't get here in time. I'm all you got. If he gets to the main street we'll lose him. I can't sit and wait for this catastrophe to happen. I can't. He's getting away and I have to go after him."

Danni ran between the cars. Minutes had passed since Kate had first seen Ali. He'd been on a pedestrian walkway then Danni thought she saw him climb the railing and disappear below the bridge.

Kate exited the van, but stood frozen next to the headlight, resisting the urge to follow. Cars honked with impatience, irritated even more when she left the vehicle.

"Get me some backup, Kate. Keep calling. Do it now." Those were the last words she heard from Danni as she bolted between stalled cars, hopped the railing and disappeared into the dark.

Kate returned to the van, tried to call Jack and Chase; her message went into voicemail, again. She grabbed the police radio mic. "Hello. Hello." What did Chase say to do if she and Danni separated? Special Ops? Tactical Ops? Tac Ops? She shrieked, "Special TacOps. Channel One. That's it!" Her fingers trembled as she adjusted the frequency setting. It didn't take long to figure out how the darn thing worked once she mimicked Danni's previous hail. "Hello. Is this Special TacOps? An officer needs assistance."

A man's voice bellowed, "Who … the hell … is this?"

"Kate Kasabian. I need FBI Agent Matt Chase. I'm with Danni … uh … state trooper … CSS … oh crap … Chase knows." She calmed herself to explain Danni was in pursuit of a known terrorist, last seen heading southbound at the Charlestown Bridge. "All approaches are blocked by traffic. You have to find another way to get here." She broadcast the GPS coordinates like Danni showed her, and asked that Chase and the Task Force be immediately notified. That was all she could do.

She exited the car, strapped on the spare vest and stood in the road feeling helpless, staring at the spot where Danni had dropped out of sight.

FIFTY

BOAT SPOTLIGHTS SWEPT ACROSS THE MIST that hovered above the channel. A dozen voices blared over loudspeakers, but it was Chase's soft-spoken command that seized attention. "Let's end this."

"I'm with you." Jack tightened his vest, checked his firearm and packed extra clips.

"Fendi?"

"Ready, sir."

They drove toward the cell tower that pinged Dante's early call to Jack and soon spotted his car. Chase twisted to compare buildings. A warehouse ahead seemed the most likely target. Right size, location, context.

Fendi killed the headlights, turned into an abandoned gas station and parked beside a broken billboard. He opened the trunk where protective gear and weapons had been stocked for the raid.

Chase grabbed night-vision goggles. "Masks, flash bombs and weapons. No grenades. We don't know what the hell is stored in there."

Fendi eased down the trunk lid. They left the lot and curled around the buildings like three feral cats on a night hunt. The warehouse was a short block down a street littered with tossed drink cups and food wrappers, newspapers and broken bottles.

Adjacent buildings were boarded. Larger structures appeared to be abandoned factories. The area likely boomed fifty years ago, but today, not even drug dealers claimed this sorry looking territory.

Chase pointed at two broken streetlights. Not coincidence. He and Jack would circle the building's west wall to check the rear, while Fendi covered the southeast corner.

Steel bay doors seemed impenetrable.

Jack said, "Dante would have kept looking." He waved around the back.

They crossed the building front to the west side alley, skirting the gloomy passage, each clinging to a side; checking grounds, windows, rooftops.

Guns drawn.

The alley was dirty and dank. The difference between old litter and new wreckage should have been difficult to deduce, yet recent carnage was evident. Torn fabric and a broken watch. Hair, blood, teeth.

Bullet casings and an empty clip. Proof of Dante's last stand.

As Chase advanced, Jack seemed paralyzed. "Hey. Keep moving."

Train tracks with I-93 beyond them bordered the rear lot; an eight foot chain link fence topped with razor wire secured the property where overgrown brush obscured the warehouse. Fendi confirmed the fence continued along the property's eastern border where he was posted.

A loading dock at tailboard height spanned the building rear with four steps at both ends. Chase and Jack crouched low as they climbed, mirroring each other's moves. Jack paused on the dock while Chase crossed from his side toward Jack, checking door locks and nailed cross boards as he advanced. Possible entry points showed no sign of intrusion.

He shined his light inside a rickety freight chute where small oval pellets plastered the floor. He pinched a clump, held it to his nose and nodded.

Jack whispered, "If Dante fit, we certainly can. I'll go."

"Stand back. I'll check for booby traps. The structure looks sturdy, but might not hold both of us so wait till I'm far ahead before you enter. How's your hand-to-hand combat?"

"Better than most." Jack hesitated. "How's yours, sir?"

"Rusty, but no one beats my firearms scores."

Chase fastened goggles, climbed in and crawled ahead. Wood creaked when Jack entered.

Chase eased down the few feet to a shipping ramp where he stooped to the floor.

When Jack emerged from the chute, Chase raised his forefinger to his lips and pointed to two men visible in the open expanse. He alerted Fendi they were inside with at least two hostiles huddled on the floor watching a small television screen.

Beside the chute, a backpack of burglar's tools. "Dante's?" Jack nodded.

Two cruisers and four bikes were parked by the cargo doors. Power lines precariously hung from ceiling struts. Near the northwest corner, a black tarp formed a mound eight to ten feet high. "Weapons stash, I'd guess." On the east wall, two small unfinished areas formed of sheetrock. "Must be washrooms." Chase radioed Fendi who confirmed one window with opaque glass, sealed with security grating. "Contact Boston PD. We've located their missing vehicles."

Air mattresses and blankets were arranged in a central living area. Jack pointed to a human shaped mass covered by a quilt. A toilet flushed. Heads snapped toward that direction. Chase raised fingers to Jack and updated Fendi that four hostiles were on site.

The shipping ramp's freight doors looked like they hadn't been used in years. "The only other way out is street side. Looks like a palm-size push release mounted on the door frame, five feet up. See it?"

Jack nodded.

Chase told Fendi to have backup come in dark and silent, and hold the front. Bomb squad, biohazard, SWAT ... everyone. "No explosives until we determine their weapons. We're against the north wall and waiting three minutes before we engage."

They checked and compared the time. 7:27 p.m. They waited.

"They're just men like us. Trust your training." Minutes later Chase signaled to split and maneuver half way around the perimeter, toss M84 stun grenades and shoot to immobilize or kill. "No shots near the black mountain. Understand? No one gets near it. Assume the cache is set to explode. Watch your crossfire and for crissake, don't shoot me."

Chase made good time to the black tarp, checked for booby traps and peeked underneath. He saw enough to know this mission could go real bad, real fast. He rounded the pile and watched Jack approach the washrooms, two-thirds the distance to his attack position, when a hostile, who'd been watching TV, headed in Jack's direction. Jack was hiding in shadow, backed against the east wall. Chase signaled by hand that when the guy left the washroom Jack should take him out, while he'd distract the others with flashbang grenades. Jack signaled, message understood.

JACK PULLED A KNIFE and tightened his fist around it. His heart thumped and blood pumped—or was it adrenaline? Breath sounds amplified in the gas mask. A far cry from working the mundane cases on his desk twelve hours ago.

The toilet flushed. The latch released and the door swung open. The man reached into his shirt pocket and pulled a cigarette pack.

Jack sneaked behind him, remembering Todd's morgue photo and Dante's broken face.

In one smooth move, he pulled the hostile's head back by his hair and sliced the blade deep across his throat. He eased the body to the floor.

Chase's flash bomb exploded, opening a brief time window of blindness and confusion. Chase had fired twice and two men went down, and he had killed a third. Where was the other? Jack was nearly sightless and though he was expecting the flash and the bang, he was thrown off his game, and off his feet.

Where was the fourth guy?

And where was Chase?

He shook his head like a dog shedding rain, trying to rattle senses back in line. Footsteps had to be Chase's, right? The hostile would run to an exit. Or he'd head toward his weapons stash. The cache must be protected and the front cargo door had to be released for Task Force entry. Two strategic objectives at opposite ends of the warehouse. Jack assumed Chase would secure the cache like he said. He made a run to the bay doors where, by the time he reached them, backup should be poised on the other side. He heard a scuffle near the northwest corner, which accounted for everyone. He bolted toward the building's front.

CHASE HAD TOSSED THE FIRST GRENADE into the living area. Its flash coincided with Jack's target collapsing to the floor. It appeared Jack had fallen backward, but Chase couldn't determine if he was unharmed.

He rushed toward the warehouse center where the hump under the blanket had not moved after its first jerk. He aimed his weapon and yanked off the quilt.

A man scowled as he struck Chase's forearm with an iron bar. Chase's weapon reeled across the concrete floor. A wild shot fired.

The man lunged at Chase, knocking him to the floor. His chin caught a powerful punch, his skull hit concrete. Now he was pissed. He hard kicked the man's groin and aimed to drive the bastard's nose into his brain, but he missed, hitting his chin instead. The man fell over, grabbing his crotch. Chase pummeled his head. Heard bones crack. He drew his extra small caliber handgun and stood over the guy.

The man crawled toward the stockpile.

"Federal agent. Stop or I'll shoot." He repeated his order in Arabic, Farsi and French, but the man didn't stop. Chase fired two rounds into the backs of both knees. "Hey, asshole. I said, stop." The man slithered toward the corner using only his hands and arms. Chase swore in Arabic, but the man kept going. Chase shook his head, fired two more rounds into his shoulders. "Jack, you okay?"

"I'm good."

"How's that door coming? My trigger finger's getting cramped."

"Aim for his head, Boss."

"The door, Jack."

"Coming right up."

Chase grabbed the man's ankles and pulled his body back to the living area, smearing a bloody trail away from the cache. He walked toward the slowly rising door. As it lifted, he could see the boots, then the legs, of an army of men and women dressed in full tactical gear, weapons aimed, laser guides sweeping the warehouse.

"One bloody SOB might be alive," he said to the Commander. "Try to keep him that way. I'll want to question him." Chase shuffled outside, eased himself to the curb to sit beside Jack. "Is CSS here? I need beauty shots. This may not be over."

Agent Fendi joined them.

Jack said, "Holy shit. It seems like we were in there for days. Fendi, you got off easy."

"I feel like I missed the whole damn thing."

"Both of you did a great job. *We* did it." Chase wiped his lip and rubbed his chin where something warm oozed down.

Fendi leaned in to see Chase's face. "I can call a paramedic."

"How's it look, Jack?"

"Yeah, at least get a butterfly on it until …"

Chase wiggled his jaw. "I don't think it's broken." He glanced into the warehouse. "We were damn lucky. Where the hell are my photos?"

"CSS is waiting for HazMat to clear it."

"HazMat!" Chase shook his head. "We were in there and we're still breathing. Fendi, shoot their damn faces. Don't make me get up."

Agent Fendi snatched a camera from a CSS tech. He entered the warehouse and within seconds, bright flashes popped. He returned in minutes and handed the camera to Chase.

Chase thumbed the button to examine one photo after another. "No. No. No. And no. Okay. Break's over."

The Commander asked, "What were you looking for?"

Jack answered, "Their leader. We don't have him."

Chase said to the Commander, "Take care of my bad guy. I want him tomorrow. Jack will grab the laptops in the morning."

The three agents left the warehouse. Fendi tossed the camera to the CSS tech as they passed. They walked back to the abandoned gas station where an ambulance was also stationed.

"We can fix that in two minutes," the paramedic said.

"Boss, let Fendi bring the car around. Get that cleaned while I check in with HQ."

"Okay but hurry, and while we're here, see what Kate and Danni are up to."

TacOps HQ relayed that both Trooper Danner and a civilian who identified herself as Kate Kasabian had called for assistance. They had located a suspect named Ali and the trooper was in pursuit.

"Thirty-seconds." Chase glared at the paramedic to prove he meant it.

The paramedic poured a bottle of antiseptic on the lower half of Chase's face and slapped a bandage on his split lip. "Get that stitched as soon as you can."

Chase ran to the car while Jack rang Kate's cell and shook his head. "Voicemail."

"Where to, Boss?" Fendi said.

Jack answered, "Charlestown Bridge. We've got people in trouble at the northbound approach. HQ warned of traffic impossible to breach."

"Get as close as you can," Chase said. "Then we'll run."

FIFTY-ONE

DANNI RAN AS FAST AS SHE COULD, which was saying a lot. She darted between stalled traffic, sure and nimble, aiming for the spot where Ali jumped the rail.

Drivers argued and honked horns, but only her last words to Kate looped in her head. "Get me some backup. Do it now." Then the words faded like the lights and the vehicles and the people. A toddler wailed and a car door swung into her path, disrupting her stride. She bounced off a burgundy Buick, dashed between two cars in the far right lane. Her soles pounded against pavement, crisp, regular and fast. Faster. She vaulted over the railing landing on loose gravel. She squatted motionless, condensing herself into the smallest mass of flesh and bone.

She'd run the Boston Marathon on the state trooper team more than once, and ran six miles a day for fun. Running wasn't her problem nor was endurance. She was night-blinded by the lights: car headlights, streetlights, spotlights on bridge struts. Her pupils must have shrunk to pinpoints. Impossible to see. They'd adjust to the new dark. All her senses would adjust.

Sweat wept from her palms. Her heart raced faster than her legs had raced before she jumped into shadows. It was taking forever for backup to arrive. No sirens wailed in the distance and she wondered whether Kate had even made the call. *She's a smart woman, she'll figure it out. Let's hope.*

"Danni, nine o'clock."

What the hell? Kate was hanging over the rail above her. She waved her to return to the van, and twisted her head left where Kate had directed. For a split second she saw movement ahead, a human shape silhouetted against a faraway street lamp. She stared at the spot. Holding her breath. Listening. Was he also still? There. There he is. Not running. Walking with slow measured steps. *He doesn't know I'm here.* Does he know we know of him? Or of his cell? Or his planned attack? He might not yet be escaping.

His plan might still be in motion. The accidents and traffic tie-ups, a rehearsal.

Danni's foot slid on loose mulch, sending chips and stones careening down the steep embankment. Her right leg slipped from under her, stretched to stress her inner thigh. Balance relied on one delicate ankle more suited to wearing two-inch pumps than rubber soled cop shoes. She rose to stand, inching her right leg closer until she regained footing. Nothing was visible beneath her where the stones had fallen. The river was down there somewhere, or she might still be above solid ground. She didn't hear the splash, but the watery bottom could be a long way down. Maybe it was better she couldn't see how dicey her position was. The dark seemed to disappear into nothingness. Perhaps she was disembodied, cruising in the spirit world like the people who wrote to Kate's Web site. She could be trapped in a nightmare, soon crashing onto her mattress, waking under her blanket.

No such luck.

Ali was ahead of her by 150 yards. On a decent surface, she could run the distance in a Marathon minute. But the surface wasn't smooth; it was loose gravel, soft mulch and slick grass. It was dark. And it was damn steep. She was in pursuit of a known terrorist to whom her life meant nothing. She had to close the growing gap between them. Above all, keep him in sight. She moved forward, her eyes locked on him. She felt for her weapon, had not lost it when she jumped nor when she slipped. She would not lose her gun—*must not* lose her gun. Her physical force couldn't restrain a ten-year-old boy despite her training.

Still no sign of backup.

Developing steep legs, like sea legs on a boat, her steps were becoming more sure, her balance more acute. She walked faster, eyes on the target—always on the target.

Each stride sounded a loud crunch. Soles against gravel. More like a two ton dinosaur than a size one frame. Wind hit her face. Good news for carrying sound from Ali to her and beyond. She'd closed by 30 yards. She heard his steps maneuvering around bridge supports. *Never lose sight of the target.*

She'd drawn her weapon only twice in her career, but didn't have to fire. Crime scenes were cleared and secured by the time she arrived. She would have warned a fleeing suspect by now—but this was different. Hell, an FBI counterterrorism supervisor had flown in, supported by global intelligence. It doesn't get bigger. But *they* weren't under the bridge, she was, and she'd gained another 40 yards. 80 yards to impact.

Where the hell was backup?

Danni's night vision had fully adjusted and Ali's form was now visible. Not an unattractive form, slender and agile, with perfectly straight posture—even his damn limp was graceful. He wouldn't look out of place in a marble palace or posed on Persian carpets in a desert tent. What the hell was he doing skulking under a Boston bridge?

She heard his every step and considered mirroring them to camouflage hers, but that wouldn't gain ground. She'd worked security shifts at the New England Patriots stadium; and last fall she'd been to a Pat's game on a date with a TV cameraman. She didn't have a second date, didn't even remember his name; she'd dated nine men after him, none past a second or third. Maybe it was her unpredictable work schedule, or her cynicism. Whatever her strengths or weaknesses, she was confident she knew the measure of a football field.

She'd closed another 15 yards, leaving 65, over half a field between them.

Backup, where are you?

Ali didn't look behind to see if he was being tailed. Soon he might hear her. Then what? Fight or flight? Either way, the disadvantage was hers. She didn't know if he was armed. She'd heard Chase's range scores were tops. She scored in the top thirty percent, but preferred to be within 30 yards for a kill shot. Wow, that was the first time she'd called it that. She had good control of her service revolver and didn't need bigger bullets to put a guy down. Her skill was capable, but when his eyes met hers, would his humanity trip her up? She revised her strategy.

Never lose sight of the target. But don't look in his eyes.

She unsnapped her hip holster strap to free her weapon, giving up on the hope that backup would arrive anytime soon. She might have heard a copter's rotor blades in the distance, but dared not look. *Eyes on the target.* Ali's pace remained slow and steady. Then he suddenly paused, glanced at the chopper, then to the traffic. Did he assume news crews had arrived to cover the mysterious tie up? He kept walking. She'd gained another 25, leaving only 40 yards between them.

She reached to her holster and drew her weapon … wished she could tape it to her hand. *Don't fall now.* Can't lose footing. Can't utter a sound.

Cannot take her eyes off the target. *But don't look at his eyes.* Must *not* drop her gun.

The copter neared, flashing a spotlight on the bridge where her CSS van was stuck. It had to be Boston PD or state police. Did the light shine on Kate? Directing them to her and Ali? She was sure of it. The light spotted Danni, blinding her; she shielded her eyes with her left arm, gun clenched in her right hand. Barrel pointing ahead. The beam swept until it tagged Ali. He looked over his shoulder, spotted Danni and ran. She couldn't lose the yardage she'd gained. No need for silent steps now. With everything in her, she ran.

Never lose sight of the target.

Don't drop the gun.

Thirty-five yards. "Stop! Police."

He didn't slow.

The helicopter hovered to her right, then swung forward beside Ali, dangerously close to the bridge as it broadcast orders. "Police. Halt. Stop." It backed away, but Danni had gained another 5 yards. At 30 yards out, she could almost smell his cologne. *Spice?* "Ali. Stop. I *will* shoot."

People were out of their vehicles and gathered on the walkway. Hundreds leaned over and peered below to see what had attracted the helicopter and the police. Another chopper approached from the same direction, and a third lit boats on the water. Boston police and fire. State police. Danni's gut burned.

The state chopper flew to the far end of the bridge, beyond Ali, where four SWAT officers rappelled onto the roofs of cars, the open backs of pickup trucks, and on the deck.

Ali watched them touch down, turned to Kate at the railing. "You?" He shook his head.

Danni froze where she stood, raised her arms and steadied her weapon. Ali looked her straight in the eye. His black eyes were intense and piercing, demanding engagement.

Danni's glance caught the movement of his hand as he reached for a detonator strapped to his waist.

He smirked at the people watching over the bridge—mothers and fathers hoisting children for a closer look.

"Don't do it, Ali."

He gripped the device.

Danni tightened her hold on the gun. Took aim. Fired.

Thirty yards out. A perfect kill shot.

He collapsed backward. His body slid and rolled down the embankment toward the water. Explosive packs bounced after him.

Kate waved off the bridge crowd. "Get back. Get down!"

Danni screamed, directing the boats to move away. "Bomb! Bomb!"

She couldn't reach a piling in time to shield herself, stooped for cover instead.

Bomb packs bounced past Ali's body—exploding before they reached the water.

The blast launched Danni, hurling her onto her back. Her gun flew from her hand. Likely landing to her right. Wood chips and gravel shot into the air and rained down, but she didn't hear them land. Chips lit by spotlights looked like snowflakes drifting toward her in slow motion.

Snowflakes in September—like Kate's dream.

She tried to sit up, recoiled with a dizzying spin. *Wait for help.*

She grew cold as consciousness withered. Quiet. Dark, darker ....

"Officer down! Officer down!"

Danni barely heard the muffled alert. She wondered if someone was hurt. *Oh ...* calls for help were for her.

A hand gripped her shoulder ...

A firm lifesaving grip ... Like that night in the woods on a dark lonely road ... the night she wasn't meant to die. A premonition of this moment? Or her life saved for significant purpose. Her destiny ... *I've done something meaningful.*

A face peered down, strong and composed, staring eye to eye. She read the SWAT Commander's lips. "Don't move. We gotcha."

"Gun." Her right hand twisted with feeble shocks, her forefinger pointing aside.

The officer grinned and reached across her body to retrieve her weapon. "I got it. Don't worry. It'll be waiting when you return to work."

Danni's lips hinted a smile of relief. Her body shivered. Ice in her veins. *Snow in September.*

"At ease trooper. You did a great job. It's over."

Danni closed her eyes.

"No. Eyes open. That's it. Stay with me. You earned the name Deadeye. Your shot hit him dead between his eyes."

She squeezed his hand. "I aimed for center mass."

He laughed. "We won't tell anyone." He sat beside her and held her hand until paramedics arrived.

FIFTY-TWO

HALF OF BOSTON must've heard the explosion. *Déjà vu.* People on the bridge watched it all, looking spellbound like the people in Prague. Two visions overlapped until they synchronized, merging into one. The bridges and the people and the lights on the water.

The walkway where Kate stood offered a clear view of the embankment, watercraft on the river, and helicopters hovering too low to be safe. Most boats had withdrawn before the blast and were drifting back; a few were hit when gravel and shrapnel fired like bullets. If copters didn't avoid damage, at least they remained in the air.

But where was Ali? And where was Danni?

Kate bolted to the van and locked it; then ran to where she last saw them.

Voices emerged from the crowd. "Oh my God!" "Did you see that?"

"Is she all right?" "Who is she?"

"What's happening?"

Most cars were now dark and silent as if they'd been forsaken in an auto graveyard, engines and headlights turned off. People hit by debris comforted each other, wiping blood from facial cuts, examining bruises and bumps. Hugging and assuring everything would be alright.

Kate squeezed through onlookers, apologizing at every push. "Sorry. Let me through. She's my partner." She leaned over the railing, her arms waving high above her head as she called to the SWAT Commander, "Hey, I'm Kate Kasabian, working with the FBI. Is Danni hurt?"

"Should be okay."

Kate took a deep breath and turned to the crowd who asked about the woman below. "She's a Massachusetts state trooper." Her eyes teared with pride. "You'll hear about it on the news. I'm sure she appreciates your concern."

Someone called Kate's name. Her head snapped in that direction, toward the beginning of the ramp. Jack and Chase were running toward her, and behind them, Agent Fendi, a team of FBI agents and Boston PD; all members of the Task Force she'd seen at the hotel.

Jack hugged her then held her at arms length, spun her around as if inspecting for injury. Chase moved behind her, his arm around her back and his hand at her waist, while he leaned over the railing above the spot where Danni lay.

Jack said, "Are you okay? Where were you when the bomb went off?"

"It was a bomb?"

"That's what we heard."

Chase nodded affirmatively.

"I was way down there, where we parked Danni's van. She warned us. I tried to move the people away from danger and we all ducked."

"Stay here. I'll check on her." He hopped the rail and slid down the embankment.

Danni waved to Kate as Jack yelled up, "I'll stay with her. Will you be okay?"

"Yes. Go. I'll stay with Chase." She leaned against him, resting her head in the crook of his neck, until she realized what she'd done. Her eyes widened. She stepped away and turned to face him. "Oh … I'm sorry. I didn't mean to … It felt natural."

"You don't have to explain. I know what you mean as evidenced by my arm around you."

Kate felt his energy shift as if it made a one eighty turn.

He cocked his head with a curious look. "What happened after we split up at the hotel? How did you get here?" He took a step backward.

She told him how she and Danni collaborated to interpret the clues. "We focused on bridges spanning the river. That's when I saw him."

"You *happened* on him?"

"No. Dreams and premonitions led us here. We were heading in this direction when a message laid out this exact location."

"I don't doubt you. You got us here, but I want to hear the whole story another time. More than the premonitions, something about this doesn't feel right."

They watched as paramedics secured Danni to a stretcher and carried it to a Fire Department Whaler, its rescue door open and waiting to receive her. Jack hopped onto the boat and shouted they were going to Mass. General.

"Let's go," Chase said.

"What are you driving?"

"Your buddy, Agent Fendi drove me and Jack."

"Danni's van is stuck in traffic down there. I locked it but …"

"Don't worry about it." He took the keys from her and called out, "Any CSS tech need a ride?" Two approached. He tossed the keys and pointed. "Take possession."

"Glad to do it. We'll get it back to her barracks."

Kate turned to Chase. "I'll grab my purse and papers, all evidence of our paranormal collusion." She winked. "I'd suggest walking if I'd worn better shoes. We could slide to a boat."

At the van, she gathered her belongings and Danni's purse. "I tried to call. Where were you and Jack?"

"Beating on bad guys."

Kate almost laughed. "Jack must have had fun with that."

"He got his hands dirty. We both did." He rubbed his chin.

"Are you hurt? Let me see." She turned his face toward a spotlight. "It's bruised and swelling. Let's go to the ER."

"I don't mind a few battle scars, but if you insist …"

"Don't fight me on this. I love your face the way it is. Who did this?"

Chase stared ahead. "Ali's cell members. Jack and I ran into four of them."

"Aren't *you* the tough guys." She slid her hand down his arm; their fingers interlocked.

"Kate, I can't pretend everything turned out right. There's something— It's serious."

"We stopped a terrorist attack on Boston. How much more serious can it be?" His expression didn't show the relief that should have come with victory.

"Chase? You're scaring me. What is it?" She stopped dead to face him. "Jack's okay, right? I mean, I saw him."

"Yes, Jack's fine. It's about Dante."

Kate shook her head as she backed away. "Oh no." She raised her hands to shield her ears, but Chase grabbed her wrists.

"Dante was killed earlier this evening. Jack wanted to tell you himself, but I can't walk along like everything's fine. It would be dishonest."

"It's my fault. I wanted to go with him, but I didn't. It would have changed the outcome." She twisted her wrists away from Chase's hold and spun around. "Dammit!" She stepped away. Chase grabbed her arm, pulled her close and cradled her head while she sobbed. "I loved that big old slob."

"I know you did. I'm so sorry."

"God, no. Jack! Dante was like a brother. I'll never forgive myself for causing this."

"Oh babe, you didn't cause this." Chase held her tighter.

FIFTY-THREE

WHEN JACK RETURNED to the warehouse the next morning, half of the Task Force had rotated shifts. Three bodies had been removed. The lone survivor didn't survive the night, and Jack was relieved he wasn't the agent who'd delivered *that* news to Chase. Likely it fell on poor Fendi, replaced at the warehouse investigation by Special Agent Jamie Herrera, who he and Danni had met yesterday morning at the field office. *Yesterday morning? It didn't seem possible that so much had happened since then.* Twenty-four hours ago he sat at his Burlington desk, watching herring gulls soar over Lake Champlain while anticipating the arrival of the legendary Matt Chase. *Whew— hell of a day!*

Jack waved to Herrera then took a walk around the outside of the warehouse. He needed to see everything in daylight, to know he and Chase did it right—that *he* did it right. Reconnaissance, entry and combat. He needed to better know the enemy.

And he needed to see where Dante was butchered.

He turned down the alleyway and scouted the building's perimeter: a windowless brick wall on one side; a chain-link fence topped with razor wire on the other. When Dante stepped into the alley, he must have known his death was inescapable.

Bullet casings littered the pavement. Scraps of fabric, hair and broken teeth lay in dried puddled blood.

Jack turned to the building's rear and climbed the loading dock steps like he did last night. He gave the freight chute a shake, then squeezed along the east wall. Back at the street, he brushed debris off his trousers and wandered inside where Herrera met him.

"Jack Kasabian, right? Tough assignment, huh?"

"Yeah. Tough."

"So what's it like in the field with Matt Chase."

Jack weighed his words before admitting what he really felt. "It's a damn rush."

"Yeah, I bet it is. I'm sorry about your friend. We'll do something special for his kid."

Jack sucked in a deep breath. "Can you update me on what you found here? I need … ah … whew—" He shook his hands and arms. "I'm still wired, you know."

"The HazMat team removed Sarin and DIC."

"What's that?"

"A stabilizer to increase Sarin's shelf life. Consensus is, that was the primary weapon. They had enough to kill half the population on the East Coast. Aerosol dispensers and dozens of small sprayers like an exterminator or landscaper might use. Can find them at any home improvement store."

"What do you think their plan was, to run through a crowd?"

"Speed, confusion, panic, it doesn't take much of a plan."

"And the main target?"

"The MBTA, we suspect. Some of the targets. The underground and the trains. They might have considered the stadium, but security's been awfully tight. We may never know. No one's left to interrogate, so look for dates on the computer and compare them to scheduled NFL games or other events that draw a crowd. The nerve gas is odorless and colorless. Painful symptoms end with suffocation. It gets ugly fast. Death follows a lethal dose in less than sixty seconds."

"Geezus, I knew it was bad, but—"

Herrera pointed here and there. "AKs, grenades, bomb triggers, suicide vests, cases of ball bearings. A pound of cocaine and about three grand in new twenty dollar bills."

Jack stared at the spot where he killed a man.

"There's something else. I can't say yet for sure, but ..."

"What is it?"

"We found crates of masks and bio-suits, more than for only five men. Six were unwrapped, but the boxes contained enough for thirty people."

"What do you think that means?"

"Me? I think the four guys here were only guarding the cache. I think the cell is bigger than this and they're on their way or already here and hiding around Boston, or Hartford, or who knows where. That's what I think. But Chase knows them best, so pass that information to him."

"Of course I will. I'm headed to the field office now, but I'm gonna take a quick walk around inside. I didn't see much in the dark."

"Take all the time you want. We've sealed the computer; it'll be at the door." He pointed to a table stacked with evidence bags, labels and forms.

Jack called Chase about the weapons count. He agreed the amount seemed excessive and he was working that angle, but needed the computer. Jack assured he'd deliver in twenty minutes.

He poked around the living quarters in the heart of the warehouse, fascinated by the firsthand insight. He'd also gained an understanding of Chase and what it took to work counterterrorism. Critical work and very exciting. He'd push for transfer even if he had to relocate. Kate would be furious, but it was time she lived her life.

He crossed the open expanse, pushed the bathroom doors and peeked in. Then he saw the bloodstained floor. His first kill should have left more of an emotional scar, and he was surprised it didn't. Anger kept hold of Todd's morgue photo and the mental picture of Dante beaten to death. That he didn't live in Boston was a relief. He'd never have to see that place again.

BACK AT THE FIELD OFFICE, Jack handed the laptop to Chase. They commandeered the interview room where the cabin crime scene photos remained on display. He could no longer bear to look and Chase agreed he pack them for Danni.

"Agent Herrera and the Task Force will be raiding several safehouses we found through phone audits. They'll be planning operations this morning."

"I'd like to be part of that."

"We're also closing in on the Bayonne cell and should move on them in a week."

"I'd like to be part of that, too."

"I pulled my agent in Warsaw to relieve Banzik just when he was about to follow a lead to Odessa."

"I apologize for my rusty geography."

"Ukraine, Jack. Black Sea. Kiev. Chernobyl." Chase shook his head. "Don't ask for part of it. I'm assigning a Russian expert, besides, I need you here. If I'm satisfied with our progress, you can work a support position with Herrera or Fendi and the Boston raids. Until you train with the Task Force, you're deciphering technology."

"I'm still buzzing from last night's rush. I'd like to get trained as soon as a slot opens."

"I get it. You did good. You kept your head, but it's not about the rush."

Jack nodded. Even poking through seized files was exciting. Finding and interpreting the pieces, forming the whole picture was a thrill and he told Chase as much.

"I hear you. Most nights I sit home running slideshows of photos, hoping to stumble on the one clue that sparks an unconventional idea."

"Are you married, Boss?"

"I was. She was hit by a car two years ago. Died instantly."

"Geezus. I'm sorry, I shouldn't have asked."

"I've come to terms with it. I'm glad we have this time to talk about something sensitive. I've spent some time with your sister and I like her. I'd like to get to know her. How would you feel about that?"

Jack smirked. "Kate?"

"Yes, Kate. Unless you have another sister I'd like better."

"No, there's only Kate. You know, she's kind of … out there."

"That's what appeals to me. She's so honest about who she is, even when she struggles with something, there's no hiding. Her complications intrigue me."

"She is unique. I don't have a problem at all. Good luck." Jack studied Chase with a curious look. "In a way, you're kind of out there, too. A different *there*, but the two of you might be well suited. I say, go for it."

"Good. Great." Chase grinned, almost glowed. It was odd for Jack to glimpse his human side, soft and flawed, like his fear of heights he tries to hide. It was also helpful to see how effectively Chase compartmentalized work from personal interests. He suspected they were alike that way.

Jack turned on the laptop and copied files onto a removable hard drive for safekeeping. "Let's see what these assholes are up to?"

They spent the better part of the afternoon opening and translating files, and viewing surveillance photos—photos of obscure landmarks located in various climates, the first clear indication of additional attacks.

Chase initiated a nationwide alert, effective until target locations were narrowed. "See, this is why we need you. We have to move fast. Can you stay on top of this?"

"I certainly can."

"Look, I don't care if you work here, in Burlington, or in New York. If you must get it out of your system, go on another raid. Observe everything. You can start most of the investigation remotely. I'll upgrade your clearance for extended server access."

"I'm already being vetted."

"Good for you. I'll see what's the holdup. I'm sure it's only backlog." Chase rose from his seat and slipped on his suit jacket. "I'm going to check on Danni then I'll probably head back to New York. If you get stuck, call my cell and I'll talk you through it. Don't hesitate. Call and ask. Got it?"

"I will. Thanks, Boss. Um … hey Chase, before you go, take a look at this entry. This was the last message posted on Kate's site. There's something hinky about it. Look at the language; the English spelling and grammar are too perfect, not like the others."

Chase tracked its route and saw it had bounced around Canada and upstate New York, but had originated in Vermont. "I wouldn't worry much about it, but we'll check it out."

"I don't know, Boss. It lays out the exact spot where the girls would find Ali. Could someone have wanted him dead more than we did?"

"Knowing they would sabotage the whole plan?"

"Ooo ..." Jack said, "Maybe it was a true premonition from an ordinary person."

They both laughed.

"I'll work here another day or two, then I *would* like to return to Burlington. I need to see Dante's wife and kid."

"I understand. Do what you have to. I'm sorry about Benard. He was a brave man. I wish I had known him."

"I wish you did, too."

Kathryn Orzech

~ *Part Five* ~

Aftermath

Kathryn Orzech

FIFTY-FOUR

VERMONT
Sunday, Early October

GULLS SWOOPED against a timid northeasterly breeze above the waters of Lake Champlain, the calmest Jack had ever seen. For the first time in years he'd slept until eight thirty, as if even his subconscious psyche resisted the duty he was to perform—facing Dante's wife and son.

Bobo, with Dante's same silly grin, ran from the back yard. "Uncle Jack!"

He stooped to lift the boy and nuzzled his neck. "Who's your favorite uncle?"

Angie stood at the home's threshold with arms crossed and a stiff scowl twisting her face. "He asked why he's dressed in his church clothes. *You* tell him." Her anger was obvious, her blame more subtle. *And she was right.* She left them in the living room and disappeared down the hall.

"Come here, little buddy. We've got man-talking to do." Bobo sat beside him, mimicking his posture with elbows resting on his knees, and eyes aimed at the darkened TV screen. "Your dad was my best friend and I'm sad he's gone to heaven."

"Mommy cries at night."

"I know she does."

"Did it hurt Daddy to get killed?"

Jack pulled the boy against his chest to shield his lying face.

"Oh no, Daddy didn't hurt. Angels gave him a ride on a nice soft cloud."

"Sometimes I forget he's gone. I wait at the window, but he doesn't come home."

Angie entered as Jack said, "He saved a lot of little boys and girls. He's a hero and we're very proud of him."

"Like a Super Hero?"

A smile escaped. "That's right. A real Super Hero."

"It's time," Angie said.

"Where're we going, Mommy?"

Her puffy eyes glared at Jack.

"We're going to the park where the Governor will read a letter from the President of the United States and all the people will know how brave Daddy was." She blew her nose. Her voice quivered. "Whadda ya' say, kiddo?"

Bobo held out his hand to Jack and said, "Let's go. We can't be late."

FLAGS THROUGHOUT THE CITY flew at half-mast and flapped from Main Street office windows. The high school band played patriotic music in the DEMOCRACY sculpture courtyard near the Federal Building, where members of Dante's former Marine unit, some from as far as Oregon, had come to pay respect.

Funerary bows of black taffeta tied the granite boundary posts of City Hall Park, and recent plantings of red and white mums, and blue creeping phlox decorated corner beds. Thousands of citizens jammed the Park and overflowed to the Battery, along with representatives of the Massachusetts state police, Boston police, and the FBI Boston team who had volunteered personal time to escort Dante's body home.

Jack and Angie held Bobo's hands as they climbed stairs to the platform where various speakers praised the "unmatched valor of their distinguished native son, Dante Benard. Husband. Father. Patriot."

Bobo straightened his bow tie as he marched along the line of dignitaries who flanked the stairway; he shook hands to thank each official.

Media photographers, videographers, and citizens with camera phones captured images bound to replay, day and night for weeks, on YouTube and TV screens in living rooms across the nation.

Jack gave no speech, nor did Angie.

After Bobo's courageous display, what more was there to say?

FIFTY-FIVE

CONNECTICUT
Monday

THE TWO-HOUR DRIVE from the Boston Field Office to Connecticut more clearly focused Chase's thoughts than a week in St. Croix, and no matter what happened with Kate, he decided this was the area where he would live. Midway between New York and Boston, and near his family.

He turned onto Summary Road, a cul-de-sac that saw little traffic, he guessed, by the way neighbors peered from windows when he passed like it was a rare event. He wasn't surprised by Kate's little Cape; it suited her and was exactly the type of house he'd imagined for himself, small enough to maintain on weekends, big enough to start a family.

She was lugging trash bags to the curb when he drove up her street. He aimed toward her driveway and she backed toward her front porch, shielding her eyes from the sun as she seemed to study the steel blue Ford Escape, his rental car. She wore jeans stained with taupe paint that matched her house, and a man's loose shirt, maybe Jack's, maybe not. She stood on the lawn, her skin as gold as autumn leaves; her hair tied in a disheveled knot he itched to unfasten.

"Chase!"

"I didn't have your phone number on me."

"Hmm. Couldn't find my number? Doesn't say much for the FBI."

He laughed. "I had to see you and couldn't risk your saying, no."

"I've used that line with Jack. Good call. I might have said, no, because … look at me. I'm tired, damp and dirty." She smiled in a flirty way. "But I wouldn't have meant it." She brushed off her arms, pulled off the band and shook dust from her hair.

Even with her smile, her demeanor remained as somber as he remembered in Boston. Despite his rusty dating skills, he projected a gentle voice. "You look beautiful." He inched closer, glancing curbside. "Looks like the heavy work's done."

"I've been cleaning all day; it won hands down over lopping shrubs and was far less destructive. Look." Bushes edging the front porch had been snipped to an inch of life. She pointed to the garage where, she said, two bags of clothes she no longer wore were stashed for pickup by the secondhand store. "And Todd's belongings filled two cardboard boxes. I stuck them in my car trunk until I see his family." She stepped nearer to him. "Clearing out old business."

"Yeah, I have a closet of old business, too."

"Dante had offered to come down and give me a hand." She winced.

"Kate, I'm so sorry." He pressed her tight against his chest as she burst into tears.

"I was doing a good job at holding back."

He cradled her head in his hand. "A brave effort, but you don't have to hold back anything."

"I never want to know how he died. No details and no photos. Can you protect me from that?"

He wished *he* hadn't witnessed the savagery. "I promise you won't hear about it from me."

They stood in the driveway holding each other until a neighbor's door opened. "Kate, everything okay?"

"I'm good. Thanks for asking."

Chase waved and the neighbor disappeared. "That's nice that you look after each other."

"Look … I'm a mess." She wiped her face with her shirt sleeve. "Come inside. I'll get cleaned up. You're staying, aren't you? Did you drive from Boston? You must be hungry. Make yourself at home. Really … I have nothing to hide. Are you on your way to New York?"

"Slow down. I took some time off." His hand ran down her back. "No hurry. No pressure. I'll take care of myself. Clean up if you want, then we'll sit and talk." His forefinger under her chin tipped her head upward. "I'm not going anywhere."

CHASE GRABBED A SLICE of pizza and a Pepsi bottle from the refrigerator, and found a small plate in the cabinet. The microwave's hum muffled the sound of the upstairs shower. The oven beeped.

In the living room, he bit into the slice as he wandered, scanning the room like he was speed-reading. "Charming." Built-in cabinets held an eclectic collection of books and exotic mementos much like his own. A great stone fireplace was centered on one wall and its damper seemed in good order.

He grinned at the family gallery displayed on the mantle. *Must be mom and dad.* Kate looked about ten years old and so serious, sledding with a teenage version of Jack. He picked a framed photo of her at Niagara Falls with Todd, who he recognized from the picture in Jack's office and from Danni's crime scene photos. "Poor kid."

Kate entered the room to his locked gaze. "His memorial service is day after tomorrow."

"I'd like to go, if you don't mind."

"Sure, that'd be nice. Jack's coming down tomorrow night, too." She rubbed her hair with a towel and tossed it on top of the washer in an adjacent room. Her teal wrap-around robe could easily pass as dress.

"You look refreshed. Feel better?"

"I do." She took his hand and led him to the sofa. "Would you just hold me for a while?"

He slid his arm around her, brushed a strand of damp hair from her eyes and kissed her forehead as if it were the most natural affection, as if they had known each other a lifetime—as if they were lovers. In his mind they *had been* lovers. He couldn't imagine himself with any other woman. He could hardly imagine he'd been with his wife. He was prepared to surrender to his feelings. Timing was right and Kate seemed right.

Her heart beat against his arm.

"Mmmm. You smell heavenly." Her shampoo's coconut scent relaxed him, stirring thoughts of clear waters lapping a hot sand beach. Palm fronds swaying in a salty breeze. The rhythm of her breaths synced with his as she slipped into sleep. And he wouldn't be far behind.

His heart, mind and body belonged to her. The most tranquil sigh escaped his lips as he watched her sleep, and like he had nearly every night, he imagined the day they would make love—knowing it would be this day.

Her eyes shot open as if his thoughts had reached her dreams. Her expression appeared more peaceful, as if she'd been with him on his imaginary beach. She rose and stood over him, extending her hand. "Want to see my room?" She winked.

He followed her upstairs and down a hallway to a corner bedroom. She pulled aside the comforter and eased onto the bed. "I've wanted this since the moment I saw you."

"I'm here now, Kate." He tugged at the belt of her robe.

FIFTY-SIX

NEW YORK
Tuesday

CHASE RELUCTANTLY KISSED KATE goodbye and drove to Manhattan to shower, grab a dress suit and sleep. He planned to meet her and Jack Wednesday morning for Todd's service, and while in the area, he'd spend a few days at the New Haven Field Office—his idea of downtime.

He dropped his keys in the lapis bowl, opened the drapes and raised a window. He hadn't been to his apartment since the morning he'd rushed to the airport, the day he first met Kate. Plans to visit his folks had tanked; he couldn't recall when he'd last seen them. The past week was a dream and a nightmare. It hardly seemed real—except for being with Kate, the dream part. A satisfied smile crossed his face.

His apartment felt more lonely than it ever had—*he* was lonesome without her—yet something bound him to this space. He no longer wished to live in a netherworld of here nor there. Even while his steamy shower rained on him, he felt he didn't belong. He was the last person at a party. The guests had left, the fun was over, and all that remained was the mess and the stink. He wrapped a bath towel around his waist and combed his hair straight back.

A few shirts, slacks and tees would be enough clothes for a stingy week; they stacked on the sofa to be packed along with two suits, ties, a few personal items, and a handful of music CDs he grabbed from his desk drawer for the two-hour drive back to Connecticut. He tugged at his weekender luggage buried in the closet rear, but the wheel caught on the plastic bag he'd shoved in the corner two years ago, purposely ignored since then.

Though he still bore the scar of his betrayal, feelings for Kate had eased the heartbreak that had prevented him from opening his wife's hospital bag. He pulled it out, sat on the bed and read the scribbled black marker notes: name and patient ID, room number and date. He opened the drawstring cinch and shook out the contents.

He tossed aside the plastic sealed blood stained clothes. Inside her purse, he found a makeup bag; a change purse and billfold with one hundred and eighty-six dollars that he set on the nightstand; a driver's license she didn't use, library card, and membership IDs to several museums. Expired credit accounts had been canceled long ago; he cut the cards into pieces. Among a fistful of notes and lists, a folded photo was stashed in the back flap of a datebook. He leaned against the headboard, squinted at the unfamiliar picture and turned on the bedside lamp.

His wife posed with a man against blue skies and a background of ancient ruins. *Who the hell is this guy?* He grabbed a magnifying glass from his desk drawer, but sunglasses and a profile view made the stranger unrecognizable, it could have been anyone cuddled against her. Was this her lover? They traveled together? *Dammit. Where was this taken? When?* Her sandy blonde hair was cut in a short bob, an experiment that had lasted a year, the year preceding her death.

Chase had rebounded from hitting his emotional bottom and nothing he learned about his wife surprised him. But even if his heart had moved on, his investigative mind wasn't free of her, and he wondered if it ever would be.

CONNECTICUT
Tuesday

LATER THAT NIGHT, Kate hung Jack's suit in the closet and stashed his overnight bag in the spare room. As soon as he excused himself to the upstairs bath, she wondered if Chase had left anything behind. Question answered. Jack stood grinning at the top of the stairs, rocking a travel-size can of shaving cream with a 'gotcha' smirk. "Oh, Kate."

She peered up to the landing. "Don't ask."

"Ohhh-kaaay." He jumped down the stairs. "Hey, your place looks great. What the hell happened here?"

"Cleared out a lot of old crap. It *does* look good, doesn't it?" She spun around feeling gratified. "I even feel lighter."

"Well, you look amazing ... like you're ... glowing."

"Who'd have thought housework would have such an effect." She winked.

Jack seemed puzzled that there was a joke in the air, but he didn't get it yet. His gaze darted in an apparent search for clues. "What time are we going tomorrow?"

"Mass begins at ten." She hesitated. "Someone else will join us. We're meeting here at nine thirty."

"Okay. So ... who's coming?"

"Well, ah, Chase will be in town."

Jack smiled, as if he finally understood the punch line. "Will he?"

"Shut up, Jack." She slapped his arm.

He fell onto the couch like he owned the place, legs crossed at his ankles as he clicked the TV remote. "Just be careful. He might be damaged."

"We're *all* damaged." She kissed the top of his head. "I'm going to bed. Have a donut if you're hungry. I locked the doors, just turn off the lights when you come up."

Kate slipped into bed and pulled up the comforter. She rang Chase's cell. "I miss you. Did I wake you?"

"I can't sleep without you ..." His whisper drew her in.

"Tomorrow will be a tough day for me. Having you near will be a comfort."

Though Chase was saying the right words, he delivered them with crisp edge, as if circumstance competed for his attention. Something had changed. She wondered if he needed a graceful way out of attending the funeral. "Maybe we should meet at the church, in case you get hung up in traffic."

"That's probably best. Did Jack get in?"

"Sound asleep downstairs. So I'll see you tomorrow at the service."

"Good night, Kate."

She turned off her cell and set her alarm for seven, though she wouldn't sleep that late.

Chase's voice forged a path to his thoughts. She cradled the pillow on which he had lain; it still held the smell of his hair and aftershave she didn't recognize—the fabric still bristled with his essence. She closed her eyes and visualized a string of light that led to him. The energy of her spirit slipped toward him like data in a fiber-optic cable, only faster and more direct. In an instant she was in his apartment with a strong and stable psychic connection. The air was so heavy with gloom, she hardly noticed the furnishings beneath the dark pall. Only his inner being flickered with light, like embers of a dying campfire.

She was in his head, seeing what he saw and feeling what he felt, being where he had been—and beyond. Their melding would be impossible if she wasn't welcome in his psyche, still, she felt like an intruder in thoughts so private.

He was visualizing a lovely woman, his wife, on a street corner. Her eyes were wide and fear paralyzed her body as a van sped through the intersection, clipping cars, before wildly mounting the curb as if it aimed directly at her.

Kate felt the impact to her torso as organs exploded. She felt the release of her spirit as it shot out of her body and rose above the pain.

Chaos calmed. Screams of witnesses faded.

The dark earth disappeared in the bright white light of a thousand suns, accompanied by the sound of metal scraping against stone—her vibration changing.

Everything went dark faster than a power outage, and Kate was back in Chase's apartment. Her spirit body stood over him like an angel monument beside a grave. He lay on his bed beside bagged bloody clothes and a stack of cash on the nightstand. A bath towel was heaped on the floor as if casually tossed, while bedcovers barely covered his naked body. His arms wrapped a pillow held close against his chest, like they had caressed her last night. His hand clutched a crumpled photo. She touched his hip running spectral fingers across his skin.

She hurt with his pain.

Kate slipped onto his bed and moved against him, tucking her body of spirit beside his sleeping frame, like her body of flesh had done last night. She felt his arm draped around her, as real as if they physically lay together.

"Sleep in peace, my love." She held him tighter. "I'll protect you."

FIFTY-SEVEN

Wednesday

KATE PERCHED AT THE EDGE of a church pew flanked by Chase and Jack. It seemed a lifetime since she'd last seen Todd's family. She hurt for his sisters and couldn't imagine her life if something happened to Jack. And his poor parents; they might have been grandparents to her children. It would be cruel to tell them how close they had come.

She introduced Chase as the FBI supervisor whose team had tracked and killed Todd's murderer, while Jack passed Todd's belongings to his older sister's husband.

She said to Jack and Chase. "My presence will only remind his family of a stolen future."

Once they had left, Jack drove while she and Chase sat in the rear. She stared out the window, not speaking to either of them and when they returned to her house, Jack hurried to leave. "I'll miss rush hour if I go now."

"Take care of yourself. Don't make me come up there." Kate walked him to his car then joined Chase on the porch.

"Do you have to get back to New York right away? Can you stay a while?"

"Yes, I can. I thought I'd hang around a few days and visit the local field office."

"We're only twenty minutes from New Haven. Why not stay here?"

"I've already busted in on you without warning. Are you sure you wouldn't prefer time by yourself? You've been through so much."

"I want you with me." Though after last night, she wasn't so sure about who needed who.

"Good, because we need to talk."

Her head cocked as she looked beyond his eyes wondering if he was aware of her spirit visit. "Did something happen yesterday? Last night?"

He settled in a chair against the front porch wall and leaned toward her.

Nervous anticipation rolled in like a sudden nor'easter. "What is it?" She jolted from her seat and backed against the handrail. "Should I be worried? Is this about us? Because I can't handle more bad news, so if you're dumping me, save it till next week."

"No. NO!" Chase's eyes widened. "We're good ... great. That's why I want your opinion about something. Please." His hand guided her to sit. "I might transfer out of counterterrorism."

"Because of this case?"

"No, I've been thinking about it since my wife was killed." He wrung his hands and pinched his ring finger.

"Two years ago, right?" It seemed too long to hold pain so close to the surface. *Trust me, I know and Coop would agree.*

His fingers fidgeted. "I really like you and I'm past window-shopping. I want more and I'm ready. I know what I feel, but you're a mystery to me."

"Don't doubt your people skills. I'm tough to get to know, but once you get through, I'm the most loyal friend or lover, forever. It's my fault if you're confused. Maybe it's a character flaw, maybe self-defense. I'm either my selfish id or my wiser spirit plugged into a bigger picture. And sometimes I go to a very dark place, but I sense it's one where you also go. We'll be great together if you can figure out which of me is home."

"We'll have to avoid being in the dark at the same time."

"We will. I'm sure of it."

"I've been offered an attractive position in the private sector, but it would mean relocating to Alabama and I wouldn't consider leaving the Northeast if it meant losing you."

Kate felt her breath slip away as she leaned back. All she could blurt was, "Wow."

"Let me finish before you respond. I'd like to know more about you and Todd. Maybe because I met his family. It's not my business and I want to put it away, but something about it seems unfinished." He leaned against the seat back, mirroring her body posture. "And I need to know what you think about leaving the area."

She didn't hesitate to admit, "I'm in the same place. Totally taken by you. Todd was a great guy, a wonderful guy. I liked him and we had fun." She stared down the road at nothing. "I *wanted* to love him, but even after years, it didn't happen." She shrugged. "That's all there is."

"Is it? I need to hear all of it, Kate. I'm in no position to judge anyone, but evading truth is a deal breaker for me." He looked with a squinting, searching stare. "You cling to Todd. I can't explain, but I feel it. What hold does he have on you?"

"You're right." She squirmed in the chair and took a deep breath. "I waited for him at the airport. If he had showed up, I might have caved and agreed to marry. Had an okay life with him. I would have tried my best. I was that close to saying yes despite knowing I was compromising my feelings. The night he walked out, I was relieved I no longer had to force our relationship, and now I feel guilty about my relief and about his death." She looked Chase square in the eye. "Todd's murder was my fault and I don't know how to let that go."

"No way does that come back to you. He was a random victim and he would've been at the cabin helping his friend, with or without you. That you were drawn into the cell's plot was because *he*—not you—was in the wrong place."

"Logically, I know you're right, but it'll take me a while to come around. I haven't forgiven myself for what I did to my best friend Coop and to Dante. It's too much."

"I understand. You have work to do with that. And Alabama?"

"I would never, ever, ask you to pass on an opportunity, and if you invited me to go with you, I would in a New York minute. No doubt. I can work anywhere." She paused, wondering which answer he wanted from her. *The truthful one.* "But if the choice were mine, I'd stay close to family and Coop and all the Northeast has to offer. I love to travel, but this is my home."

"My folks are here, too, and I love it here." His mouth crumpled. "I'll decline their offer. Maybe someday I'll do my own thing. But frankly, I'm not ready to leave the bureau quite yet, but I have to get out of New York. I want to and it's overdue. I'm going to request assignment in New Haven."

"That would be perfect. You could live here." Her hands sealed her mouth. "Oh my God. I said that out loud?"

"I'm guessing that was your id speaking. It's a brilliant idea."

"Chase, what are we doing? Are you sure you're ready for this?"

"I am, so I'm going with it until we hit a wall. Listen, Thanksgiving is coming fast and my parents have been asking if I'm bringing anyone special to dinner." He blushed. "My mother is especially hopeful. Will you come with me?"

"If I'd follow you to Alabama, I'd certainly go to your parents' dinner. Tell your mom I look forward to meeting her."

"I have to warn it might be awkward. They loved my wife and I haven't told them the sordid version of what really happened."

"What *did* happen? I want to know because, honestly, sometimes I feel like a dingy bouncing in her wake."

He cleared his throat. "She was with her lover when she was hit. An accident investigation officer at the hospital shared his witness statements. A male witness said they *appeared* to be together, standing on a Manhattan street corner whispering to each other, but a woman at the scene said they were 'definitely kissing, and for sure were a couple.' I visited the woman and talked to her myself. Her sympathy for my ordeal made her very cooperative. She said in previous months she'd seen them in the neighborhood; said she'd swear to it. The guy's 'piercing eyes and elegant stature' had caught her attention, and the woman 'dressed to the nines' so she remembered her. She wondered if they were a celebrity couple."

"That must have been difficult to hear."

"Yesterday I found something that raised new questions. I'm not sure what to believe."

Kate knew otherwise, but didn't say: You *are* sure and that's what hurts. But it's over.

Is it?

"An unidentified van raced toward them. A witness reported the guy tried to shove her aside, but another claimed he had pushed her in its path, yet another said the van had aimed at the guy. One witness said it aimed at her. I might never know the truth. Anyway, *he* ran off and she was dead."

"Oh ... babe. I'm so sorry."

"Until then, I thought we were happy. Being so blindsided makes me doubt my judgement. I didn't have the slightest suspicion about her affair, if that's what it was, until I arrived at the hospital and talked to the cop.

"When they asked me to identify her body, I couldn't make myself enter the room."

She ran her hand down his back. "I know what *that* feels like."

"They had to show me a morgue photo. Kate, I wanted to kill her. I was so angry she was already dead. Sounds crazy, huh?" He rubbed his hands. "I've said too much." His eyes met hers. "Not literally kill her. I was frustrated. I wanted answers and knew I wouldn't find them. That's all I meant."

"I understand." Kate twisted in the chair and caressed his hands, the strong hands of a man weakened by a wounded heart … hands that made her flesh ache for their touch. "I can promise this, if I'm ever unhappy about *any* little thing, you *will* know it. As you can guess, it takes a lot to intimidate me."

"Any complaints now?" He seemed relieved to get out of his story.

"Just one." She snuggled onto his lap and whispered, "We both can't fit in this chair, and I feel the neighbors' eyes remain on us, so let's go in."

He lifted her in his arms, carried her inside and dropped her on the sofa, where she bounced. His stare seemed to penetrate her soul.

"Get down here." She grabbed the bottom edge of his tee-shirt and pulled him beside her.

FIFTY-EIGHT

VERMONT
Mid-October

IN THE DAYS AND WEEKS following the failed attack, munitions, explosives and chemicals were removed from the warehouse. Seized computers held a stunning trove of communiqués indicating three major cities, stretching to the Pacific, would also be attacked. Jack's analysis helped uncover sleeper cells, and in a subordinate role, he assisted other teams as they doused Eastern Flame.

He had found his calling.

He'd been on the road more than he'd been home and it felt good to be back. A take-out sandwich sat on the counter, his luggage stashed in the spare room. He changed the clothes he'd worn since yesterday and slipped on fleece pants and a sweatshirt, grabbed a beer and planted himself on the sofa in front of a Giants game. *Heaven.* He would check three weeks of phone messages at half time, expecting at least a few from Kate and a couple from Mom.

Someone knocked on the door just as he bit into a meatball grinder. *Dammit.* No one from work would dare intrude, and with a dusting of snow on the ground and a few more inches due, an impromptu visit from Kate was unlikely. He wouldn't see her till the spring thaw if he was lucky.

He checked the security peephole. *Whoa! Definitely not Kate.* The gorgeous young woman was 5'8, maybe 130 lbs., athletic, with hazel eyes and light brown hair tied in a pony tail. *Drop-dead gorgeous.* He opened the door and said hello, wiping tomato sauce from his lips while holding the grinder in his other hand.

She glanced at the sandwich and with the slightest southern twang, she said, "Sorry to interrupt your dinner, but I wanted to meet before you left again."

"I'll be hanging close to home for the next week or so. Pardon my appearance, I just walked in and wasn't expecting company."

"Allow me to introduce myself. I'm Daryl, Dr. Daryl Kincaid, your neighbor across the hall." She pointed to her door. "I moved in last weekend, but haven't seen you around."

"Hello Daryl. Jack Kasabian." He fumbled to shake hands, but they were full. His foot shoved open the door. "Do you watch football?"

"Some. I'm hoping to acquire more of a taste." She walked by the picture window where city lights twinkled below. "Lovely view you have on this side. I look out to a parking lot." She sat on the sofa, crossed her legs and leaned back like she owned the place.

"Make yourself at home." Jack checked the refrigerator. "Can I offer a beer, or a … ah … light beer? I haven't restocked groceries."

"Why thank you, Jack. I'll have a light. Have you lived in Burlington long?"

"A few years. Been moving around Vermont a lot longer. I like it." He handed her the bottle, a glass and a paper napkin.

She gazed with a curious look. "I can't quite place your accent. It's not Vermont."

"My family's from Connecticut. Where're you from?"

"The Deep South. Left after the storm. I've been chasing jobs farther and farther north. It's cold up here."

"Do you want a blanket?"

"No, I'm warming up now." Jack nearly choked. She continued, "I don't know what I'll do when the snows come."

He grabbed a small plate, knife and fork from the kitchen; sat beside her and cut the grinder in half. Somehow sharing food with Dr. Daryl Kincaid wasn't as annoying as sharing with his sister. "You become accustomed. Try to stay active 'cause it's too easy to fall into a cabin fever type of thing."

"I can see where it would be. I've been working out at the hospital's fitness center when I can steal a few minutes. I'd like to run when I'm home, too, but I haven't found a good route and it gets dark so early. I don't know where it's safe to jog alone. Do *you* have any ideas?"

It was all Jack could do to keep a lecherous expression off his face. He had a zillion ideas for Daryl, a few even related to jogging trails, but his new neighbor was a doctor and probably too smart to fall for his lame lines. Had he known she would drop by, he would have planted a few cerebral props like coffee table books about the Louvre and saving the rain forest, but short of that, he'd have to resort to sincerity. "I jog mostly every day along the waterfront. Why don't you join me and see if that works better for you?"

"Why, thank you, Jack. That is so sweet of you to offer."

"It's nothing. We should watch out for each other. It's the neighborly thing to do."

FIFTY-NINE

CONNECTICUT
Late October

CHASE HAD LIVED at Kate's house for the past two weeks; moving clothes and a couple of small boxes from his apartment. Merging him into her life had been the easiest thing she'd ever done, and though he'd said the same, she felt an obstacle to his total commitment. It sometimes seemed his walls were higher than hers, and capped with razor wire. She was patient because her sixth sense warned of more to come—for him and Jack and ….

He spoke quietly on his cell, pacing from the kitchen to the living room and back, likely settling something at the office by the look on his face. His hair mussed from sleeping, he ran a hand through it with a smooth stroke. A gray tee-shirt hugged his chest and shoulders. Loose pajama pants hung on his hips. She couldn't take her eyes off him, afraid that if she did, she'd awake from the best damn dream of her life.

Sunlight filtered through white pines and silver maples stripped of their leaves. Enough of an autumn chill justified building a fire, if she had wood to burn. They'd planned a lazy Saturday morning, but late last night, FBI tech specialists had returned her computers, scrubbed of messages from foreign servers. Her site had been offline and would not be live until she posted the backlog of new stories and updated pages back to normal. *Or paranormal.*

Chase ended his call. "I hope we didn't mess with your data."

"My data?" she chuckled. "This is my data: Ghost Stories, Premonitions, and client photos. I need to organize my files." She glanced his way, then back to the screen. "Everything okay at the office?"

"Personnel changes. We ruffled Massachusetts when we offered Danni a forensics position. She declined, but accepted a transfer to state police detective."

"Good for her. I'd like to stay in touch. We bonded."

He ran his hands along her shoulders. "Anything interesting?"

"E-mail." She looked up from the screen. "Jack's dating someone new. A doctor, a real southern belle, he writes, who moved in across the hall. He's never talked so openly about his feelings for a woman. It's scary. She could be *the one*. I'd warn him not to rush into anything, but I live in a glass house."

"Oh yeah, he's done. But he's a big boy." He took her empty cup to the kitchen and returned with two coffee refills. "Jack is about to be a happy guy."

"About the doctor?"

"Well, yeah, there's that ..." He set her cup on the taboret. "But I was speaking of his transfer."

"I wish I could see his face when he gets the news." She brushed her hand against his. "You didn't have to do that, you know."

"Jack did it. I simply expedited paperwork."

Later that afternoon Kate set a bag of groceries on the dining table, and was hanging her coat in the hall closet when the back screen door slammed shut. "Chase?"

"Only me. I can fix that."

"My burglar alarm? I like it that way … reminds me of grandma's house."

He entered the dining area cradling a stack of firewood. "I didn't hear you come in."

"Where'd that come from?"

"The wood? Out back, littering your forest floor." He stacked the logs on the hearth.

"I missed seeing you chop wood?" A sly smile crossed her face.

"It felt good." He stretched his arms over his head and back. His chest protruded.

"You're killin' me, Chase …." She moved against him and whispered, "Next time you're outdoors being a manly man, I want to watch."

"Oooh … the woman has a visual trigger." He tickled her sides till she giggled. "Later, I'll be in the shower."

"Asking for trouble." Her arms quivered with an electric charge.

"Cold?" He briskly rubbed them. "I'll light a fire before dinner."

"Sounds perfect." She pulled a bag of onions and a pack of carrots from the grocery bag. "I stopped at Westwoods while I was out."

"Good. How's Coop, today? Any change?"

"None that I can see, but we talk, regardless." She tilted her head. "I feel she's so close to a breakthrough I want to reach inside and yank her out." She demonstrated with grasping fists.

"I'm sure she knows you're with her. Be patient. The body is capable of miraculous healing."

As is the soul.

"I told her …" Kate suddenly felt outside of herself and eased to a dining chair, "… about you."

"Kate? What's happening?"

"When I first spotted you at the airport, I saw something in your past that draws you to a dark place. I had only a flash of it. In Afghanistan, right?"

Chase dropped to sit. Every muscle seemed to go limp as if he no longer carried weight.

"I don't *ask* for these insights. I wasn't poking around your aura looking for trouble. The vision came to me. Like it did just now."

"I was close to catching Ali. I should have anticipated his moves, but he slipped away and people died."

"I beat myself, too, about Coop. Some events have to play out."

"I can't accept that. We have to fight … protect ourselves. Protect each other."

"Yes, we do. Consider that fate dictated success at *this time*, but not years ago."

"That predestination theory is too tidy for me."

She laughed. "It's anything *but* tidy. Free will mucks it up every time."

"I've thought about destiny. Explain again how you and Danni found Ali. You said it was fate."

Kate didn't answer. She froze and stared at Chase as she ran in her mind a primer on Paranormal Activity. There didn't seem to be a way to tell him that didn't sound too weird. And part of her was miffed about his obsession with Ali—it remained an obstacle to their future. The guy was long dead so what was haunting Chase? His ghost? *Too bad this conversation wasn't going to be about that.*

"I've told you. Everything matched my premonitions." She rose and swung her arms. "And then we read a new posting on my site directing us to Ali's exact location. That's when Danni jumped out to catch him. But what you don't know is that her

life had been saved by a force, or something from the other side
—saved, I'm sure, to execute her predetermined fate.

"Danni was destined to kill him."

Chase's brow furrowed. "You lost me. Where are you going
with this?"

"There's more to the story." She told Chase about her attack
dreams and LittleEv's visions from six weeks *before* Todd
walked out, *before* Prague and Yusuf and Ali—*before* all this
began. "Dead-on accurate predictions that can't be explained
away.

"Every detail of the attack … identical. My bridge dream,
even Ali's damn limp … identical."

"Now *that* is interesting. But it makes me wonder if reading
those very stories inspired the idea to hijack your site. It doesn't
dismiss my assumptions, it reinforces them."

Kate shook her head. "I was afraid those stories might be
too inciting. I didn't upload them. Our dreams and
premonitions were never online."

When Chase walked away, she recognized he needed space
and hoped he'd ponder her viewpoint.

Premonitions routinely accompanied mindless tasks, like
now, deleting old e-mails. After all that had happened in
Boston, she should have sensed relief, but dread remained like a
minor infection that had to fester before symptoms appeared.

This isn't over.

Was that a premonition or logical sense? It hardly mattered.

She released a deep sigh as she organized CDs, none of
them labeled. As mindless a task as any. She slid each one into
her iMac, but on several discs the file names were unfamiliar. *A
few of Chase's music CDs could have mixed on the table with
hers.* She double clicked to open. No sound files, only images.
Hers, a client's—or Chase's? She viewed several JPEGs.

With sunny skies over ancient stones, a man and woman stood among the ruins of Ephesus. She recognized the Temple of Diana from her visit to Turkey four years ago on a Mediterranean cruise. The woman in the photo was a few years older than she was. A few pounds lighter, maybe. Sandy blonde hair was styled in a short bob. Nice clothes. Striking green eyes.

Must be one of Chase's CDs. And from his past description, the woman would be his wife. *She* was *his wife.*

Oh my God! The man!

She blinked and squinted. The camera caught his back, but it looked like him. She opened more photos. His face avoided the lens in every shot except one—a beautiful photo souvenir of a romantic getaway. Kate glanced over her shoulder through the living room, dining area and kitchen—no Chase—and back to the screen. The way the woman looked at him and held him … she clung to his body like a lover would.

Oh crap!

Geezus. Ali *was her lover.*

The back door slammed. Kate jolted. Her head snapped toward the noise.

Chase was in the kitchen, again on the phone.

She studied the photo. Her throat tightened and her skin prickled. He looked different. Heavier. Shorter hair. Big smile. But he definitely *was* Ali. She checked the image date stamp—the timing fit, as best she knew. Her mind was spinning.

Should she tell Chase? She jumped up and paced with her hands cupped over her mouth as if she'd witnessed something bad. It was bad. Devastatingly bad. She sat again with her fingers readied on the keyboard, glancing in Chase's direction as her anxiety grew.

All he had asked of her was honesty. Her promise seemed easy when she had nothing to hide. But now …. This would be a knife in his heart. *Sleep in peace, my love. I'll protect you.*

Rest in peace, dead wife.

How could she spoil their perfect journey? Their relationship might not survive the blow.

He might run.

She wished she hadn't seen the damn pictures.

She could pop out the CD. Hide it or destroy it. Ali was never coming back, so who would know. *Really, who would know?*

Damn him. He must have targeted Chase to spy on counterterrorism methods, where Chase spent time and what interested him. Chase had warned against *her* making new friends. He warned about pressuring him to discuss his work. Don't ask questions. I'll say where I'm going if I can, he'd said.

Ali had used her and Todd like he'd used Chase and his wife.

Maybe her death *wasn't* an accident. What might that investigation do to Chase's psyche?

If she hid this secret, he wouldn't suffer the hurt. She was strong enough to hide the truth for a lifetime. She'd carried bigger burdens. As soon as he left the house, she could search and label every CD—demolish this one. He'd never have to know his arch enemy and his wife's lover were one.

Chase's call ended. His footsteps left the kitchen. She had to decide. Her eyes teared as she called toward the living room, "Have you been to Turkey?"

"I planned to, but canceled because of a work emergency. My wife went anyway. Why? Want to go? I do, someday." He bent to the hearth, stacking logs. "This is going to be a ripping fire."

A minute or more passed. Her stomach felt sick when she took a deep breath, knowing she would come to regret her decision.

Lie? Don't lie? Show him? Eject?

Her hand hovered over the key as his footsteps neared.
Tell him? Don't tell him? Tell ...
"Hey, hon ..."

SIXTY

FLORIDA
Late February

FOUR MONTHS LATER, a handsome elegant man dressed in a fine silk suit disembarked a plane from Athens. He answered questions posed by the immigration officer regarding the purpose and length of his stay. "Business, perhaps a little pleasure." He smiled while gazing into her eyes, his fingers sweeping hair off his forehead. "Ten days."

She stamped his Ukrainian passport. "Welcome to Miami."

He draped the strap of a laptop case across his chest as he exited toward ground transportation, glaring at a security camera with a defiant expression. A warm humid breeze brushed his face when he stepped outdoors.

Across the road, a man waved and pointed to a nearby parking lot and his private car.

Ali's replacement had arrived.

He nodded at the driver as he pulled a cell phone from his pocket and punched two digits to speed dial his contact. "Doctor?" His lips shaped a satisfied smirk. "Good work in Boston. It was wise to bounce your message through Canada."

"Too bad about Ali."

"Yes, our loss of his talents was unfortunate, but his loyalty was flimsy. His group has served purpose, an effective diversion."

"We remain covert."

He smiled at her response.

"Daryl, it's good to hear your voice again."

~ END ~

AUTHOR'S NOTE

The attack premonitions in this story are entirely fictional. However, the following excerpts are true paranormal stories submitted to Dreamwatch.com by people like you and me:

The spirit body of a loved one slipping into bed

Meeting the spirit of a living friend on the other side

The story of the child's crystal spirit

and

The State Trooper's lifesaving experience

***

The idea for the Dreamwatch website came in a dream.

For *true* stories about psychic dreams and visions, predictions and premonitions, spirits and ghosts, or if you have a spooky story to tell, visit:
www.Dreamwatch.com

ABOUT THE AUTHOR

Kathryn Orzech, a New England native,
is a seasoned world traveler with interests in
geopolitics, sociology and culture, earth sciences
and psychic phenomena.

On line since the 1990s, her website,
Dreamwatch.com, true paranormal experiences
of ordinary people, was the inspiration for
PREMONITION OF TERROR.